THE SCHOOL MISTRESS

Emerson Pass Historical Series, Volume One

TESS THOMPSON

Praise for Tess Thompson

The School Mistress of Emerson Pass:
"Sometimes we all need to step away from our lives and sink into a safe, happy place where family and love are the main ingredients for surviving. You'll find that and more in The School Mistress of Emerson Pass. I delighted in every turn of the story and when away from it found myself eager to return to Emerson Pass. I can't wait for the next book." - *Kay Bratt, Bestselling author of Wish Me Home and True to Me.*
"I frequently found myself getting lost in the characters and forgetting that I was reading a book." - *Camille Di Maio, Bestselling author of The Memory of Us.*
"Highly recommended." - *Christine Nolfi, Award winning author of The Sweet Lake Series.*
"I loved this book!" - *Karen McQuestion, Bestselling author of Hello Love and Good Man, Dalton.*

Traded: Brody and Kara:
"I loved the sweetness of Tess Thompson's writing - the camaraderie and long-lasting friendships make you want to move to Cliffside and become one of the gang! Rated Hallmark for romance!" - *Stephanie Little BookPage*

"This story was well written. You felt what the characters were going through. It's one of those "I got to know what happens next" books. So intriguing you won't want to put it down." - *Lena Loves Books*

"This story has so much going on, but it intertwines within itself. You get second chance, lost loves, and new love. I could not put this book down! I am excited to start this series and have love for this little Bayside town that I am now fond off!" - *Crystal's Book World*

"This is a small town romance story at its best and I look forward to the next book in the series." - *Gillek2, Vine Voice*

"This is one of those books that make you love to be a reader and fan of the author." -*Pamela Lunder, Vine Voice*

Blue Midnight:
"This is a beautiful book with an unexpected twist that takes the story from romance to mystery and back again. I've already started the 2nd book in the series!" - *Mama O*

"This beautiful book captured my attention and never let it go. I did not want it to end and so very much look forward to reading the next book." - *Pris Shartle*

"I enjoyed this new book cover to cover. I read it on my long flight home from Ireland and it helped the time fly by, I wish it had been longer so my whole flight could have been lost to this lovely novel about second chances and finding the truth. Written with wisdom and humor this novel shares the raw emotions a new divorce can leave behind." -*J. Sorenson*

"Tess Thompson is definitely one of my auto-buy authors! I love her writing style. Her characters are so real to life that you just can't put the book down once you start! Blue Midnight makes you believe in second chances. It makes you believe that everyone deserves an HEA. I loved the twists and turns in this book, the mystery and suspense, the family dynamics and the restoration of trust and security." - *Angela MacIntyre*

"Tess writes books with real characters in them, characters with flaws and baggage and gives them a second chance. (Real people, some remind me of myself and my girlfriends.) Then she cleverly and thoroughly develops those characters and makes you feel deeply for them. Characters are complex and multi-faceted, and the plot seems to unfold naturally, and never feels contrived." -
K. Lescinsky

Caramel and Magnolias:
"Nobody writes characters like Tess Thompson. It's like she looks into our lives and creates her characters based on our best friends, our lovers, and our neighbors. Caramel and Magnolias, and the authors debut novel Riversong, have some of the best characters I've ever had a chance to fall in love with. I don't like leaving spoilers in reviews so just trust me, Nicholas Sparks has nothing on Tess Thompson, her writing flows so smoothly you can't help but to want to read on!" - **T. M. Frazier**

"I love Tess Thompson's books because I love good writing. Her prose is clean and tight, which are increasingly rare qualities, and manages to evoke a full range of emotions with both subtlety and power. Her fiction goes well beyond art imitating life. Thompson's characters are alive and fully-realized, the action is believable, and the story unfolds with the right balance of tension and exuberance. CARAMEL AND MAGNOLIAS is a pleasure to read." - **Tsuruoka**

"The author has an incredible way of painting an image with her words. Her storytelling is beautiful, and leaves you wanting more! I love that the story is about friendship (2 best friends) and love. The characters are richly drawn and I found myself rooting for them from the very beginning. I think you will, too!"
- Fogvision

"I got swept off my feet, my heartstrings were pulled, I held my breath, and tightened my muscles in suspense. Tess paints stunning scenery with her words and draws you in to the lives of her characters."- **T. Bean**

Duet For Three Hands:

"Tears trickled down the side of my face when I reached the end of this road. Not because the story left me feeling sad or disappointed, no. Rather, because I already missed them. My friends. Though it isn't goodbye, but see you later. And so I will sit impatiently waiting, with desperate eagerness to hear where life has taken you, what burdens have you downtrodden, and what triumphs warm your heart. And in the meantime, I will go out and live, keeping your lessons and friendship and love close, the light to guide me through any darkness. And to the author I say thank you. My heart, my soul -all of me - needed these words, these friends, this love. I am forever changed by the beauty of your talent." - **Lisa M.Gott**

"I am a great fan of Tess Thompson's books and this new one definitely shows her branching out with an engaging enjoyable historical drama/love story. She is a true pro in the way she weaves her storyline, develops true to life characters that you love! The background and setting is so picturesque and visible just from her words. Each book shows her expanding, growing and excelling in her art. Yet another one not to miss. Buy it you won't be disappointed. The ONLY disappointment is when it ends!!!" - **Sparky's Last**

"There are some definite villains in this book. Ohhhh, how I loved to hate them. But I have to give Thompson credit because they never came off as caricatures or one dimensional. They all felt authentic to me and (sadly) I could easily picture them. I loved to love some and loved to hate others." - **The Baking Bookworm**

"I stayed up the entire night reading Duet For Three Hands and unbeknownst to myself, I fell asleep in the middle of reading the book. I literally woke up the next morning with Tyler the Kindle beside me (thankfully, still safe and intact) with no ounce of battery left. I shouldn't have worried about deadlines because, guess what? Duet For Three Hands was the epitome of unputdownable." - *The Bookish Owl*

Miller's Secret

"From the very first page, I was captivated by this wonderful tale. The cast of characters amazing - very fleshed out and multi-dimensional. The descriptions were perfect - just enough to make you feel like you were transported back to the 20's and 40's.... This book was the perfect escape, filled with so many twists and turns I was on the edge of my seat for the entire read." - *Hilary Grossman*

"The sad story of a freezing-cold orphan looking out the window at his rich benefactors on Christmas Eve started me off with Horatio-Alger expectations for this book. But I quickly got pulled into a completely different world--the complex five-character braid that the plot weaves. The three men and two women characters are so alive I felt I could walk up and start talking to any one of them, and I'd love to have lunch with Henry. Then the plot quickly turned sinister enough to keep me turning the pages.
Class is set against class, poor and rich struggle for happiness and security, yet it is love all but one of them are hungry for. ......Where does love come from? What do you do about it? The story kept me going, and gave me hope. For a little bonus, there are Thompson's delightful observations, like: "You'd never know we could make something this good out of the milk from an animal who eats hats." A really good read!" - *Kay in Seattle*

"She paints vivid word pictures such that I could smell the ocean and hear the doves. Then there are the stories within a story that twist and turn until they all come together in the end. I really had a hard time putting it down. Five stars aren't enough!"
- **M.R. Williams**

Also by Tess Thompson

CLIFFSIDE BAY

Traded: Brody and Kara

Deleted: Jackson and Maggie

Jaded: Zane and Honor

Marred: Kyle and Violet

Tainted: Lance and Mary

Cliffside Bay Christmas, The Season of Cats and Babies (Cliffside Bay Novella to be read after Tainted)

Missed: Rafael and Lisa

Cliffside Bay Christmas Wedding (Cliffside Bay Novella to be read after Missed)

Healed: Stone and Pepper

Chateau Wedding (Cliffside Bay Novella to be read after Healed)

Scarred: Trey and Autumn

Jilted: Nico and Sophie

Kissed (Cliffside Bay Novella to be read after Jilted)

Departed: David and Sara

Cliffside Bay Bundle , Books 1,2,3

BLUE MOUNTAIN SERIES

Blue Mountain Bundle, Books 1,2,3

Blue Midnight

Blue Moon

Blue Ink

Blue String

THE SCHOOL MISTRESS

Emerson Pass Historical Series, Volume One

TESS THOMPSON

A note to readers

Dear Reader,

Thank you for joining me for the first book in my new series. This series is a bit of a departure for me, as it will combine both historical and contemporary romances. I know, a little weird, right? All I can say is that I woke up one morning with Quinn Cooper, Alexander Barnes and his five children begging me to write their story. Later, another idea came to me about a contemporary Emerson Pass recovering from a forest fire. If you've read my Cliffside Bay Series, then you'll remember the ski town of Emerson Pass was the setting for part of Stone and Pepper's story.

There will be five historical novels with the stories of the Barnes family, taking place between 1910 and 1930. The contemporaries, of which there will be another five novels, will be about the descendants of the characters you meet in this first book. For more information on the series and to see family trees, please head over to my website, https://tesswrites.com/.

I love to hear from you. Don't hesitate to write me at tess@tthompsonwrites.com.

Much love,
Tess

For Anita and Tony Horton, my dear friends.

THE SCHOOL MISTRESS

Quinn

Had I known of the ways in which Emerson Pass would test my character, I might not have had the mettle to step off the train that autumn day in 1910. Then again, perhaps I would have. The path to our true places, our northern lights, are circuitous. We cannot predict the joys and sorrows that await us on this journey through life. Courage is our only map.

My journey began when we lurched to a stop at the train station with a terrible roar and release of steam from the engine. As I had during the entire way from Denver to Emerson Pass, I wondered if the passenger car would remain in one piece. During our trek higher and higher into the Rocky Mountains, through tunnels and over tracks built on stilts over deep canyons, I'd feared we'd never reach our destination. My wild imagination had run amok envisioning the train falling from the track and killing us all. Would I die in the unforgiving mountains after making it all the way from Boston to Denver?

I cleaned the window and pressed close, hoping to catch a glimpse of the former mining town that was to be my new home. I'd expected golden leaves of the famous aspens this time of year.

Instead, I saw nothing but snow flurries so thick it was as if I were peering into a closely knitted white blanket.

I slipped into my wool coat, frayed and tattered from withstanding six Boston winters, and squared my shoulders. Courage, just then, was a shadow buried deep within me. Even more so than the day last week when I'd pressed this same nose to a different window to catch one last glimpse of my mother and sister as the train pulled from the station.

Next to me, the baby asleep in her mother's arms woke and began to howl. Her diaper was full. The odor mixed with that of human perspiration and the greasy hair of my companions might have turned my stomach, but I was too tired and hungry to care. Third-class was not for the fainthearted. I gathered my suitcase and rose unsteadily to my feet. I waited for the couple with the baby to exit first, then the two men dressed in overalls and heavy work boots with whom I'd been sure to avoid eye contact. For a woman, traveling alone was not wise. For those like me, without funds or a companion, I had no choice but to set out alone.

I held my long skirts high and stepped from the train down to the platform and lifted my face toward a sky the color of smoke. Daylight was nearing its end. Snowflakes as big as quarters caught in my lashes. Grime and soot swirled about me as I tromped onto the platform. The covered area was a relief, although the wooden planks were icy. Behind me, the train groaned as if it too were happy to have arrived. *Here at last*, it seemed to say.

The trip had taken almost a week to get from Boston to Denver. Long days with the scent of oil and unwashed men. When we reached the plains, blizzards, ice storms, and harrowing wind that howled like a tortured animal had chased us all the way to Denver. "Unusual this time of year," the porter had said to me, probably in response to my terrified expression. After a night spent in Union Station in Denver, unable to sleep for fear of being murdered for my meager possessions, I'd boarded the train that took us up the mountains to my final destination.

A gust of wind swept under the train station's awning and threatened to lift my hat from my head. I gripped the brim between gloved fingers. This hat with its wide black bow was no match for the gusts of wind and snow. It did not matter. I was off the godforsaken train. I was alive, despite nature's relentless attempt to make it otherwise.

I would have dropped to my knees and kissed the ground if I hadn't been concerned with decorum. Truly, with no thought to my only gloves and second-best dress, I'd have dug through the snowdrifts that were as tall as my five-foot-two-inch frame and given the ground a big smooch as if it were my beloved. Instead, I sighed with great relief and stuck a pin through my hat, fixing it more securely into my masses of honey-blond hair.

My thick, silky hair was my only vanity. Some women needed wigs to make their buns appear thicker, but mine needed no enhancements. I'd once hoped my golden tresses compensated for my lack of figure. Even with my corset pulled tight, I had no curves. My hips were narrow and my chest flat. Combined with a quick mind that suffered no fools, and a teaching degree instead of a dowry, my fate was clear. Spinsterhood.

Alexander Barnes had written that he would send a man to fetch me and take me to the boardinghouse in town where I was to live. Clutching my suitcase, I searched the platform but saw no one. I exhaled, long and slow. My warm breath made a cloud in the frigid air. Only a few seconds off the train and I couldn't feel my toes. Dizzy and light-headed, I felt as if I were drunk. Was it the altitude?

What if no one came for me? What if coming out here all alone to this place that was truly the Wild West was a terrible mistake? Emerson Pass was a town of prospectors, mostly men and probably heathens. One tiny woman named Quinn Cooper who had never set foot outside of Boston until a week ago was sure to fail.

I gave myself a stern lecture as I stood shivering on the platform. What was needed were the skills of a fine actress and the courage of a lion. For Mother and Annabelle. Images of their thin faces wavered before me like apparitions. Under my gloves, there were cracks between my fingers from the frigid nights without heat. I was their remedy and their hope. This work would save them. I'd live frugally with the barest of necessities and send everything else to them. Soon, I would have enough to send for them. We could all be together. Or I would return home.

No looking back. I can do this. I will do this. I was a young, educated woman about to teach at a newly built school. Lord Barnes had written of its brick construction and shiny wood floors. A dozen students, he'd said, who needed an education. I might be headed to spinsterhood, but I was a good teacher. Having my own school was a dream. *Remember how blessed you are,* I reminded myself.

I'd be plucky, like the characters in the novels I loved so much.

Please, someone come. Don't leave me to freeze when I've finally reached my destination. As if I had conjured him, a young man appeared from the curtain of snow. He had dark eyes with thick lashes and a red mouth, which smiled at me. Brown curls sneaked out from under the back of his newsboy cap.

"Miss Cooper?"

"Yes, yes." Relief flooded through me. I was saved.

"It's Harley, Miss Cooper. I'm sorry to be late." I detected a slight accent. French, perhaps? "This storm came out of nowhere this afternoon and made traveling slow. Our horses don't like it. We have a twenty-minute drive to town in the sleigh, but I have blankets."

Harley took my suitcase, and I followed him outside where a sleigh waited, hitched to two brown horses. One whinnied and grinned at me with his large teeth. "Hello, lovely." I stroked his nose. He nudged at me, most likely wondering if I had an apple. If I'd had one, despite how much I loved animals, I would not have shared it with him. I hadn't eaten since the morning. Although my room and board would be covered, I'd had to leave most of the traveling money Lord Barnes had sent with Mother. They needed it to survive until I could mail my first paycheck. Which meant that I'd had to get by on one meal a day.

"Careful now," Harley said, helping me into the sleigh. "We'll have you there by suppertime. Mrs. Winslow makes a fine stew, and the boardinghouse is warm." Had he hesitated before the adjective *warm*? What else was it besides warm? Was warmth all it had to brag of? And Mrs. Winslow's stew? I thought of Mother's meals. Although made of meager provisions, somehow, they always tasted delicious, if not altogether filling. Bread filled the spaces between our bones, my mother sometimes said when the soup was mostly broth.

I ached with a sudden homesickness. They would be sitting by the fire by now with their knitting or needlepoint. I was not there to read to them as had become our custom since my father passed two years ago.

No, I must not succumb to self-pity. This was an adventure. An opportunity. Traveling across the country to this beautiful, uninhabited land. A newly built schoolhouse and children who craved learning. I'd read the letter from Lord Barnes so many times I had it memorized.

The children here need education and refinement. The West lacks in proper guidance for young ladies, especially. Our hope is for your good breeding and manners to influence and educate a new generation of Americans. These are children born of adventurous and hopeful men, who have longed to provide better lives for their children. Alas, with this effort comes the wild.

Five out of the dozen children in town were his own. He was the board of education for their community, he had written. *Not because I'm fit for the vocation, but because there was no one else.* He did not mention a wife in his letters. I felt certain she was dead, as he'd referenced a nanny who cared for his children, but never a mother.

It was how he'd spoken of education that had touched my heart.

We raise them to be tough here, but at what cost? Surely culture and art must be taught, no matter that the gold rush has given birth to a new West?

"Please take off your hat or you might lose it," Harley said.

I undid the pins and stuck them into the band, then handed the hat to him. He set it under a blanket in the back, along with my bag. "And wrap this scarf around your head and face."

He tucked several blankets around me. On top of those, he laid a fur of some kind that smelled of oil. I lifted my scarf over my nose, which still carried the scent of home, and tried to relax. Bells around the horses' necks made a merry song as Harley drove us away from the station. It was slow going for the horses through the high snow, but they clopped at a steady pace.

"Thank you for picking me up," I said.

"It's my pleasure, miss. I work for Lord Barnes. I take care of the animals and the garden, and whatever else needs doing. My little sister, Poppy, and I live in the servant's cottage on his property."

"I thought the train station would be closer to town."

"Back during the gold rush, the train stopped at the mining site," he said. "As the town grew, they realized building in the valley between the two mountains made more sense."

"Have you been here long?"

"A few years, yes. My parents were French. They came out here chasing gold, like most. They died three winters ago from the flu, and so now it's just Poppy and me."

"Poppy? What a sweet name."

"She's thirteen. Same age as Miss Josephine, Lord Barnes's oldest daughter. She can't wait to start school. Until my parents died, we spoke mostly French, so she's anxious to learn to read in English."

"Does Lord Barnes live in town?" I asked.

"No, his estate's a few miles from town."

Estate? Estates were large with servants and fine meals. What did I expect from a man with the title Lord in front of his name?

"Lord Barnes owns at least a thousand acres, including the land in town. There was a fire in the late nineties and most of the residents left. Lord Barnes bought up all the property and rebuilt the town. This time in brick."

"He owns everything?"

"That's right. He rents the buildings to local businessmen for a fair price. His aim is to civilize this place." Harley laughed, clearly fond of his boss. "If anyone can, it's him."

Normally, I would have been fascinated to learn more. I'm curious bordering on nosy. People are like books. I can't wait to turn the next page to learn what happens next. But I felt sleepy, lulled by the rhythm of the sled across snow. I blinked to try to stay alert, but between the falling snow and dimming light blocking the view, in combination with the warmth of the fur some poor animal had sacrificed, I drifted to sleep.

The sound of a shotgun jarred me awake. Both horses jumped and neighed and then began to run. Harley called to them and tried to rein them in, but to no avail. They were afraid. As was I. Another shot rang out. The horses ran faster. The sled seemed to be several inches above the snow, as though we were flying. We were out of control. I could feel it in the way the sled shimmied. One of the horses reared back, and the sled yanked hard to the left. We flew over an embankment. A large tree loomed close. I screamed as I flew from the sled. Everything went black.

Alexander

❧

A pounding on my front door pulled me from a particularly moving passage in a Henry James novel. Startled, I looked at the clock in the corner of my library. Six on an evening? Who would call without notice? The children were all upstairs with Nanny Foster having baths. My belly was full of Lizzie's hearty stewed chicken and potatoes, and I'd just settled in with a glass of whiskey for a deep read.

The knocking turned loud and fierce. I rose from my chair, alarmed. This was not the typical timid tap of tradespeople or visitors, but urgent, almost frightened, as if something was terribly wrong. A shiver crept up the back of my neck. Jasper's efficient footsteps passed by the door of the library, all *click-click* on the hardwood floors.

I crossed the room and into the hallway just as Jasper yanked open the front door. Wayne Higgins stood on the steps, holding his hat in his hands. Behind him, snow dumped from a hidden sky.

"Mr. Higgins, are you all right?" Jasper asked.

"Yes, sir. I'm sorry to bother you." Wayne nodded to me as I came to stand next to Jasper. "Lord Barnes, Harley's had an accident. He and the schoolmistress were coming from the station.

Someone fired a gun and the horses got spooked and somehow the sled got unattached and it went over the embankment just yonder." He pointed toward the road. "Clive and I saw the whole thing. We hauled them up from the bank, sir." A layer of snow had already covered his white-blond hair and glistened in the lamplight.

Harley had gone to get Miss Cooper an hour ago. "Are they hurt?" I asked.

"Harley's all right. We dropped him at the cottage so his sister could clean up a gash on his hand. He was bleeding pretty good. The teacher hasn't opened her eyes or made any noise. We thought it best to bring her here so we could call the doctor."

"Of course, yes, come in," I said. From the darkness, Wayne's brother, Clive, appeared, carrying a woman in his arms. She was a tiny slip of a thing, not much bigger than my thirteen-year-old daughter. Her boots were well-polished, but the soles were thin, and the sleeves of her dark coat tattered. Fair curls had come loose from her bun and dangled over Clive's arms.

"Evening, Lord Barnes." Clive shared the same light blue eyes with his brother. Tall and broad, made from German stock, they owned the butcher shop in town. The Higgins Brothers Butcher Shop was clean and well-run. They sold their cuts of meat at a fair price. I'd known them from the first day they moved here. I happened to know, too, they gave away scraps and day-old meat to the hungry.

"I think she's bumped her head real good."

I stepped forward. "I'll take her."

"Yes, sir." Clive transferred her to me. I gazed down at the lovely face that belonged to Miss Cooper. This was not the old lady spinster I'd expected. For one, she was a young woman. And my, she was a beauty, with alabaster skin and delicate bone structure. Her cheeks, flushed from the cold, were the color of cherry blossoms in the spring. She had long dark eyelashes and hair the color of wheat. A small mouth suited her small oval face.

Clive and Wayne hovered by the front door, holding their

hats in their hands. "We sure hope she's not hurt too bad," Clive said.

"Would you like to come in?" I asked. "Lizzie can get you something warm to drink before you go back out in the cold."

"No, sir. We best get back into town and send the doctor out," Wayne said.

"This time of night he'll be at the saloon," Clive said.

"Thank you. It's very kind of you," I said, holding back from making a comment about the doctor's gambling and whiskey habits.

"One more thing before we go," Clive said. "The shots sounded like they were down by the Coles' place. It might be best to send someone out there in the morning to make sure they're all right."

Samuel Cole and his family lived on the other side of the creek that separated our property. He and Rachel were good friends and neighbors. I doubted there was anything amiss. Samuel knew these parts better than anyone. The shots were most likely from him. He hunted or trapped almost all their meat. Deer were particularly abundant this year.

"Thank you. We'll take care of it," Jasper said as he clasped his hands behind his back. A habit from the old days when he'd been trained as a footman on my father's estate.

"Yes, sir," Clive said, without making eye contact.

At first glance, one wouldn't have thought Jasper to be intimidating. He was quite ordinary-looking—tall and slim with sandy-colored hair and light blue eyes. It was the unfortunate way his lips often puckered, as if he smelled something foul, and his posh British accent that made him seem haughty and disdainful.

"Thank you. That'll be all," Jasper said to the Higgins brothers.

The young men put their hats back on and inched backward before escaping into the night.

Jasper shut the door as I headed toward the library with Miss Cooper.

My cook, Lizzie, appeared, poking her head out of the door that led downstairs to the kitchen, bringing the scent of garlic and butter with her. "What's all the commotion?" She placed her flour-covered hands over her round cheeks. "Who is that?"

"The new schoolteacher. Harley had an accident on the way back from the station," Jasper said. "Don't worry, he's all right." He often anticipated a question before it was asked. "But he's got a gash on his hand. Can you send Merry over to check on him?"

Merry, who had appeared from downstairs before she could be summoned, nodded and scuttled to the closet for a coat. "Yes, yes. I'll go right away." Not that I would have discussed such a topic, but I assumed I wasn't the only person in this house who'd observed young Merry's crush on Harley. In fact, the only person who seemed oblivious to the pretty Swedish immigrant's devotion was Harley himself. If he didn't come to his senses soon, I couldn't imagine the strong, tall woman with golden skin and hair would remain single for long. The town was full of men only too happy to entertain her.

As Merry bounded out the door, I headed into the library, Lizzie and Jasper close at my heels.

I set Miss Cooper on the east-facing couch. In the lamplight, she looked even younger. She couldn't have been much older than twenty. In our correspondence, Quinn Cooper had never mentioned her age, but I'd assumed she was an old maid—a spinster with a silver bun and a long nose with a wart.

Jasper had already fetched a blanket. I grabbed one of the square pillows from the settee and placed it under Miss Cooper's head.

Lizzie, never exactly calm in normal circumstances, stood over Miss Cooper, tutting and fussing. "Is she breathing?" Short and round with curly brown hair that was forever springing from her bun and freckles that covered her fair skin, Lizzie looked very much like her Irish mother. Both her parents had worked for my father at our country estate. When I left for America, she and Jasper had asked to join me. Initially, I brought only Jasper but sent for her as soon as I was settled here in Emerson Pass. She'd been making delicious meals ever since.

I knelt at the side of the couch and picked up one limp arm to feel Miss Cooper's pulse. "Strong," I said.

"Shall I fetch tea?" Lizzie asked, looking as if she were about to burst into tears. "For when she wakes?"

"Yes, and smelling salts," Jasper said. "We need smelling salts."

"And loosen her corset," Lizzie said. "God knows that'll help."

Jasper coughed and turned red.

"Let's try smelling salts first," I said, almost laughing despite the gravity of the situation.

Lizzie nodded and flew from the room and down the stairs to the kitchen.

"I had no idea she was young," I said to Jasper.

"It's not proper for her to travel alone," Jasper said. "Americans have no sense of propriety."

At times, I found Jasper's reluctance to accept America's ways irritating, but this time I agreed with him. A wave of shame washed over me. Why hadn't a companion accompanied her? It *wasn't* proper. Every young woman should travel with a companion. I should have paid for someone to chaperone her. Dangers lurked around every corner on a train headed west. Not to mention here in Emerson Pass. Rough and lonely men would do terrible things to her if given the chance. How could I have possibly suggested she stay at the boardinghouse? She wouldn't be safe there. Miners and prospectors stayed there, forever enraged that the gold they hoped for never appeared. They stumbled home at night from the saloon, drunk and violent. It would be fine for an older woman who had more than likely seen a thing or two, but this innocent woman would be in constant danger.

She would have to stay here in the house. We had more than enough rooms to accommodate her. I'd built this house with three extra bedrooms, hoping for family and friends from England to come for extended stays.

I heard the clamor of my children filing down the stairs. They'd come to say good night. Would seeing their teacher splayed out upon their couch scare them? I feared it might. Especially after what had happened to their mother. I glanced at Jasper, who uncharacteristically seemed as rattled and unsure as I. Before I could decide upon a diversion, the children burst into the library. All five of them. Wearing their flannel nightgowns, they looked clean and shiny and smelled of lavender soap. I loved them after their baths.

For once, the children seemed stunned into silence. They gathered around the prone body on the sofa and stared.

Flynn, one of the nine-year-old twins, not unusually, found his voice first. "Who is she, Papa?"

Before I could answer, Cymbeline, only six years old but particularly articulate, stepped closer to Miss Cooper and whispered, "Is she a princess from a faraway land?" Cymbeline's dark curls, still damp from her bath, stuck to her rosy cheeks.

Nanny Foster, from behind, spoke in a sharp voice. "Cymbeline, don't get too close. She might be sick."

"No, it's all right, Nanny," I said. "She's only bumped her head."

"Is she a stranger, Papa?" Josephine asked in a voice much too old for only being thirteen. "Have we taken her in from the cold?"

"No, this is our new teacher. Harley had an accident in the sleigh."

"The small sleigh?" Flynn asked.

"What does it matter?" I asked.

"I'm just wondering," Flynn said, grinning. "Because if the

larger one is wrecked, then we wouldn't be able to go into town for school."

"You're out of luck. It was the small one," I said.

Fiona, my smallest daughter, slipped her hand into mine. At three, she still looked like a doll, with dark ringlets and round blue eyes that could melt the heart of the fiercest man. Especially her father. "Papa, I'm scared."

I lifted her into my arms. "No need to be afraid, my darling. Doc's on his way. He'll fix her right up."

"What if he can't?" Theo asked. The quiet, worried half of my twin set didn't have to explain his question. He would be thinking of his mother, who had walked into a blizzard and died when Fiona was a baby. Theo had been the one to find her. The doctor had come then, too.

"Let's not worry ourselves," Nanny Foster said in her brisk, unemotional way. "This looks like a strong but rather foolish young woman."

I wasn't sure how a bump on her head made her foolish, but I'd learned not to follow up with Nanny Foster's observations unless I wanted a few more paragraphs of her opinions.

The children all gathered close, inspecting our patient.

Fiona wriggled from my arms, forever worried she'd miss something her older siblings were privy to.

Jasper appeared with a piece of ice wrapped in a cloth and placed it gently on top of that mound of shiny hair.

Miss Cooper's eyes fluttered open. I took a step backward, stunned by the beauty of those eyes, brown and shiny as polished stone. They widened with alarm as she took in her surroundings. Here we were, staring at her like she was part of the circus. "Children, step away. Give Miss Cooper some room to breathe."

"Oh, dear," Miss Cooper said. "What's happened? Where am I?"

Quinn

Five sets of eyes peered at me. Was I in heaven? Dead at the mercy of a horse and sleigh on my very first day in Colorado? With five child angels surrounding me? Yet, no. The pain in my head and midsection told me I was still very much on earth. There was no pain in heaven.

Nevertheless, these children indeed looked like angels. The two smallest possessed adorable cherubic faces with brown ringlets and eyes the color of the ocean on a summer day. There were two boys, identical twins, I quickly gathered. Their faces seemed carved from the finest birch tree, pale and smooth. They had dark hair like their sisters, but their eyes seemed almost black in the dim light. I might have had trouble telling them apart, except that one had a scar above his left eye. Ridges from a comb in their damp hair and glowing skin told me they'd just come from a bath. The oldest child, a girl, was the only one with fair hair and light green eyes. She was slighter than the others, daintily built, as if a slight breeze could knock her over. She held a book to her chest and gazed at me with a somber, inquisitive expression. A reader. This was my favorite kind of child. Well, they were all my favorites, really, other than the spoilt or mean ones. However, the world was to blame for those. Most children were born sweet.

A man appeared in my sight line. A particularly handsome man with high cheekbones and a mouth that naturally curved upward so that he appeared to be smiling even though his eyes were serious. Faint laugh lines around his eyes were evidence of a life lived.

And those eyes of his. They were a spectacular shade of dark green and seemed to exude intelligence and curiosity. At the moment they were fixed on me, holding my gaze. He was obviously the father of these children. Other than their brown eyes, the twins were the spitting image of him. I could imagine him as a boy, which made me like him immensely before he even opened his mouth. The twinkle in his eyes contributed some too, I suppose, other than they seemed to be laughing at me. If eyes could laugh. They can't. They're only meant for seeing or producing tears.

"Miss Cooper, we do beg your pardon for this most inauspicious meeting." A deep, resonate voice and, God help me, an English accent. "It seems you've had an accident. The Higgins brothers brought you to the closest home. Ours. We're the Barnes family. I'm Alexander Barnes. We've corresponded, as I'm sure you remember."

Silently, I groaned and fought an outward wince. *This* man was Lord Alexander Barnes. How unfortunate he was handsome. I mustn't let my romantic mind get the better of me. I'd been prone to that kind of behavior before. Daydreaming of a love that existed only as a figment of my imagination. Charles, whom I'd been in love with since I was a little girl, loved my friend Betsy, not me. I'd never told a soul of my longings. For which I was grateful. At least the humiliation was only in my mind, not out for the world to see. I shoved that thought aside and focused on the scene in front of me now.

"Do you remember? Or has the bump on your head given you amnesia, like in a story I read?" the oldest girl asked.

I managed a smile, even though my head throbbed. "Yes, not to worry. I remember everything, other than the moment after I flew from the sleigh." I closed my eyes as images from those last terrifying moments flooded my consciousness. Harley shouting to me to hold on and I'd thought, *hold on to what exactly?* and then the cries of the horses. "Are the horses all right? And Harley?"

"All fine," Lord Barnes said. "You seem to have taken the brunt of it."

I sat up and winced from the pounding in my head. Black dots danced before my eyes. "I'm sorry to cause trouble at our first meeting."

The second-to-smallest girl stepped forward with a distinctly disappointed look on her round face. "You're *not* a princess, are you?"

"Cymbeline, hush, child." I looked in the direction of the voice to see a plump, middle-aged woman with silver hair and a thin mouth.

Cymbeline. The name suited her.

"Yes, Nanny Foster," Cymbeline said.

The smallest one drew close enough that I caught the scent of soap on her skin. "I'm Fiona. I'm the baby." She picked up a lock of my hair. "Pretty, like Josephine's."

"Josephine?" I asked.

Fiona pointed to the oldest daughter. "My sister. She has hair like yours."

Josephine curtsied. "Hello, Miss Cooper. I'm pleased to meet you. I can't wait for school."

"I'm pleased to meet you, Miss Josephine," I said.

"Fiona," Nanny Foster said. "Step away." I could see right away that Nanny Foster had a most unpleasant disposition. Why did women who hated children become nannies and teachers? "We don't touch other people."

"It's all right," I said.

"No," Nanny Foster said. "Obey me, Fiona, or you'll be sent to bed without a cookie."

Fiona backed away but not without a conspiratorial glance toward Cymbeline.

I stayed quiet, glancing behind the children to take in the dark walls and plush furniture. Rows and rows of books lined the shelves. A roaring fire warmed the room. For the first time in ten days, I started to unthaw. I unbuttoned my coat.

"Jasper, please help her with her coat," Lord Banks said.

Jasper, who was obviously the butler or valet or some kind of fancy servant, leapt forward. I moved my feet to the floor and then tried to stand, but the room seemed to tilt. I sat back down, shrugging out of the coat and handing it to Jasper.

The door opened and another woman entered, carrying a tray with a teapot and, glory be to God, a stack of cookies that smelled of butter and sugar. My mouth watered, accompanied by a loud growl of my stomach. I glanced around to see if anyone heard, but they were all fixated on the cookies.

"I've brought tea and biscuits," the woman said. She also had an English accent. Cornflower-blue eyes gazed at me with such sympathy I immediately wanted her to be my best friend. "You poor dear. I'm Lizzie, the family cook. You've given us quite a fright." She said all this as she set the tray on the table in front of me. I tried not to feel jealous of her curves and glowing ivory skin peppered with freckles, but I didn't quite manage it. "Are you hungry? You look half starved." Her white cap hung lopsided over corkscrew brown hair that escaped from its bun. A white puff of flour wafted from the front of her apron as she leaned over to pour the tea.

"Allow me, Lizzie," Jasper said.

"Yes, right. Of course." Lizzie straightened and touched her pink cheeks with the palms of her hands. "I'm quite undone. We don't often have visitors."

"Especially ones with a broken head," said the twin with the scar as he squinted and moved closer. "Does it hurt?" Given the sparkle in his eyes, he appeared quite thrilled over the turn of events. I half expected him to pull out a notebook and start jotting down field notes about the strange woman who had appeared in their library. A curious child. I felt certain I would adore him even though he was obviously a rascal.

"Didn't they feed you on the train?" Lizzie stacked a plate with cookies and thrust them into my hands.

"I was on a strict budget," I said before I could stop myself. This Lizzie was a woman who wrapped you in a warm blanket, fed you hot tea and biscuits, and made all your secrets spill forth.

"Sugar, Miss Cooper?" Jasper asked.

"Yes, two please." If someone offered free sugar, one should take it.

Jasper poured the tea and added two scoops of sugar from a bowl on an ornate silver tray, then stirred with a different tiny spoon. Two spoons for one cup of tea? I was in a new world compared with the one from which I'd come. "Here you are, Miss Cooper." He set the cup and saucer on the table in front of me.

I took a grateful sip. "Thank you, Jasper and Lizzie. Everyone. I'm sorry to have interrupted your evening."

"My sister thought you were a princess, but I could tell you were too plainly dressed," said the twin with the scar above his left eye.

"And your shoes are old," Cymbeline said.

"Cymbeline," Lord Barnes said. "That's impolite."

"I'm sorry, Miss Cooper," Cymbeline said.

"It's quite all right. My shoes are old." I smiled through my embarrassment. My poverty shamed me even though I knew it had nothing to do with my character. I'd found over the years that it was impossible to hide how poor my family and I were. Shabby clothes and shoes were out there for everyone to see. Regardless, they couldn't see the inside of me. In there, I was rich with dreams and imagination and my big heart. No one could ever mock those or make me feel inadequate. They were mine. "True enough. I can assure you I'm not a princess." Far from it. From the appearance of this elaborate house and almost as many servants as children, I had a distinct impression the members of the Barnes family would not have the slightest understanding of the scarcity from which I'd come. As if in agreement, my empty stomach growled again. I put my hand over the front of my dress, praying no one had heard.

"Ah, biscuits aren't going to do it now." Lizzie shook her head and tutted. She must have good hearing. I willed myself not to blush, but it was too late. My cheeks burned. Why did embarrassing incidents always happen to me? Who flew from a sleigh into a tree and was rendered unconscious during the first thirty minutes of arrival in a strange place? I knew the answer to that. Me.

"May I warm up some of my chicken stew for her?" Lizzie asked.

My mouth watered so much I was afraid I might drool to add to my embarrassment.

"Yes, yes, of course," Lord Barnes said. "Fix her a tray. I don't think we should let her up just yet."

"Agreed." Lizzie beamed. "I've fresh bread too, Miss Cooper. It'll put some meat on your bones." Lizzie swept from the room, her long black skirt whirling around her ankles.

Lord Barnes cleared his throat. "Before we get you a warm meal, Miss Cooper, allow me to introduce you to the Barnes children. Line up now."

The five arranged themselves in a neat line—oldest to youngest, like stairsteps, other than the twins, who made an even landing.

Lord Barnes stood behind them. "As you've heard already, this is Josephine, age thirteen."

"Good evening, Miss Cooper," Josephine said.

"Hello, again. What're you reading?" I asked.

"*The Wonderful Wizard of Oz*," Josephine said. "For the second time."

I let out an exaggerated sigh. "I love that book. I've read it at least a dozen times. How lucky you are to have a copy of your very own."

Josephine smiled shyly, then glanced up at her father. "Papa knows the publisher."

I was too shocked to think of a response and simply nodded dumbly.

Lord Barnes continued. "This is Theo and Flynn. They just turned nine last month." He put a hand on each of their heads. "This is Flynn on the left."

Flynn had the scar. He was the wild one of the two, probably always getting into scrapes. Whereas the other seemed cautious and scholarly. Flynn looked me directly in the eyes and spoke in the high-pitched voice of a young boy. "How do you do, Miss Cooper?" His mouth twitched as if he were trying not to smile.

I smiled at him, and I was rewarded with a grin that rivaled the brightest spring morning. "It's a pleasure to meet you."

"This is Theo," Lord Barnes said. "Say hello to Miss Cooper, son."

Theo stared at the floor rather than me and mumbled a version of his brother's greeting. Or at least I thought so. I wasn't able to decipher exactly.

Lord Barnes moved to stand behind the second-to-youngest. "This is Cymbeline. You have to watch out for her. She's almost always looking for mischief, and her tongue has a mind of its own."

"I'm sorry you're not a princess." A clumsy curtsy in mimic of her sister caused Cymbeline's dark curls to bounce. "But you're pretty so I don't mind as much as I normally would."

"Is it true you're always looking for mischief?" I asked.

Cymbeline bit her lip and looked downward before returning my gaze. "I'm spirited." She drew the word out as if she'd over-heard an adult say it and wasn't exactly sure what it meant. I suspected she'd heard it from her father, perhaps in defense of her to the grumpy nanny.

"More like sassy," Josephine said.

Cymbeline shot her sister a dark look before returning her gaze to me.

"And finally, Fiona," Lord Barnes said.

Fiona's curtsy more closely resembled a bow. "I don't get to go to school."

"Not yet, but soon enough," I said.

"I'm a sweetheart," Fiona said. "Everyone loves me the best."

I bit the inside of my lip to keep from laughing.

"Fiona, hush now," Nanny said. "Boasting is not acceptable."

"Papa says I am." Fiona crossed her arms and stuck out her bottom lip.

"I do, yes." Lord Barnes scooped Fiona into his arms and kissed the top of her head. "But you must obey Nanny and remember to be humble."

"How?" Fiona asked.

"This child," Nanny Foster muttered.

Fiona's eyes flashed with temper before she buried her face in Lord Barnes's shoulder.

"And this is the woman who takes care of these mischief-makers. Nanny Foster," Lord Barnes said. "Like you, she's from back east."

"It's a pleasure to meet you," I said.

"Likewise, Miss Cooper," Nanny said. "Good luck surviving the winter."

I swallowed, unsure how to react.

"Our mama died," Cymbeline said.

"I'm sorry," I said. "My father died."

"Are you sad?" Cymbeline asked.

"I am. But he's in heaven now," I said.

"Like Mother," Josephine said, then promptly flushed pink.

Nanny Foster had crossed her arms over her chest. Her complexion now resembled a purple turnip. I wasn't sure of the offense, but clearly the children were not behaving as she wanted them to. She also disapproved of Lord Barnes's lack of formality with his offspring. It *was* unusual to see a man so outwardly affectionate. I suspected it was even more uncommon for an Englishman.

However, Lord Barnes was both mother and father.

"It's time for the children to go to bed," Nanny said. "You may each take one cookie and head upstairs."

"Yes, off you go," Lord Barnes said as he held out his arms. The children, one by one, kissed him and filed out of the room.

Seconds after they left, Jasper announced the arrival of Dr. Moore.

My head *did* ache. Still, I wished the doctor hadn't been called. All this fuss was unnecessary. I'd wanted to give a good impression, one of an independent, educated woman, and now I was in the library of an actual English lord looking like a complete fool as well as a frail damsel in distress. Where was my plucky inner heroine when I needed her?

"Let's take a look at you," Dr. Moore said. He set his doctor's bag on the floor and asked me to lie back against the couch.

"I'm really fine, Dr. Moore." Regardless, I did as was asked of me.

The doctor picked up my arm and felt the pulse at my wrist. Embarrassed to be touched, I peeked at him through my lashes. His white hair and neatly trimmed beard gave him the appearance of an esteemed doctor. However, his hard gray eyes and a strong odor of alcohol on his breath did nothing to instill my confidence in his abilities.

The doctor placed his hands on my scalp and felt around.

I yelped as he pressed his fingers into the bump.

"Does that hurt?" he asked.

I nodded. "Did my cry of pain give you a clue?"

"Be gentle, Moore," Lord Barnes said from somewhere in the room. "Miss Cooper's been through enough."

"She has a bump the size of an egg," Moore said in a tone that implied it was my fault. If only I had a head strong enough to withstand a collision with a tree.

He asked me to follow his finger back and forth. "No troubles seeing, then?" he asked.

"No, Doctor."

"Double vision?"

I shook my head.

"Excellent. My diagnosis is you have a large bump on your head. Nothing to worry about, but I'd suggest a good meal and a decent night's rest, and you'll wake up right as rain."

His assessment didn't give me complete faith in his scientific qualifications. My mother could have identified a bump and advised bed. However, his recommendation of a meal warmed me to him somewhat.

The doctor pulled out a vial of white powder. "Give her this in some brandy," Dr. Moore said.

I wasn't certain what the brandy was for, but I didn't want to cause further attention by asking.

As the doctor was leaving, Lizzie came in with a tray of food. "Do you feel well enough to eat?" she asked.

"Always," I said.

Lord Barnes instructed me to sit at a small round table with two chairs near the fire. A checkerboard occupied the center, but Lord Barnes moved it to the mantel to make room. Lizzie set the meal down as Jasper led me over to the chair all the while looking at me with a mixture of concern and disdain, as if my unfortunate incident had him worried about my abilities to teach a school full of students along with my general character.

"Lizzie, this smells delightful," I said, hoping to sound sophisticated when all I wanted to do was wolf it down as fast as I could.

"Thank you." Lizzie stood there, beaming at me. I had the distinct feeling that Lizzie wanted to be my friend.

Jasper cleared his throat. "That will be all, Lizzie. You may retire for the evening."

"But what about clearing away the dishes?" Lizzie's brows came together, making her pretty face surprisingly intimidating.

"I'll take care of it," Jasper said. From what I'd gathered thus far, other than his pursed lips, Jasper's facial muscles weren't capable of movement. His eyes, however, told the story of his mind. When they looked at Lizzie, I detected complex feelings of love, fear, impatience, and a need for control. Of what, I wasn't sure. His own feelings or her obedience? How very English they all were.

Lizzie's hands clenched into fists at her sides, as if she'd love nothing more than to smack his condescending mouth. "Yes, sir." She made an exaggerated curtsy and then headed out with her head held high.

I exchanged a glance with Lord Barnes, who hovered near the fire. He lifted one shoulder in a half-shrug and smiled.

Jasper set a short tumbler of brandy on the tray. I wasn't in the habit of a brandy before or after supper—my family were lucky to have a meal, let alone a drink—but I had to admit the potent smell gave a hint of its warming abilities.

I thanked him. He nodded before moving away to stand on the other side of the room.

"May I sit with you, Miss Cooper?" Lord Barnes asked.

Strangely, this request made me flush with heat. "Please."

He set a glass of brandy on the table before taking the chair opposite me. When he crossed one leg over the other, I noticed his fine black leather boots and the expensive wool material of his suit.

I crossed my ankles. These old boots tattled my tale too well.

"Please, eat," Lord Barnes said. "We'll talk after your stomach is full."

I couldn't resist any longer. As politely as I could, I scooped the savory stew into a spoon and took a bite that tasted of butter, garlic, and rosemary. To my embarrassment, a groan of ecstasy erupted from my chest.

Lord Barnes chuckled. "Lizzie's chicken stew is enough to make a grown man weep with happiness."

I nodded and wiped my mouth, then picked up the brandy

and took a sip. Holy God, what poison was this that made my throat burn thus? I gasped, then coughed so hard that my eyes watered, and I had to clench my butt cheeks together to keep from tooting. The very last thing I needed was eruptions from my nether regions to escape in front of my new employer. Speaking of embarrassing body function, I wondered if I'd drooled while unconscious. Why, why, why had this happened?

Lord Barnes had scooted to the edge of his chair during my coughing fit, his brows knitted together. "Are you all right, Miss Cooper?"

"Yes, thank you. I'm not used to brandy. I had no idea it was awful."

"It's an acquired taste." Damn those laughing eyes. They were most certainly laughing at *me*. Any attempt at acting sophisticated was now impossible. I'd embarrassed myself since the moment I entered this house. I decided to finish my meal in silence and without another sip of brandy.

I took another bite of a carrot so tender it melted on my tongue. A chunk of chicken was next. When had my chewing become so loud? I swallowed, self-conscious. Lord Barnes watched me with amusement mixed with apprehension.

"I'm fine now, Lord Barnes."

"Are you quite sure? I can't have you almost dying on me for the second time in one night."

"I'm hardly dying despite your attempt to murder me with that foul liquid."

He slapped the tabletop and laughed. "Miss Cooper, you're nothing if not unexpected."

Unexpected? I could say the same for him, I thought, as I shoved more stew into my mouth.

He put several more logs on the fire and returned to his chair, gazing into the flames with a reflective expression.

Thankful he was no longer worried about my death from brandy, I took a good look around the room. Dimly lit with gas lamps and the fire, it was impossible to pick out titles of the books that lined the shelves. I'd have to sneak a peek later. Just the idea of this many books in one home took my breath away. What would it be like to have access to them any time one wanted?

The fireplace was made from river rock in shades of gray. Portraits of two women hung on the wall, one fair-haired with a thin face and enormous green eyes, the other robust with the black hair and eyes like Lord Barnes. I guessed them to be of his late wife and his mother, respectively. If I were correct, Josephine looked very much like her mother.

The hardback chairs where Lord Barnes and I sat had cushions made of soft brown leather. After the hardness of the train seat, my bony bottom appreciated them even though they were too tall for me. I had to sit on the edge so that my feet could touch the floor. A large desk took up one corner of the room. Two couches, one of which had been my area of recuperation, faced each other over a coffee table. In all my life, I'd never been in a finer room.

"I brought the books from my home in England," he said, as if I'd asked. "I collect more during my trips to Denver and Chicago."

"What brought you here?" I blurted out.

"This will sound strange to you, no doubt. Although, as eldest son I was set to inherit my father's title and estate, I knew from the time I was young that I would have to find my own way. I gave it all up to come to America. My younger brother happily took my place. He was better suited for the life. I wanted adventures. Jasper and I left for America, landing in New York, where we spent a few months exploring. While there, I read about a former mining town in the mountains that had burned to the ground. I decided to come out here and see about buying property for investment purposes. When we arrived, it was a summer day and the sky a brilliant blue against the white tips of the mountains." He chuckled, shaking his head. "It was like falling in love. I had to have her. The land, that is. I decided to build a town for honest, hardworking families to have an opportunity to own businesses or farms. So I did."

"But how? I don't understand."

"I put an advertisement in the Chicago and Denver papers, offering to build and lease buildings or farmland for anyone willing to come here. Even with the train from Denver able to bring supplies, it behooved us to be self-sufficient. Therefore, farmers willing to raise cattle and fresh produce on my land in exchange for keeping the profits outweighed much of the risk."

"And they came?"

"Not all who applied were accepted." He shrugged. "It was a rather laborious process."

"What about the people who were already here? The ones before the fire."

"Many left before I could offer them work, but those who stayed were able to make enough to live better than they had before. You'd be surprised how many men it takes to build a town from nothing."

I nodded, thinking about the construction I'd witnessed in Boston as I walked from the slums to the wealthier neighborhoods.

"Anyway, the men who came to open businesses brought families. Those children are why you're here."

I watched him, interested to know more—to know everything about him. The only thing I knew for sure was that the man sitting across from me was a soul made of complex layers. "What would make you want to do something like this? Build a town?"

"I wanted a community for my children. We are stronger as a team of people rather than acting entirely alone. Truth be told, I craved a village. I'm a pasty Englishman at heart."

I laughed. "There's nothing pasty about you, Lord Barnes." The moment I said it, my cheeks burned. I could almost hear the gasp from my mother if she'd been here.

"I'll take that as a compliment." He smiled in a way that

was closer to a smirk than a grin. My fingers twitched with a sudden need to touch that mouth, to feel the hardness of his lips.

I focused on my food, reminding myself that it was best when I kept quiet. When I was done, I set down my spoon. "Thank you for supper."

"You're welcome." One of Lord Barnes's eyebrows raised as he cocked his head to one side. I shuttered my eyes and looked away, shy. Something in his gaze gave me a prickly, raw feeling, as if I were naked. Not that I'd ever been undressed in front of a man. If I had, I imagined it to feel like this—exhilarating and terrifying.

Jasper swooped over to collect my tray. His silent, swift movements were disconcerting. Had he been in the room the entire time?

"Would you like anything else to eat or drink? More brandy?" Lord Barnes asked, deadpan.

"I would. However, I'm cutting back on the amount of poison I consume in one sitting."

A low rumble of laughter came from deep in his chest. "As long as you're sure."

"Quite sure." I lifted my chin and allowed myself to smile back at him. I'd eaten so much the bones of my corset were pressing into my ribs, making it hard to breathe. My head continued to ache. I grazed the bump with my fingertips. Yes, it was still the size of an egg.

"I'll be forthright, Miss Cooper. I thought you were older."

I pressed into the palm of my hand with my nails. Correspondence regarding my age and experience had been misleading. I'd done it purposely, hoping he would assume I was older, given my description of myself as a spinster. "Are you disappointed?" My mouth dried. I unhooked my hands to sip from the water glass Jasper had left for me.

"Not at all. However, it produces a problem."

I pressed my nails harder into my hand, praying that he

would not send me back. Going home now would be the end of every hope I had for the future.

Lord Barnes tugged on his ear. "How can I put this delicately?"

I waited, heart pounding.

"I have a predicament." He cleared his throat. "You see, there are men here who are coarse—uncouth and uneducated and angry that their hopes for gold or silver are squelched when they arrive to find the mountains and rivers stripped of their former bounty. There aren't many women. If you were an ancient schoolmistress, I wouldn't worry." He rose from the chair and crossed the room to a table with various decanters of alcohol and poured himself another drink.

"Worry?" I squeaked the word out of my dry mouth. What did he mean?

"Yes, Miss Cooper." He sat across from me once more. "I'm afraid that a lovely young lady will not be safe at the boarding-house. In good conscience, I cannot allow you to live there."

I swallowed tears. If he made me go home, I would die. Yes, die. How could I fail so miserably already? I cursed myself. I should have told him the truth about my age during our corre-spondence. "I'm tougher than I look, Lord Barnes." My voice wavered, defying my argument.

"Miss Cooper, I'm sure your moral toughness is unparalleled. Your grit has been demonstrated by making the journey alone without funds to eat properly. However, given your...your appear-ance...it's simply not possible for you to live at the boarding-house. We have one woman to eighty men. I wouldn't sleep at night."

I reached for my water glass but instead picked up the one with brandy in it and took a large swallow before I realized, which caused another terrible coughing fit. By the end of almost hacking up a lung, I wished the floor would simply open up and consume me. So much for the lion or the plucky heroine. They'd both died a quick death. My vision blurred with tears from the fit and the panic that surged through me. "Please, don't send me back. I need this job desperately."

He put up his hands, obviously alarmed by my tears. "No, no. I'm not suggesting that at all, Miss Cooper. I was honest with you in my letters. I've been trying to get a teacher out here for years."

"I'm here. I don't want to go home."

"Yes, we're in agreement. I don't want you to go home, either. Thus, you will live here with me and my family. This way I can rest easy that you're safe and well taken care of."

"Stay here?" I couldn't possibly. A family lived here. I didn't belong in this posh mansion with an English lord and his beautiful children. "I'm not someone who should live in a house like this."

"Why would you say that?" The laughter had left his eyes. He stared at me with what appeared to be genuine curiosity.

"I'm... Well, look at my shoes." Like an utter oaf, I lifted one foot from under the table. "Two weeks ago, I was scrubbing floors to keep my family from starvation."

His mouth opened, then shut, then opened again. "Miss Cooper, the state of your shoes has nothing to do with your merit. You've come all this way, exposed yourself to danger and hunger, which is all I need to know about your character. This house is big enough for all of us. Please, this is the only solution."

My heart beat so fast I was afraid it might explode. He wasn't sending me away. He wanted to keep me safe. Lord Barnes was a gentleman with a warm heart. I gushed, the words tumbling out of my mouth. "If you want me here, then I'll stay. I'm sorry I didn't tell you about my age. I was afraid you'd discard me because of my lack of experience. I left out a few details, which was wrong of me. It's that I'm desperate. My mother's sick, and my sister's only sixteen. They need my salary."

"Consider it no more."

I breathed for the first time in more than a minute. "I promise I won't be a disappointment."

"I've complete confidence in you."

I murmured another thank-you and studied my hands as fatigue settled on me as heavy as the falling snow outside the window.

"May I ask what's wrong with your mother?"

"It's something with her lungs. The city air makes it hard for her to breathe." I stopped talking, afraid I would burst into tears if I said much more.

He was quiet for a moment before he said, "It's all right to miss them, Miss Cooper. I hope, in time, your sadness will lessen. We'll keep you busy enough that perhaps you'll be distracted."

"So far, it's proven to be an adventure." I let my gaze stray to his face. "I've already been thrown from a sleigh, awakened on a stranger's sofa with the eyes of five little angels staring at me." I found myself smiling at the memory. "Not to mention the kind offer to let me stay at your magnificent house."

He looked away as a smile crinkled his face. "I have one more thing to discuss with you."

"Yes?"

"In our correspondence, I wasn't completely forthright, either. The job I'm asking of you is not as simple as teaching children. Not in the conventional sense, anyway. We have a great deal of men here who have come from other places and cannot read or speak English. I'd like you to teach them as well."

"Adult men?"

"I understand it's a bit unusual." He swirled whiskey around his glass without looking at me. "I'll pay you double if you conduct night school twice a week."

"Double?" Double pay would mean I could save as much as I sent home. I could reunite with my sister and mother sooner.

"You'll be safe," he said. "I'll make sure you have a male escort during the lessons to and from the house."

"Why do you care so much?" I asked.

His eyes narrowed as he tapped one finger against the arm of his chair. "The men have come here for a chance to better their lives. When they're cheated and stolen from because of their ignorance, I'm angered. Education provides them a weapon."

I clasped my hands together under the table. "You and I share a common passion, Lord Barnes." I looked at the book-shelf instead of him so that I could speak actual words. "The power and importance of literacy—of books. For anyone to have much of a chance for improving their circumstances, reading is essential. I've been poor all my life. Without education, I would not be here right now speaking with you of such lofty notions. It's not only that there are few choices of occupations for a woman that I chose teaching. I'm not likely to ever be important or rich or powerful, but to have taught one human to read, I will go to God in peace."

"You're right, Miss Cooper," he said, low and throaty. "We share a common passion."

My stomach fluttered.

"You're an unusual man." A rich white man who cared about the plight of the less fortunate was most unusual. At least as far as my world was concerned. No one had cared about my family. It was up to me to save us.

"I'm going to take unusual to mean uniquely wonderful." The corners of his mouth lifted into a gentle smile.

"I think that's a proper assessment."

"Then you'll do it? You'll teach the men?"

"Under one condition." I smiled back at him. "I'd like women to be welcomed as well."

"Without question," he said as if it were nothing. "You must be exhausted. We'll work out the rest of the details tomorrow."

We said our good nights, and I followed Jasper up the gleaming mahogany stairs to the third floor. At the end of the dark hallway, he opened the door to a bedroom. I walked past him into a room with a large poster bed, dresser, and secretary desk. A cozy fire roared in the stone hearth. A girl dressed in a black smock with a white apron was finishing up making the bed.

"This is Merry," Jasper said. "Anything you need, simply ask."

I opened my mouth to let him know a maid was unnecessary but thought better of it. Discouraging what was obviously a household tradition would be rude. I'd talk with Lord Barnes in the morning and make sure he knew a maid was not necessary.

The air seemed lighter the moment Jasper left the room. He made me nervous with his piercing gaze and all that British formality. My suitcase had been opened and all of my items hung in a wardrobe. A washcloth and towel were waiting on the dresser. My flannel nightgown was strewn over the bed, like a friend waiting for a midnight chat.

"Miss, may I help you undress?" Merry wore her butter-scotch-hued hair in a braid twisted around the top of her head. Shy hazel eyes peered at me from an oval face.

"No, thank you," I said, smiling in what I hoped conveyed a relationship of equality between us. "I've been undressing myself since I was three."

Merry's mouth twitched, but she didn't smile. "I've drawn you a bath." She pointed toward a closed door. "The bathroom is between this room and the nursery. It's the same bath the children use, but they're all fast asleep by now, so take your time."

"A warm bath?"

"We have hot water in this house," she said.

"Have I come to heaven?"

This time she smiled. "Lord Barnes had this house built with only the finest things. You'll be happy here, I hope."

"I shall be." Even if I was homesick for my mother and sister. A bath made up for a lot. "The train ride was horrific. I haven't had a proper scrubbing since I left home."

"I came from Chicago two years ago," she said. "On the train from Denver, I thought the whole thing was going to fall off those rickety tracks and I'd be killed and my mother would never know what happened to me."

I laughed. "I thought the same thing."

We shared a smile before she bustled over to the fire and adjusted the grate. "I've just put a few logs on the fire, so it should keep you warm until you fall asleep. There's a feather comforter on the bed. It'll keep the heat in."

The logs flamed high from behind the iron grate. Suddenly, I was so tired I could scarcely keep my eyes open. I doubted I'd be awake long enough to see the fire die. "I'm not sure I wouldn't sleep like the dead out there in the snow."

A look of alarm crossed over her features so quickly I wasn't sure I'd truly seen it. "Is there anything else I can do before I go?"

"No, thank you."

Merry gave a little curtsy and left the room.

The moment she was gone, I wished she'd return.

A lantern on the bedside table and the fire shed a dim light. Still, the corners of the room were dark, and I was in an unfamiliar place all alone. I'd never slept in a house where my sister or mother was not near. I sat on the edge of the bed and took a deep breath into my aching chest. Homesickness really did make one feel ill. It was a terrible emptiness that couldn't be filled with anything or anyone but the people I loved. What were my sister and mother doing now? Had they already gone to bed? Had the bitter Boston weather crept into Mother's bones and made her tired body hurt in addition to her breathing problems? Was Annabelle keeping up with her schoolwork without me there to nudge her in the right direction?

I willed myself over to the dresser and looked into the mirror. There were no ghosts here. Nothing could harm me. I stared at myself. My hair was askew and the smudges under my eyes were dark as coal. What Lord Barnes had thought of me, I could only guess.

My hat. I'd forgotten my hat in the sleigh. It would most likely be ruined, and what would I wear into town and to work?

I put that thought aside to figure out tomorrow. There was a bath waiting. I opened the door with trepidation, half expecting one of the children to be in there despite Merry's assurances. To my relief, the room was empty, and a deep, claw-foot tub held more steaming water than I'd ever seen in my life. I undressed, peeling my dress off my tired body and then loosening my corset and tossing it onto a shelf. The bathroom was mostly white, with round tiles on the floor. I looked at my bare torso in the mirror above the sink. If anything, I was skinnier than before I left. My collarbones stuck out, and my face was more skin on bone than flesh. Lizzie was right. I needed fattening up. I had a feeling she was the one to do it.

I lowered into the tub and let out a little sigh of pleasure. The temperature was just right. On a small table next to the tub, bottles of various soaps were lined up in a row. With a washing cloth Merry had left and a brown slab of soap, I lathered up my skin.

When my skin had pinkened from scrubbing, I let my hair down from its stack. The golden strands reached the middle of my back and tickled my sensitive skin. With my fingertips, I touched the bump on my head. The egg had not gone down in size but hadn't grown, either. I used the liquid soap from a glass bottle labeled "shampoo" that smelled of lavender and washed my hair and scalp, then rinsed in the water.

Only exhaustion and yearning for a bed kept me from staying longer in the bath. After I lifted the plug to let the water run out, I used a towel to dry myself as best I could. Then I sprinted back into the bedroom, locking the bathroom door behind me. Shivering, I slipped my flannel nightgown over my head and pulled on the wool socks my sister had knitted as a gift before I left home.

Merry had set my brush on the dresser. I combed my hair, gently at first to untangle the inevitable knots and avoiding the bump. While I did my one hundred strokes, I blinked at myself in the mirror. I was no worse for wear, really. A little old bump on the head wouldn't keep me down for long. My father always said I was born tough. Small but mighty.

Bluster aside, I didn't feel particularly mighty just then. In fact, the opposite might be a better description.

The fire was dying down. A chill as sharp as a knife sliced through me. Clamping my teeth shut to keep them from chattering, I turned slowly around the room. Besides the bed, dresser, and wardrobe, there was also a small desk between two windows. The two windows reflected the firelight, giving no hint of the dark night. Was it still snowing? I grabbed the lantern and crept to the window. Holding the light near the glass, I watched the flakes of snow tumble from the sky. The vastness of this strange place might swallow me whole.

I tiptoed across the hardwood floor to the edge of the rug, then, careful not to trip, set the lantern on the bedside table. Throwing back the thick down comforter, I inspected the sheets. There were no spiders. For some reason, I thought Colorado might have a lot of spiders. Didn't a lot of trees mean a lot of spiders? I'd ask Merry about that in the morning.

I blew out the lantern and hurled myself into bed. The sheets were cold on my bare calves. I rolled onto my side and brought my knees up to my chest. With the comforter tucked under my chin, I stared into the dying embers.

Without the soothing sounds of my sister's breathing next to me, the darkness crept closer. We'd slept together in our small bed in the closet of a room, and I missed her warmth. I missed her. Annabelle with her flaming red hair and petulant mouth and dancing eyes. My sister could make me laugh harder than anyone in the world. I closed my eyes and said a silent prayer for strength.

Alexander

fter Miss Cooper left for bed, I remained in the library, strangely comforted by the movements of my new houseguest in the room above me. It would be a lie to say the unexpected visitor had not lifted my spirits. Since my wife's death, life had been easier for me and the children. The days and months were predictable without the ups and downs of Ida's mental illness.

In the three years since her death, I hadn't contemplated having a woman in my life ever again. For some, perhaps, one terrible marriage was enough. The nightmare of living with Ida in the last five years of our marriage had made me cautious. Women were not always what they appeared to be. There was darkness hidden in some. Darkness that no amount of love could squelch. I'd tried.

Lately, though, I'd thought more and more about finding someone with whom to grow old and gray. However, the idea of a woman was a concept not born from reality. No one had piqued my interest. Alas, there were no women to choose from here in Emerson Pass. Most single women were the kind who charged for their attention and probably carried various diseases. Not exactly the sort I'd bring home to my children. Some men paid for brides to make the journey west, promising marriage in exchange for a warm home and enough to eat. These women were desperate, having lost husbands or fathers who could support them. Much like Miss Cooper, I supposed. Hiring a teacher, however, was different from ordering a bride. How could a man be sure of what he was getting, having corresponded only through letters? For that matter, I'd thought Miss Cooper was an old maid. When she appeared, young and beautiful, I was quite taken aback.

Was I mistaken that there was a spark between us? Or was I simply a lonely man taken in by her beauty? Anyway, she probably would think me too old for her and that I had way too many children.

"May I have a word with you?" Jasper asked from the doorway. I hadn't heard him enter the room, so absorbed with thoughts of Miss Cooper.

"Yes, yes. Have a seat. Pour yourself a drink."

"No, thank you, lord."

For fifteen years, Jasper had been a steady force in my life and home. Through all the heartbreak with Ida, he'd never faltered or wavered in his devotion to me or the children. That said, he would never consider loosening his grasp on the ways of our old world. A world in which a butler would never have a drink with his employer.

When I'd given up everything to my brother and we'd come to America, Jasper had refused to call me anything other than Lord. He'd called me that since we were small. I figured it didn't matter much. In America, no one cared that I would not be called that if we were still at home. Keeping with some of our old traditions gave Jasper a sense of security.

Lately, though, Jasper changed. Subtly, of course. His movements seemed heavier, more labored. It was as if something had snatched the joy from him, leaving him flat and stiff. Something troubled him. I was certain of that. The reasons for his sadness, I couldn't fathom.

"Jasper, are you feeling well?"

"Yes, thank you."

I searched his placid, unreadable features for hints. "Has something happened?"

"Yes, sir. It appears that Nanny Foster has given her notice."

"Notice?"

"She's going back home to live with her sister. Something about frigid winters, spoiled children, and tea."

"Tea?"

"I'm sorry, lord. She didn't elaborate." He cleared his throat. "She's leaving in the morning."

"But she's only been here six months." I said this knowing Jasper was quite aware of how long this latest nanny had been employed. We should have known better than to hire her in the summer when the skies were a brilliant blue and birds sang from trees and everything smelled of pine needles and wildflowers.

"I'll contact the agency back east to see if we can find someone suitable," Jasper said.

"Yes. I suppose that's our only option." I rubbed my forehead, hoping this wasn't a foreshadowing of what would happen with Miss Cooper. Would she be able to withstand the winter and such a difficult assignment? Would she miss city life in Boston? I had already seen the sadness on her face when she talked of her family.

"Lizzie and Merry have both offered to help with the children," Jasper said. "But with a new houseguest, they'll be stretched a little thin."

"It's kind of them, but I agree. Are you sure there's no one in town who would be qualified?"

"Absolutely not."

I smiled at his horrified expression. Jasper was alternately appalled and fascinated by the lives of the women of ill repute and the rough men who closed down the saloon every night. He wanted me to round them all up and send them away. I'd tried many times to explain to Jasper that I was not allowed to dictate the lives of others, regardless of how much money I had.

"Jasper, do you think the children are spoiled? Is this the problem with the nannies?"

Jasper's brows lifted. "Absolutely not. They're precious children. Nanny Foster doesn't seem to understand that children have a need for exercise and games, not just sitting still for hours looking pretty."

"All right then." Jasper's quick defense and loyalty to my children never ceased to both amaze and warm me. "I worry. Since Ida..." I trailed off, unable to explain and knowing Jasper understood anyway.

"The children will be fine," Jasper said. "They'll be going to school now that Miss Cooper's come. All but Fiona, who can keep Lizzie company in the kitchen."

"Speaking of Miss Cooper. She's agreed to teaching a night school several evenings a week."

Jasper frowned. "May I speak frankly, sir?"

"Of course."

Jasper coughed before speaking. "Given her appearance, I'm worried about this idea. Will she be safe?"

"I share your concern. One of us or Harley will have to accompany her."

He nodded, obviously satisfied by my answer. "Will you need anything else, sir? I've prepared your room."

"No, thank you. That'll be all for the night."

"Good night, my lord."

It was nearly nine. Time for my nightly habit of checking on my offspring. I'm not sure what it was, but I liked to see them snuggled into their beds. I took a lantern and walked up the stairs. As was my routine, I checked on the girls first, setting the lantern on the table by the door so I could get a good look at them. They slept in twin beds lined up in a row. Cymbeline slept on her stomach with her arms flung out to the sides. She'd managed to kick off her quilt. I tucked that around her as best I could without waking her. If she woke, it might be hours before she fell back to sleep. My tempestuous, sassy Cymbeline, as turbulent and untamed as the mountains that rose above us. She was as tough as any boy and her competitiveness unparalleled, other than in her brother Flynn. They could make a game out of any situation and then try as hard as they could to win. Like Flynn, she seemed made of this place.

Fiona, with her dark lashes splayed against her full cheeks, slept on her back with her arms around Teddy. My baby. The only child of mine who had not known her mother. Ironically, given what had almost happened, she was the only one undamaged by Ida simply because she never knew her.

I kissed Fiona's forehead and stayed for a moment, begging my memory to remember her exactly this way. What I knew about fatherhood could be boiled down to two things. My heart was forever changed the moment I first held baby Josephine in my arms, and their childhoods went way too fast. The passage of time for a bachelor sifted through fingers like sand. Shoes and clothes outgrown, fat baby cheeks that turned into cheekbones, first words that became sentences and then paragraphs, made the constant movement of time impossible to ignore.

Next, I knelt by Josephine's bed. She was asleep with a book open on her chest. I took it from her, ever so gently, but my eldest had a sixth sense when anyone tried to pry her away from a book. Her eyes fluttered open. "Hi, Papa."

"Hello there. I'm sorry to wake you," I whispered, conscious of the other two.

"It's all right." Her green eyes stared at me with her usual intensity. "Has Miss Cooper gone?"

"No, I've invited her to stay. I didn't think the boardinghouse was the best place for her. She's in the guest room on the other side of the bathroom."

"Will she live here all the time?" Josephine asked.

"For the winter, most likely," I said. "Until she can find a suitable place. A young lady isn't safe on her own."

"She's pretty, isn't she, Papa?"

"I hadn't noticed, really."

She looked up at me with widened eyes and a hint of a smile. "It seemed you did—the way you couldn't stop looking at her."

My daughter had sensed my attraction to Miss Cooper. Well, I've never been accused of being a subtle man. "I wasn't staring at her, you little goose." I tweaked her nose, knowing full well she was onto me.

"It would be all right if you liked her," Josephine said. "We'd like to have a mother."

"You would?" This struck me in the middle of my throat, as if someone had punched me. They'd never once said anything about a new mother.

She nodded. "We all discussed it. I don't really need one, but the others do."

I smiled despite the pang in my chest. My sweet Josephine needed a mother most of all the children. I'd spent the last several years watching her try to step in as a mother to the little ones when she should have been enjoying her own childhood.

"Is it true that Nanny Foster is leaving?" Josephine asked.

"You know about that?" Surprised, I inched backward to get a better look at her.

"I heard her talking to Jasper. She was very rude to him, and she said horrible things about Cymbeline and Flynn. She called them wild animals."

"That was very rude," I said. Damn that woman. Jasper's assessment was correct. She had no idea of how to look after children. Yes, they were untamed, but only because they'd grown out of the earth. The forests and meadows had mothered them, taught them their ways. Fresh air and exercise had made them robust and strong.

"We all hated her anyway," Josephine said.

"Darling, that's not nice to say." I felt something akin to hatred toward Nanny Foster, too, but kept that to myself.

"Sorry, Papa." Josephine pressed her lips together as if it were a great sacrifice to hold her tongue.

"Good night, my love. No more reading."

"Yes, Papa."

I kissed her on the forehead and unfolded my long legs to stand. At the doorway, I picked up the lantern to take one more look. Josephine had curled onto her side and closed her eyes. She looked young and vulnerable there in the flickering light, and I wished for the millionth time that she had less of a burden.

The boys' room was across the hallway. They slept in twin beds pushed just inches apart, preferring to mimic what it must have been like in the womb. Each morning, Nanny moved the beds farther apart. Somehow, they were back together by the time the boys fell asleep. Tonight, their hands touched. I had no idea if they started this way or if they naturally gravitated to each other in sleep. They were quite different in temperament and interests, yet their bond was more profound than any discrepancies of personality. This was another understanding that had come from fatherhood. Love was both immense and simple, mysterious yet clear.

I pulled the covers up from where they had fallen to the twins' mid-chest, then kissed them both on the forehead and crept silently from the room.

I passed by Miss Cooper's room. The space between the door and floor was dark. Hopefully she was warm and able to rest. I hesitated for a brief time, fighting the urge to stand guard at her door. Miss Cooper didn't need my protection here in my home, yet I felt responsible for her.

In my room, I undressed and put on my wool pajamas. The nights this time of year were frigid. Without my wife to warm my bed, I often woke cold, having thrashed about and knocked off my quilt.

I blew out the lantern and lay on my back. The fire shed some light into the room, enough that I could make out objects. So many nights I lay awake, wishing for sleep that never came and watching the fire die down slowly until it was nothing but red embers.

Tonight, I could sense the presence of another person in my home. It sounds odd, but I could almost hear Miss Cooper's breathing. I turned on my side and fluffed my pillow under my cheek. Never mind that, I told myself. Miss Cooper was here to teach, not fall in love with me. I was too old for her. She would want a young man. One without five children. Surely, she'd want her own children—not all the work of someone else's without the love. Even if I were younger and handsome, the burden of five children wouldn't be appealing to a woman like Miss Cooper. The sooner I got that through my head, the better.

I'D JUST DRIFTED TO SLEEP WHEN A TAP ON THE DOOR followed by Jasper's voice brought me fully awake.

"My lord, I need you downstairs."

Alarmed by the high-pitched, panicked tone of his voice, I leapt from bed and grabbed my robe from the end of the bed.

"What is it?" I whispered to Jasper as we sprinted down the hallway.

"It's Mrs. Cole. Something's happened."

We reached the stairway. Rachel Cole, her dress covered in blood, stood inside my foyer. Her brown skin, which normally glowed from health, appeared sallow. She had her arms wrapped around her slim waist and was hunched over as if in pain. This was not the straight-backed, unflappable woman married to my neighbor and friend Samuel.

I rushed down the stairs. "Are you hurt?" I asked, fearing the worst. In the light I could now see that the entire front of her dress was covered with blood.

"It's Samuel. He's dead," she said. "Someone shot him."

A chill started from the pit of my stomach and spread

throughout my body. Gunshots close to their place had startled the horses.

Rachel leaned against Jasper as if her legs wouldn't hold her. "I tried to save him but there was just so much blood."

"How?" I asked. "Who?"

"I don't know. He'd gone outside to bring in more firewood. I heard two shots near the house. I thought, no, it can't be anything to do with us." She choked as tears streamed from her eyes. "But it was. Someone shot him dead."

"Come sit." I was numb and operating outside of my body, as if I were dreaming the scene instead of living it. Samuel Cole, larger than life, broad-chested and built like a lumberjack. He relied on no one but his own strength and intellect, hunting and trapping most of their food even though he was a wealthy man. I'd once seen him fell a twelve-inch trunk of a pine with three swings of his ax. It was impossible to imagine him as anything but fully, loudly alive.

Jasper helped Rachel into the library and eased her into the chair closest to the fire. I added logs to the dying embers as he poured her a tumbler of whiskey and set it in her hands. "I went out to the woodshed. He was sprawled on the snow. Covered in blood. His chest ripped open."

Eight years ago, he'd gone to Chicago to conduct some business. His father had been one of the first men to find gold in these mountains. Gold had made him a rich man. Clever investments had made him richer. As the only heir, when his father died, everything went to Samuel. Thus, once or twice a year, he took a trip to the city to conduct business, returning months later. This time, he brought a woman with him. Rachel.

I couldn't help but wonder if his choice of a wife had gotten him killed.

I remembered the summer day I first learned of Rachel as if it were yesterday. I'd been outside with the twins and Josephine, watching them run in our meadow of wildflowers, when I spotted Samuel traipsing across the meadow. He'd been in

Chicago for a few months. I knew he'd have good stories of his antics: drunken brawls, women of the night, and various other scrapes. The fact that I'd never participate in such activities did not diminish my enjoyment of his tales of debauchery.

Thus, I was not prepared for what he said next.

"I've brought a wife home with me," he said.

"What's this? I thought you were a sworn bachelor."

"I saw her, and I knew." He grinned. "I'm a married man."

"I thought a rake like you would never succumb to a domestic life. Who will I live vicariously through now?"

He laughed and tugged at his long beard. "It's a damn shame, but love sure smacked me upside the head."

"You'll have to bring her by," I said. "Ida's not well right now, but hopefully soon she'll feel up to visitors."

"Sorry to hear," he said.

He knew nothing of Ida's real problems. No one outside of my household knew of the weeks she could not get out of bed or the cycle of mania where she would be up for night after night. Samuel thought she was merely sickly.

"There's something you should know about Rachel." He looked up at the sky, hesitating before he spoke. "Rachel's the granddaughter of slaves."

I stared at him as the significance of what he said made its way into my mind. *The granddaughter of slaves.* My heart thudded between my ears. He'd brought home a black woman.

"We can't marry under the law. But I sure as hell will do what I want in my own home and on my own property. My father left me this land so I could live free, and you can bet your ass that's what I'm going to do."

I took my hat off and slicked back my hair, buying time to formulate a response. There are few moments in life that are as perilous as the one I found myself in just then. My words would shape our relationship for years to come.

"Barnes, what say you?" he asked, softly.

I'd never seen him vulnerable before, and it scared the bloody hell out of me. "You're my friend. Nothing will ever change that. And you know I could care less about the color of anyone's skin. I'm not sure about the rest of the town. Am I afraid for you? A little, yes."

He shoved me in the shoulder. "Nah. Nothing to be afraid of. You know folks are scared of me. The wild mountain man and all that. Most people aren't even tough enough to get here, let alone mess with me. No one can hurt us here in Emerson Pass."

I'd last seen him a few weeks ago when he'd shown up unexpectedly at my door. Over a whiskey, he asked for a favor so unusual it left me speechless. "I need you to agree to handle the finances for Rachel if something should happen to me."

Rachel wouldn't have the right to own property. Instead, he would have to leave all assets and money to me. "I trust you to keep it safe for her to use as she wants," he'd said. "She knows everything about our finances. You'll own it all in name only." I'd agreed, somewhat reluctantly. It was a big responsibility. However, no one had ever seemed less likely to die than Samuel Cole.

"You're too much of a scalawag to die," I said.

Had he sensed his own death? I wished I'd asked him.

And now, here I was, standing before his wife with his blood all over her. My friend gone. Someone from within this community I was so proud of had killed. Was it because of Rachel? Or was it something else? There had been hints of trouble over the years, but we'd always been able to quash it. Samuel, with his frightening presence, had only to look crossways at someone and they backed down. But this was a sneak attack after dark. Someone had lain in wait for him.

"I dragged him into the barn," Rachel said. "I didn't want the children to see him."

The children. Oh God, the children. Two little sons and a daughter. All under eight.

"Are they at home?" I asked.

"Yes. With Susan." Susan was their longtime housekeeper.

She'd been with the Cole family for forty years. "They don't know yet." Rachel folded in half, weeping over the whiskey glass.

Jasper and I exchanged glances. "Get Sheriff Lancaster out of bed," I said to Jasper. "Bring him out to the house."

"The sheriff?" Fear replaced grief in Rachel's eyes. "Is that necessary?"

"Your husband's been murdered," I said. "The sheriff needs to know so he can find out who did this."

"We have to bury him." Rachel's tears had subsided, and now she sounded numb. "He wanted to be next to his parents."

I knew the spot. It was a small family burial ground with two white crosses. Now there would be three.

"A hole will have to be dug, and the ground's covered with snow." Rachel stared blankly at the wall. "I have to tell the children, but I don't want them to see his body. Not the way he looks. We have to bury him before morning."

"We'll find a way," I said. "We have to."

Quinn

My first morning in Colorado, I woke to the sound of knocking. Bleary-eyed, I sat up, unsure for a moment where I was. Ah yes. I'd arrived in Colorado. I was now sleeping in this beautiful house in my own room in this tall, soft bed. In the light of day, I could see more clearly the gleaming floorboards and braided green-and-red rug. The furniture was a rich mahogany, thick and sturdy. Snow had accumulated outside the windows like a white frame to the world.

"Miss, are you awake?" Merry's voice came through from the other side of the door.

"Yes, come in," I said as I straightened the covers around my legs.

She inched inside, seeming apologetic for her presence. "I've come to build your fire."

"Thank you. That's so kind of you." At home, I was the first up and always built the fire.

Merry crossed over to the fireplace and quickly started a fire from a few pieces of kindling. When that was going, she tossed logs from the bin into the flames.

"Are you feeling well?" Merry asked. "How is your head?"

I felt my head. The bump had reduced considerably. "I'm completely recovered. Nothing to worry over."

"Breakfast is downstairs in the dining room," Merry said. "Lord Barnes and the children always eat at eight. He asked that you join them."

"Thank you, Merry." That's right. It was Sunday. All days had merged together during my long trip.

"My pleasure, miss." She gestured toward the wardrobe. "May I take your dirty underclothes to wash?"

Merry was washing my clothes? At home, my sister and I did all the wash on Saturday, using two tubs of water that took hours to heat on the stove, and then strung everything across the front room to dry.

I went to the wardrobe and picked out my underclothes. Ashamed, I handed them to her. I'd worn the same ones for days. They probably smelled horrific. Merry seemed undaunted. "What about the dress?" she asked.

"It's exceedingly dirty," I said, pulling my plain gingham dress from the wardrobe where I'd hung it the night before. Dirt and grime had soaked into the bottom, despite the ankle-length hem.

"I'll take care of it, Miss Cooper." She smiled, seemingly pleased.

After she left, I dressed by the fire in my Sunday best. My sister had sewn a dress in a light blue wool serge with a gray trim from a pattern she'd borrowed from a neighbor. Between that and my teacher uniform, we'd used the last of the money I'd set aside for my wardrobe. There had been none left for a new coat, but the dress was beautifully sewn. What I would do when the weather warmed, I was uncertain. I'd decide when the time came.

I fixed my hair, enjoying how clean and shiny it felt as I wrapped it into a bun at the base of my neck. What a luxury to have fresh hair. I hadn't felt as rested or good since the day before I left home. I still had no idea what I was going to do about a hat. Had Harley been able to rescue it from the accident?

By this time, the clock said it was five minutes to eight. I examined myself in the mirror, not displeased with my reflection. The smudges beneath my eyes had lightened. My cheeks were pink from the chilly room and my eyes bright.

As I came out of my room, Flynn came barreling out of his. "Last one downstairs is a rotten egg." Theo followed shortly thereafter, holding a book against his chest.

He smiled shyly at me. "Good morning, Miss Cooper. Flynn thinks everything's a race."

"That's quite all right," I said. "Does anyone ever race him?"

"Only Cymbeline," Theo said. "But she never wins. One time she slipped and sprained her ankle."

"Dear me."

"Someday, when I'm a doctor, I'll know how to fix an ankle and the bump on your head."

"You want to be a doctor?" I asked.

"Yes, Miss Cooper. A good doctor that fixes people." A shadow crossed over his face. "Even ones where the sickness is the kind you can't see, like my mother had."

I practically had to put my hands around my own neck to keep from asking a follow-up question to this first hint about the late Lady Barnes.

The girls tumbled from their room, wearing dark blue dresses with white pinafores. Fiona's and Cymbeline's dark curls were pinned back with a white bow. Josephine wore her long blond hair in a braid down her back.

"Hello, Miss Cooper," Cymbeline said, grinning. "Josephine helped us dress because Nanny Foster ran away."

"She did?" I asked Josephine, deferring to the oldest child.

"She's gone back to the east," Josephine said, looking solemn. "She didn't like us."

"We didn't like her," Cymbeline said.

I hid a smile. I hadn't liked her much either.

"Who are you?" Fiona asked, her eyes wide.

"That's our teacher," Josephine said. "Don't you remember her from last night?"

"Oh, yes. The fainting lady," Fiona said. "I forgot."

"Are you going to live here now?" Cymbeline asked.

"For a while anyway," I said. "Is that all right with you?"

Cymbeline shrugged. "I guess so."

Falling into step with Josephine, we followed the little girls down the hallway. "Will you have a new nanny?" I asked.

"We don't need one," Josephine said. "They have me."

"You did a wonderful job dressing them this morning," I said.

"Thank you, Miss Cooper," Josephine said, beaming up at me. "I love church."

"Me too." I held on to the railing as we headed down the stairs to the main floor.

"Come on, Miss Cooper," Cymbeline said. "I'll show you where breakfast is." She held out her hand and I took it.

"I want to show her." Fiona stomped her foot.

I stretched my other hand out to her. "I have two hands."

Fiona lit up, then plopped her warm, chubby hand into mine. "Your hands are cold."

"I'm sorry about that," I said. "Isn't it lucky I have yours to warm me up?"

We entered through double doors to the dining room. Lord Barnes was already there, slumped over a cup of coffee and reading a book, with an untouched plate of eggs and bacon in front of him. He was dressed in an elegant suit, and his hair was damp and slicked back. He looked ready for church. However, there was a quality about him this morning that seemed completely different from the man I'd met the night before. I imagined a cloud hovered over him.

Lord Barnes stood to greet us. His eyes were puffy, and there were several nicks on his chin from shaving. His complexion looked green, like Mr. Jones who lived down the street and often stayed out all night drinking. I'd often seen him stumbling home in the early morning when I was on my way to work at the bakery where I assisted Mrs. Caper with the morning batches of bread.

I caught a whiff of his shaving soap. "Good morning, Miss Cooper. Girls."

"Morning, Papa," the girls said, in perfect harmony.

"Good morning," I said.

"You're all looking lovely." He sat back in his chair, rubbing his temples.

"Papa, what's wrong?" Josephine asked. "Are you ill?"

"No, darling. I had a terrible night's sleep. I'll have to have a nap after church."

I breathed a sigh of relief. If Lord Barnes had proven to be a drunk, I'd have been extremely disappointed to learn that my first impression was wrong.

Fiona and Cymbeline led me over to the head of the table. "This is where you should sit," Cymbeline said to me. The table was set with places for seven, with shining silver utensils and delicate china painted with a pattern of pink roses.

"But first you have to get a plate of food," Josephine said.

The boys were at the buffet with Jasper, who was scooping scrambled eggs onto their plates.

"Have whatever suits you for breakfast," Lord Barnes said.

My stomach rumbled in response. The scent of bacon and coffee had me salivating and light-headed. Taking a cue from the girls, I loaded my plate with eggs, bacon, and slices of toasted bread spread with butter.

Now that I looked more closely at Jasper, he also looked tired and sad. What had happened after I went to bed last night?

The boys had already taken places on either side of their father. A chandelier made of glass hung over a rectangular dining table. Dark walls and almost crude-looking furniture, including a buffet and hutch, seemed rustic and rich all at once. A bank of windows looked out to a world covered in a white blanket. Thin winter sunlight filtered through the glass.

Outside, sparrows leapt between pines and firs with branches laden with snow.

As directed, I sat at one end of the long table. My eyes met Lord Barnes's briefly before I directed my gaze toward the two little girls who were squabbling over who was granted permission to sit next to me.

Lord Barnes returned to his coffee and book. This house did not seem to have rules about children being seen and not heard. Perhaps this was part of Nanny Foster's concern? Myself, I liked to hear children's voices and thoughts, even if this wasn't really the way of most households.

"I'll sit between you." I patted the places on either side of me. "One here. One there. Will that do?" I asked.

They both nodded and climbed onto the chairs. Josephine shot me a conspiratorial look as if to acknowledge how naughty the "children" were. She took the chair next to Cymbeline.

To my alarm, the Barnes children dived into their food. Weren't we going to say grace? And why was Lord Barnes reading at the table? Children being allowed to talk was one thing, but this was quite another.

"Are you not hungry, Miss Cooper?" Josephine's fork was poised midair as she peered at me.

Flynn, with a bite of toast in his mouth, mumbled something I couldn't decipher to Theo. Fiona hummed softly and swung her legs under the table while spreading jam on her toast. Cymbeline pushed her eggs around her plate, presumably to make it look as if she'd eaten.

Lord Barnes looked up from his book. "Miss Cooper? Is something wrong?" He looked so utterly done in and sad I lost my will to educate them on proper breakfast behavior.

"I don't know if I should say," I said.

"No, please. If something's troubling you, just come out with it," Lord Barnes said.

I cleared my throat and used my best schoolteacher voice. "First, one shouldn't read at the table during meals. Secondly, grace should be said before anyone even thinks about picking up a fork. Third, Flynn, we don't talk with our mouths full."

A flicker of guilt mixed with amusement crossed Lord Barnes's face as he closed his book and set it aside. "Anything else, Miss Cooper?"

"Not at the moment," I said, emboldened by the way the children had all paused in their fevered consumption to stare at me.

"You're quite right on all counts," Lord Barnes said. "Would you do the honors, Miss Cooper?"

I nodded. "Put down your forks and bow your heads."

To my surprise, the children did as I asked. There was a great clattering of forks against china before they all bowed their heads obediently.

"Dear Lord, thank you for the bounty we're about to enjoy," I said. "Please watch over us today. Amen."

A chorus of "amen" came from around the table, before the enjoyment of the meal resumed.

I took a bite from my toast and almost fainted at the divine taste of freshly churned butter on warm bread.

Flynn's head tilted to one side. "Miss Cooper, how come people can't talk with their mouths full?"

"Because it's rude," I said. "Bad manners."

"Nanny Foster told us that already," Theo said to his brother.

"I never heard her," Flynn said.

Lord Barnes lifted his gaze toward me. "You're looking well-rested, Miss Cooper."

"Thank you. I am. The bed in my room was the most comfortable I've ever slept on." I had to hold back my praise of the indoor plumbing. Instead, I ate from the creamy eggs on my plate.

"Were you warm enough, Miss Cooper?" Josephine asked, sounding much too grown-up for thirteen.

"Oh yes. The feather comforter kept me cozy," I said. "Merry ran a hot bath for me, which was heavenly." I leaned close to Fiona and whispered, "I was able to wash my hair."

"I like your hair," Fiona whispered back.

"I like *your* hair," I said. There was a spot of red jam in the middle of her chin. I reached over with my napkin to swipe it away. "But we can't have a sticky face now, can we?"

Fiona giggled. "I love jam."

"Jam is one of life's best things." She was so dear. The child had no mother, no woman to love her and nurture her.

Jasper approached with a silver coffeepot in one large hand. "May I offer you coffee, Miss Cooper?"

I almost squealed with delight. "Oh my. I haven't had a decent cup in ages. Yes, please." Jasper poured a steaming cup for me. The rich, toasty aroma filled my nose as I took a happy sip. An appreciative grunt escaped before I could censor myself. "Oh my, that's delicious."

I looked up to see Lord Barnes smiling at me from over his own cup. "I see you enjoy your coffee as much as your food."

Laughing, I set the cup back into its saucer. "This was worth the train ride."

I'd just finished my second piece of bacon when Lizzie came into the room with another tray of toast and set it in the middle of the table. "The boys always want more toast," she said, glancing in my direction. "Hollow leg, these two."

She winked at me, and I smiled back. In the light of day, I could see she was older than I'd first thought. A sparkle in her eyes and the quick way she darted around a room made her seem youthful. I guessed her to be somewhere in her thirties, although her fair skin was virtually unwrinkled and her hair untouched with gray. Faint lines around her eyes hinted of a more mature woman. She wore a plain gray dress with a large white apron over the top. I'd have given a lot to fill out a dress in the way Lizzie did.

"How will we get to church?" I asked. Before I'd agreed to stay at the house, I assumed I'd walk everywhere. Now I wasn't certain, especially given the massive amount of snow on the ground.

"We'll go in the sleigh," Lord Barnes said. "Just as we will tomorrow morning for the first day of school."

"What about me?" Fiona asked. "What will I do when everyone's at school?"

Lord Barnes frowned. "You'll stay with Lizzie."

"I want to go to school." Fiona stuck out her bottom lip. "Everyone has fun without me."

"You're too young, love," Lord Barnes said. "We've been over this."

Tears welled in the child's eyes, and her bottom lip quivered. "I want to go."

"Can she go for me?" Flynn asked.

"And me?" Cymbeline asked.

"She may not," Lord Barnes said. "It's a privilege to go to school. One in which I've invested a lot of money and effort on your behalf. You'll go, and I'll hear no more about it."

I suspected Lord Barnes wasn't often stern with them, because the twins exchanged a nervous glance and Cymbeline busied herself with a piece of toast.

"Eat a bite of eggs," I said to Cymbeline.

Her big eyes widened, then hardened. "I don't like eggs."

"They're good for you," I said. "They help grow your brain and make you strong and fast."

"They do?" Cymbeline asked.

I nodded and motioned toward her untouched piece of bacon. "Bacon too."

"I can't eat that," Cymbeline said, shuddering. "It's from Harry."

"Harry?" I asked.

"Our pig," Josephine said. "Our pig who was *not* a pet."

"He was raised for food," Theo said, speaking for the first time. "But Cym loved him. She loves all animals." His tone was serious, as was the concerned wrinkle of his forehead. "There are two types in this family. Those who like books and those who like animals."

"Papa likes both," Josephine said. "And we don't yet know about Fiona because she's too little."

"I'm big." Fiona scowled as she held up three fingers. "I'm this many."

"You're a very big girl," I said. "And big girls don't make a fuss."

Fiona continued to scowl but consoled herself with another piece of toast and jam.

Cymbeline tapped my forearm. "Do you see this?" With her other hand, she raised her fork to her mouth and took a bite of eggs.

"Good girl," I said. "I can practically see you growing."

Cymbeline grinned and took another bite.

"And you?" I asked Josephine. "Books, I'm guessing."

"That's correct." She lifted her pointy chin and granted me a prim smile. "One can go anywhere in a book."

"In case you want to know, I'm the animal type," Flynn said. "And the type who doesn't want to go to school when there's adventures out there." He pointed toward the window.

"School can be an adventure," I said. "Learning new things brings adventure, anyway. You can't expect to go out into the world without knowing how to read, write, and do arithmetic."

Flynn sighed. "If you say so."

"I like books," Theo said. "Animals do not smell good. I have a sensitive nose."

I laughed. A sensitive nose? Where had he heard that from?

"What about you, Miss Cooper?" Flynn asked.

"I happen to like both," I said.

"Just like Papa," Josephine said. "What a great coincidence."

Alexander

After breakfast, I shooed the children out of the dining room. I needed to talk to Miss Cooper about last night for several reasons, the most important of which was to ask if she remembered seeing anything before or after the gunshots. Harley had not, remembering only the shot and then trying to control the horses. The Higgins brothers had come along minutes after the crash. They'd been at the station to pick up an item sent from Denver. Harley had seen them arrive as he left with Miss Cooper. This kept them from being suspects in the murder of Samuel Cole.

I looked at Miss Cooper from across the table, helpless as to how to start. Weariness washed over me like a series of waves. I wished for my bed. I wished I didn't have to go into town and tell everyone at church that my neighbor was murdered in his own yard. I wished Miss Cooper would remain ignorant of the dark undercurrents of our community.

Just tell her directly, I thought. *She's not a child.* "The gunshots that scared the horses were directed at my friend and neighbor. He was found by his wife minutes later dead near his woodshed. Two bullet wounds through his chest killed him."

Her hand flew to her mouth. "No."

"He left behind a wife and three young children. Someone in this town murdered him."

"But why? Who would do such a thing?" she asked.

"Do you remember seeing anyone during the drive?"

"No, it was dark, and I was sleepy. I didn't wake up until the shots rang out." She hesitated. "They did seem close, though."

"You were near his place. If the weather hadn't been so bad, you would have seen the lights from his house."

"I wish I could help," she said. "When did you find out?"

I told her about Rachel showing up at my door. I left it at that. She didn't need to know how we'd spent the night shoveling away snow and then digging into the cold ground.

"I don't want this to scare you," I said.

"I'm not scared." She blinked several times but squared her shoulders. "I am, however, grateful to be living here at the house. Thank you, again."

"No need, Miss Cooper. It sets my mind at ease to have you with us."

After church, I'd have to go out to see Rachel. For now, I needed to get the children loaded into the sleigh and off to Sunday service.

Quinn

✦❧✦

Merry helped the girls and me get bundled up in coats and scarves and hats. When ready, we went out to the covered awning on the side of the house where a horse-drawn sleigh waited.

Flynn and Cymbeline were already outside, tossing snowballs at each other and making a great deal of noise. Harley, with his left hand in a bandage, stood near a different set of horses from the night before, petting their noses and speaking softly into their ears. Next to him, a little girl in a gray cloak waved to us.

"That's Harley's sister, Poppy," Josephine said.

"They're our friends," Cymbeline said.

"I met Harley last night," I said.

"Merry likes him," Josephine whispered.

"But he doesn't know I'm alive," Merry said under her breath.

Harley held up a hand and reached into the sleigh, then held up my hat. "I've saved it, Miss Cooper."

"Thank goodness," I called out to him. "I was about to make my debut in town hatless."

He sprinted over to me, presenting it like a crown.

I snatched it from him and happily set it upon my head, securing it with the pins.

Harley took off his cap, revealing a head of wavy brown hair. "Little ladies." He bowed to them, causing them to giggle. He straightened and nodded at Merry.

"Hello, Merry."

"Hi, Harley." Merry's cheeks flushed bright pink.

"Miss Cooper. Are you feeling all right?" he asked me. "I feel terrible about what happened."

"It wasn't your fault," I said. Knowing what I did now, I was sure this was true. "Are the horses well?"

"Yes, they were fine," Harley said. "You took the brunt of it—popped out of there like a ball from a cannon."

I laughed. "I should never have fallen asleep."

Poppy had come up behind him, peering around his waist. "This is Poppy," Harley said. "My sister."

"Nice to meet you, Poppy," I said.

She bowed her head. "Nice to meet you."

"How old are you?" I asked.

"Thirteen," Poppy said.

Her answer surprised me. She was small for a girl her age.

"Poppy's my best friend," Josephine said as they clasped hands.

Harley placed his bandaged hand on top of Poppy's knit cap. "We're lucky to have such good friends and employers."

Poppy and Josephine exchanged a smile.

Flynn and Cymbeline ran up, out of breath and glowing from the cold and exercise. Snow dusted their coats and boots. Behind me, the door opened, and Lord Barnes joined us.

"Have you met Oliver and Twist, Miss Cooper?" Lord Barnes asked.

"We're giving Prince and Pauper the day off," Harley said. "Since they had a scare."

Flynn patted Twist on his neck. "He's a good boy, this one."

"Papa named them," Theo said. "After the Dickens character."

"I had a suspicion," I said.

The children clambered into the sleigh. The boys squeezed into the back seat while Harley helped the three girls into the middle. Lord Barnes held out his hand to assist me into the front row, behind the driver's seat. As Harley jumped up, Lord Barnes smoothed a blanket over my lap.

The children were a jolly bunch by the time we set out from the house. Laughter and high-pitched chatter mingled with the jingle of the horses' bells as we glided through the snow. With the sky a bright blue, brilliant against the white backdrop, it was hard to believe that a blizzard had come through hours before. I turned back to take a good look at the house. Made of red brick, with two large pillars in the front, the house was as pretty as any I'd ever seen, even in the most expensive parts of Boston.

"However did you build such a beautiful house in this remote place?" I asked Lord Barnes.

"One brick at a time," he said. "It took me several years. I brought Ida out from New York after that. She didn't want to come out here before it was completed."

Being this close to him gave me a strange sensation—excited and safe at the same time. Drifts of snow had settled in his dark eyebrows, making them appear white. Fortunately, my arms were firmly tucked under the blanket or I might have been tempted to brush them away.

I looked away, toward the white field and red barn. "This is like a painting." I said this as a way to break this magnetic pull between us. Even so, the statement was true. I'd never seen a prettier landscape than the one before me now.

"Do you like it?" he asked.

"Very much. There's something so calming about the snow, don't you think?"

He nodded, but his eyes lost focus, as if he had slipped behind a curtain. "My late wife hated the snow. She never adjusted to our winters."

Oliver and Twist neighed cheerfully as we turned right onto

what appeared to be a road of packed snow, made slick by the passing of other sleighs.

"Ida was from New York," Lord Barnes said. "She couldn't understand my love of this place. The way the air is so crisp and sharp and the sky this remarkable blue, even in the winter."

"It's a remarkable blue," I said.

A second later, I spotted the smoke from several chimneys before I saw town. "Oh, it's lovely," I said, surprised by the quaint brick buildings that lined both sides of a street. Granted, there weren't many, but enough to make up a town.

"What did you expect?" he asked.

"I don't know." This wasn't exactly true. I didn't want to insult him by explaining my perceptions. The town was personal to him. He was invested in Emerson Pass in a way one is when they've helped to make something out of nothing. What I'd imagined was a dirty street and a collection of haphazardly constructed buildings, everything centered around the mining operation.

Beside me, Lord Barnes sighed. "I'll have to see the pastor before service and tell him what's happened to Samuel." The muscles in his face contorted before he hung his head. "I can't believe Samuel's gone."

Tears came to my eyes at the mournful tone of his voice, the heartache of loss in every word. "Oh, Lord Barnes, I'm sorry."

Grief was like this. Out of nowhere, the reality of one's loss crushed and shoved aside all other thoughts. Seeing a grown man, especially one as dignified yet playful as Lord Barnes, crushed by his grief tore at my heart. I wished there were something I could do. Having lost my father, whom I loved so dearly, I knew there was nothing, short of bringing the person back to life. Still, I asked the question. "Is there anything I can do?"

His eyes softened. "You have a kind heart, Miss Cooper— crying for a man you never knew."

"I know *you*," I said. "And it's obvious what a terrible blow this is. That's enough to make me cry."

He looked away. "I have to find out who did this to him."

"Is there a sheriff?" I asked.

"Yes. Joseph Lancaster. He's new. Our governor sent him out here."

"Why is that?" I asked.

"We've had our share of trouble."

I had the distinct feeling there was something Lord Barnes wasn't saying. As much as I wanted to ask, I stayed quiet. If he needed me to know, he would tell me. Otherwise, I would keep my curious nose to myself.

The horses went from a gallop to a walk as we entered town. Emerson Pass was nestled between two mountains that rose majestically toward the cerulean sky. I did a quick assessment and discovered a drugstore, dry goods store, post office, and butcher shop on one side of the street. The other had a saloon, the boardinghouse, and restaurant. They were all built of brick and in the same height and style. Attractive streetlamps were placed in front of each building, making a line of soldiers on each side.

We turned down a side street and there, positioned at a slightly higher elevation than the businesses on the main street, stood a brick schoolhouse. There was a skinny front porch with a bell that hung from the rafters. My chest swelled with pride at the sight of the double doors. "Lord Barnes, it's perfect."

"I think so too."

"Will I get to ring the bell?"

His eyes twinkled at me. "Every morning at nine. After church, we'll stop by and take a look inside. You can see if there's anything I've forgotten."

We continued past the school and stopped in front of a white church with a tall steeple. The walkway had been shoveled, and people were headed inside the red doors. "Did you build this, too?"

"The men who worked for me did, yes. Do you like it?"

"I can't think of a prettier church."

"Thank you. We're proud of it." He lifted the blankets from our laps and offered his hand to help me down from the sleigh. "Would you mind getting the children settled inside while I talk to Pastor Lind?"

"With pleasure."

He tipped his hat. "Thank you, Miss Cooper. You've come just when I needed you."

The children had all jumped down by then. Poppy and Josephine waited by the front steps with Fiona between them. Flynn and Cymbeline were over by a tall snowdrift with their heads together, as if discussing their plan for escape. Only Theo remained near. He offered his arm to me. "I'll walk with you. It's slippery."

I smiled down at him. "Thank you, kind gentleman."

He beamed up at me. "You're welcome, Miss Cooper."

Alexander

I knocked on the door to Pastor Lind's office. "It's Barnes, Pastor Lind. May I have a moment?"

"Come in, come in."

Taking a deep breath, I entered, then closed the door behind me. Lind sat behind his desk. He was a small, round man with thick white hair that sprouted from his head in unruly clumps. He had a handlebar mustache and thick eyebrows and wore a pair of round wire-framed glasses that perched on the end of his nose. The office smelled of coffee from the cup next to a notebook containing his handwritten sermon. He claimed it made him a better orator if he consumed a cup right before services began.

"Lord Barnes, to what do I owe this pleasure?" His hazel eyes gazed at me from over his glasses. I always had the urge to push those flimsy glasses up to where they belonged. They agitated me, perched like that on the bulbous part of his nose.

"I'm afraid I have bad news," I said.

He tutted as he leaned forward over the desk. His thick brows came together to form a long white caterpillar. "What's happened?"

Simon Lind and his wife, Pamela, were in their fifties and had

spent most of their lives building churches in small towns like
Emerson Pass. Lind had wanderlust. Pamela had told me he
could never be happy in one place. Once the church was built
and the flock firmly settled in the pews every Sunday, he grew
restless. When they'd come through here to visit, looking for a
new place to build a church, I'd made him a deal. I'd help them
build a church and rectory and pay him a decent salary even
during years when donations were scarce, but he needed to
commit to staying. His wife, worn out from the years of moving,
had convinced him to take my offer. Five years later, it was as if
they'd always been here. She'd made the rectory across from the
church into a pretty home, with flowers and a vegetable garden
during warm months. Pam Lind had such a green thumb she
kept half the town in tomatoes and beans during July and
August. She'd told me once that her inability to have a child had
fueled her need to grow living things. "Cucumbers and tomatoes
are no substitute for a child, but they can at least feed other
women's sons and daughters," she'd said to me once.

Now I turned my hat around and around in my hands. To say
the words would make them real, and I suddenly wanted to put
that off for as long as possible. "Samuel Cole is dead. Someone
shot him last night."

Lind snatched his glasses from his face and rose to his feet.
"Do we know who?"

"No idea. I can't help but think it has something to do with
Rachel."

Lind walked behind his chair and wrapped his hands around
the back as if he might fall. "Has there been recent trouble?"

"Not that I know of." I told him about my conversation with
Samuel regarding his will. "Maybe he was worried about
someone trying to harm him. Why else would he have come to
me now? He wasn't a man who thought about his mortality."

Lind chuckled. "No, he was more concerned with living than
what came in the hereafter." He quickly sobered. "Poor Rachel.
How is she?"

"Bloody devastated and terrified." I apologized for my rough language, but Lind brushed it aside. A preacher on the frontier couldn't be too particular about his flock's crusty ways.

"I can imagine she would be," Lind said. "If this is about race, then we're going to have to do what we can to protect them."

I leaned against the wall and rubbed my tired eyes. "She and Susan are all alone out there." Other than Susan, Samuel had never trusted anyone enough to hire help. "Rachel will have to pay three men to do the work Samuel did alone." I thumped the back of my head against the wall. "He kept them isolated out there. Samuel didn't want her or the kids to leave their property and go into town. He'd never admit it to me, but he was afraid for them." I looked back at Lind, who watched me with sympathetic eyes. "He should've been more careful. He should have come to me for help."

"A man like Samuel doesn't want his friend harmed because of his own trouble. He most likely was trying to protect you."

I took my handkerchief and pressed it against my stinging eyes. "It's hard to imagine him anywhere but traipsing about the woods."

"I'm sorry," Lind said. "For you and for Rachel and those kids."

"I have to figure a way to protect them."

"Tell me what you need. Pamela and I are here."

I thanked him, even though I knew deep in my bones that trouble waited around every corner for Rachel now. All she had was me to protect her, and I wasn't sure how to do that. No amount of money can fix hatred.

70

Quinn

T he simple church pews and pulpit that hung over it
were made of pale fine-grained wood. Whitewashed
walls with tall paned windows framed the winter scene
outside. The floor was made of wide planks of oak. A spectacular
cross made of a dark wood hung over the front. A faint scent of
wood shavings hung in the air.

"Is the church newly built?" I asked Josephine as we walked
down the aisle toward the front.

"No, Papa had it built for Pastor Lind five years ago," she
said. "But the cross is new. Harley made it from a fallen tree he
found last summer."

The Barnes children and I took over the entire front row of
the left side with a space left for Lord Barnes. I had the two
little girls next to me. Josephine and Poppy were on the other
end with the twins between us. As we waited for service to
begin, Fiona and Cymbeline started poking each other.

"Stop it," Fiona said.

"You stop it," Cymbeline said as she poked her sister on the
shoulder for the third time.

Fiona began to cry. "That hurt."

I lifted Fiona onto my lap. "You'll both keep your hands to yourself from now on or you'll be punished."

Cymbeline crossed her arms over her chest and glowered. Her legs, too short to reach the ground, swung back and forth. A small act of rebellion, I thought. This child was strong-willed and stubborn. I hoped to someday see how she changed the world. Whether for good or evil was still undecided, I thought, smiling to myself.

Fiona was warm and soft and smelled like a sugar cookie. She snuggled against me with her cheek on my shoulder. "Miss Cooper, is this what mamas do?"

"What do you mean?"

"Have laps to sit on."

My eyes stung. I tightened my hold on her. "Yes, this is what mamas do."

"It's nice."

"I agree."

Cymbeline unfolded her arms and jutted out her chin. "I'm not a baby like Fiona. I don't need a lap."

I smiled down at her. "If you ever do, mine is available."

She narrowed her eyes, inspecting me as if I were a liar.

Lord Barnes joined us then, taking the place next to me. "Everything shipshape?" he asked with a pointed glance at Fiona.

"Yes indeed," I said. "Fiona just needed a snuggle."

"Hi, Papa," Fiona said.

"Hello there." He kissed the top of her head, coming so near I breathed in the scent of him, shaving soap and the outdoors. When he drew back, our eyes caught and held for a moment longer than they should. We were in church. I'd known him for less than twenty-four hours. His friend had been murdered. Yet all I could think of was naming the exact color of his green eyes. Emerson Pass and Lord Barnes were going to lead me straight to hell.

Pastor Lind's sermon was blessedly short. Not that I heard most of it, what with the warm child on my lap and her father inches from me smelling delicious and having to give Flynn a stern stare for all his fidgeting. Afterward, we went out to the fresh air, and Lord Barnes introduced me to the Johnsons, who owned the dry goods store. Anna and Sven Johnson had two daughters who would be my students, named Martha and Elsa. Anna Johnson was tall with golden hair and a wide smile. She shook my hand with a firm grip. "We're grateful you've come to the wilderness. You let me know if you need anything at all. I've been here amongst all these men for too long." I suspected she could do a man's work on the farm or field and not break a sweat.

"How long have you been here?" I asked.

"Five years or so," she said. "We came from Minnesota. My girls went to school there. Since then, I've done my best to teach them myself. They're both keen to learn, and Martha would like to be a teacher someday."

Sven had jet-black hair and broad shoulders. He spoke with a Swedish accent and was too shy to meet my eyes.

I was introduced to Pastor Lind and his wife, Pamela, next. Slightly plump and pink-cheeked, Pamela glowed from within.

"Oh, dear me, you're a pretty one," Pamela said. "No wonder Lord Barnes has you staying at the house."

"Thank you," I said, with a self-conscious giggle.

"Come inside for a moment so we can talk." Pamela took my arm and we strolled back into the church. "Simon told me about poor Mr. Cole. I hope you won't be too concerned. This isn't typical."

"It's a terrible thing," I said. "Did he tell you about the gunshots that spooked the horses?"

"He did. How's your head?"

"Much better," I said. "Other than my embarrassment at causing so much trouble, I'm fully recovered."

Pamela led me over to a pew, where we sat. "I can't believe this has happened. We have fights in town from the men who drink too much, but nothing like this."

"Was he a very good friend to Lord Barnes?"

"Samuel was the type who kept to himself, but if he had a friend, it was Alexander." She fiddled with the brooch at her neck. "He was very loyal to Samuel, even when things were heated here in town over Rachel."

"What about Rachel?"

"Oh, you haven't met her?"

I shook my head.

"She's brown-skinned," Pamela said. "And you know how people can make such a fuss."

This truth smacked into me hard. Samuel had been married to a black woman. *Making a fuss* was certainly one way to put it. Mixed marriages were illegal back east. I'd assumed they were here as well. "Were they married?"

"Not legally," she said. "But they lived as if they were."

"Do you think someone would kill him because of that?"

"I hate to think so, but maybe. The situation was tolerated because folks were afraid of Samuel. He was a bit of a legend around here."

My thoughts tripped over themselves as I processed this information. Had Samuel been killed because of his wife? If so, what about her and the children? This town was full of white men. Lord Barnes had indicated many were rough and uncouth. Back home, there were so many prejudices against Jews, Catholics, and anyone with dark skin, even though the North had fought for slaves to be free.

"I'm sorry this happened just as you've come," Pamela said, interrupting my contemplations. "Lord Barnes has been talking about your arrival for weeks now. Our expectations are quite high that you'll elevate our community. However, you're not what we expected. We had you pictured as a little old lady like me."

I flushed, guilty. "That's my fault. I didn't mention my age because I was afraid he would think me too young for such a big responsibility."

She patted my hand. "You'll be fine."

Somehow her words didn't match the worry in her eyes. Was there something more?

"Did Lord Barnes tell you about night school?" I asked.

"He did."

Again I couldn't decipher from her tone if this was a worry to her. "Do you think anyone will come?"

"I'm not certain." Her gaze darted to the cross. "Please, Quinn, be careful. There's darkness in our pretty town. Be diligent."

My stomach fluttered with nerves. "I'll do my best."

"And you come by and see me any time, all right? I always have the kettle on and a jar of cookies."

"Two of my favorite things," I said.

A FEW MINUTES LATER, LORD BARNES AND I WALKED FROM the church lot over to the schoolhouse. Someone had shoveled a walkway between the two, as well as the school's porch. Lord Barnes fetched a ring of keys from his pocket and unlocked the doors, then stood aside for me to enter before him. My breath caught at the sight of the twenty wooden desks arranged in four rows. A shiny blackboard covered most of the front wall. The teacher's desk was plain but sturdy with a hardbacked chair. In one corner, a potbellied stove would warm the room.

I wandered around the room, practically dancing with excitement. "Lord Barnes, it's a dream come true. My very own classroom."

"I'm pleased you're pleased." He smiled as he looked around the room. "Harley will come early in the morning and get the fire going so it'll be warm by the time you arrive."

"I'm grateful." I knew most rural teachers had to do that themselves. I'd assumed it would be my duty.

I took a quick assessment of supplies. A stack of slates and textbooks were stored on a shelf next to the desk.

"The children will have to share books," Lord Barnes said from behind me.

I turned to him. "I'll make do."

Lord Barnes pointed toward a coatrack. "For tomorrow, the students can hang their coats and scarves there when they come in unless it's too cold for the stove to keep up. If the temperatures drop, I'd ask you to grant permission for them to wear their outer layers."

I nodded. This seemed reasonable. "Do I have a roster of children?" I asked as I walked over to the desk.

"No, you'll have to collect their names and ages as they arrive."

"I cannot wait to meet them." Tomorrow would be a day for assessing abilities and combining them into learning groups. I had a feeling there would be an eclectic mix of ages and abilities.

He met my gaze before walking over to the set of windows that looked out to the schoolyard. "I'm afraid your time here is going to test your very soul, as it has mine."

I came to stand beside him. His sadness seemed to emanate from his body. I absorbed it as I might a scent. This man and his family should mean nothing to me, but they lived inside me already.

Lord Barnes put his hands into the pockets of his coat. "Opening a school has been a dream of mine for a long time. Now, however, I wonder if it cost Samuel his life?"

"Why would you say such a thing?" I asked.

"Because I made it clear in town that the Cole children would be attending right along with all of the others."

"I see." Somehow, this had not occurred to me when Pamela Lind and I were speaking. Had Lord Barnes's stance on this been the reason for Samuel's murder? And if so, what did that mean for Rachel and her children? What did that mean for me? "How come you didn't tell me?"

"Frankly, it didn't occur to me."

I sorted through what this meant as we stood there looking out the window. The Barnes children were building snowmen. Three frozen men stood in a row, like guards of the school. Was it a premonition of what was to come?

I couldn't turn away any child, regardless of the color of their skin. Not from my classroom. If I'd been born a different color, I'd still be the same inside. People who didn't understand that baffled me. Growing up poor with uneducated parents had marked me. I knew what it was to be set aside, thrown away, as if my life didn't matter because I was poor.

"You won't turn them away, will you?" he asked.

My eyes stung as I turned to face him. "I can hardly call myself a teacher if I'm unwilling to teach anyone who wants to learn."

"Because you know how it feels to be kept out."

I stared at him, probably looking like a hooked fish with my mouth hanging open and my eyes wild. "How did you know I was thinking just that?"

"Your expressions betray your thoughts," he said. "This face of yours is like reading a book."

"I won't take up poker, then," I said.

He gave me a sad smile. "Do you know what I thought when I first came to America?" He didn't wait for an answer. "I thought here the circumstances of your birth don't matter—everyone had the opportunity to make the life they wanted for themselves. Except it's not true, is it? If you're poor or the wrong skin color, there are no opportunities."

"America's a contradiction of ideals and actual practices," I said.

His face twisted with emotion as he took in a ragged breath.

"I underestimated people's hatred. I'm afraid I've gotten my friend killed over my ideals."

"Then we mustn't let them win by succumbing to their will."

He swept his finger across the windowsill. "Miss Cooper, you're either brave or foolish."

"My father always said God had no use for a coward," I said.

A low chuckle came from his chest as he wiped the corners of his eyes. "Harley and I will keep watch during the day." He gestured toward the main street of town and accidentally brushed my shoulder. "I work in an office just over there."

Even through my coat and dress, my skin tingled from his touch. I had to stay focused on what was important. A man was dead, most likely because of bigotry, and here I was wondering what Lord Barnes's mouth would feel like on mine. I'd only ever been kissed once, nothing more than a chaste brush of lips that had left me unmoved. I strongly suspected I would like Lord Barnes's kiss. He was my employer, I reminded myself. A man of money and prestige. I was a poor schoolteacher, at the mercy of his kindness. *I must remember this and not let my romantic mind wander.*

The children had finished their snowmen and were now giving them faces with pieces of bark and fir branches.

"When I think about Samuel's children, I feel like I can't breathe." Lord Barnes choked on the last part of the sentence and stopped to gather himself. "I promised Samuel I'd make sure they were all right, and I intend to do so."

Involuntarily, I brushed the sleeve of his jacket with the tips of my fingers. "Is it hard to carry the weight of the world, Lord Barnes?"

He tilted his head to look at me. "Yes. But as you say, God has no use for a coward."

I wanted to say, *Let me carry the burden with you.* Instead, I smiled up at him, hoping to convey more courage than I truly possessed. "We're stronger together. Let them bring their hatred. We'll fight it with love."

He nodded as if he agreed, but I could see by the sadness in his eyes that he did not believe. I would have to believe for both of us.

Alexander

When we returned from town, I saddled up Twist and headed out to the Coles' place. The sun glistened on the newly fallen snow as I crossed the meadow toward the thicket of trees that hid his house. Our valley dwelled between the sister mountains, making the ideal spot for a town. There was no better view of the white-shawled mountains than the one from my own meadow. When I reached the end of the flat land, the terrain dipped into a creek bed. Samuel had built a covered bridge over the high, wide creek that divided our properties. Twist trotted right in and through to the other side. About a hundred feet from the bridge, a deep pool provided both a swimming and a fishing spot.

From the time I'd moved here, Samuel and I had come to the creek to talk through troubles or share gardening advice or just be quiet while we fished. He was the better gardener and fisherman and knew this land like the back of his hand. I'd learned much from him.

The first time we'd met, he'd looked me up and down and shaken his head ruefully. "You won't last a winter."

"Watch me," I'd said. By spring, I'd earned his respect and his friendship.

Fighting the weight of my grief, I nudged Twist to continue into the trees. The dense forest made this section of the property dark even in the afternoon sun. In the summer, the shade from the trees served as a respite from the heat. This time of year, under the branches laden with heavy snow, the temperature seemed to drop. Despite my gloves, the tips of my fingers were numb. Twist shook his mane and neighed when we came out of the trees. He knew where we were and that an apple was probably waiting for him in the barn. Samuel had loved his horses and mine.

The house that Samuel's father had built from logs and river rock sat on a flat section of land. A covered porch ran the length of the front of the house. Puffs of smoke rose from the chimney.

I put Twist in the barn with the Coles' horses, Lucy and Bell. They whinnied to Twist as if he were a long-lost friend. Samuel kept a bucket of bruised and fallen apples from his orchard in the shelf near the stalls. Had anyone thought to give one to the horses since yesterday? God, I thought, who is going to take care of these animals and the rest?

His place had been a source of pride with Samuel. No one worked his land but him. Things had changed in the second that bullet entered his chest. His desire for complete independence could not be continued without him. We would have to hire a man. Maybe two. Samuel had done the work of at least that many.

I gave Twist and Bell apples and nuzzled their noses. When I offered one to Lucy, she ducked her head and made a mournful noise. Did she know Samuel was gone? Or was she asking where he was?

I took off my hat and leaned against her strong neck as a wave of grief nearly knocked me to my knees. We stood like that, the magnificent horse and me, as tears from my eyes bled into her mane. She whinnied again and in that high-pitched cry, I heard a message as if she'd spoken words to me. *He needs you to take care of his family.*

"I'll do my best, old girl." I gave her one last stroke and let go. "Thanks for the talk." I put on my hat and walked outside.

The world seemed too still. I had the eerie sensation of isolation, as if I were the last man left in the world. I walked past the woodshed where Samuel's blood stained the snow. Averting my eyes, the images from the night before played through my mind. Samuel with a hole where his chest used to be. Rachel keening over his body. Harley arriving with a coffin he'd made in an hour attached to our sleigh. Jasper leaning against the shovel, panting from the exertion of digging a grave in cold dirt.

Rachel had refused to leave Samuel. While we dug through the snow and then the frozen ground, she'd sat beside him in that cold, dark night. It took us hours to make a shallow grave. We'd lifted Samuel from where he'd fallen and placed him inside wrapped in a quilt his mother had sewn from scraps of his baby clothes. "He'll want it for the journey to his mama," Rachel had said.

I fought against the awful ache in my gut. The living needed me. I had to get on with things. I knocked on the front door and waited. Susan opened it a minute later. Small and quick, Susan had kept the Coles' house since it was built. At sixty, she'd lost a few inches of height, and gray had replaced the brown in her hair. Still, she moved around like a young woman. Today, her eyes were red and puffy.

"Good afternoon, Lord Barnes. Come in." Susan twisted her hands around and around. "She's in his study. She won't eat or sleep."

"Did she tell the children?"

Susan nodded and dabbed at her eyes with a hankie. "Terrible thing. They all just sat there lined up on the bench and didn't make a peep. I'm not sure they understand."

A memory came to me of Josephine at the bottom of the stairs when I'd brought Ida's body in from the snow. She hadn't moved a muscle, her expression stoic. "She's dead then?" Josephine had asked.

I'd nodded and stood there, helpless with my wife's body in my arms until Jasper came inside carrying Theo.

Theo. My little boy who had found his mother frozen to death ten feet from the house.

The living. Take care of the living.

"Can I see her?" I asked Susan.

"She's expecting you." Susan lowered her voice.

I thanked her and went to the study. Wearing black, Rachel was as straight-backed and elegant as always. The woman with the blood-soaked dress was not visible today.

"Alexander, you didn't have to come."

"Nonsense."

She patted a book on the desk. "He left notes about everything in here, along with his instructions for you and me."

"Is there anything I can do?"

"He left instructions for the children to go to school," she said. "Can you believe what a fool he is?"

I sank into the chair opposite the desk. "He told me as much. You don't agree?"

"I did not agree. We fought about it the day before he died."

"Do you think he suspected trouble?" I asked. "Had someone threatened him?"

"I've no idea." She placed her hands on the desk as if she needed an object to ground her to the earth. "We had an agreement from the first. I didn't leave the property. When the kids came, I made the same rule for them. If he hadn't gotten this stupid idea that they should go to school, we would not be here today." Her eyes flashed with anger. "If it weren't that I'm obligated to go through you for what should be rightfully mine, then I'd ask you to leave my house and never come back. I blame you as much as I blame him. You and your righteous indignation."

I flinched, as if her rage were a physical blow. "Rachel, I'm sorry. Samuel wanted them at school. No one could have convinced him otherwise."

"He was the most stubborn man that ever lived. That quality got him killed."

"He was a man of principle. It mattered to him that his children were treated the same as the others. Do you really disagree?"

"I surely do. My children's safety is more important than a damn principle."

"If we don't fight for what's right, who will?"

She made an impatient noise in the back of her throat. "I don't give a damn. This is my house now. My money. My children. I'll do as I please." She stood and smoothed her hands over her skirt. "I'm not sending them to that school to end up the same way as Samuel. People forget what they don't see. I want them to forget we're even out here."

I could hardly argue with her. What other conclusion could she come to? If it were my children in danger, I would do the same. Protect them within the walls of my home. Anyway, she blamed me for Samuel's death, and she was probably right to do so. Advice or interference from me was the last thing she wanted.

"You need to hire someone to take care of the place," I said.

"I'm sending for my brother. He's the only one I trust." She slid an envelope across the desk. "This is a letter for him. Will you mail it for me?"

I agreed with a nod of my head.

"Rachel, I'm sorry."

"It's too late for that. When Wilber arrives, I'll send him over to meet you. I'm having him take over the running of the estate. I don't want to have to look at you ever again."

"After everything we've been through together, you're dismissing me from your life?"

She glared at me with cold, angry eyes. "That's right. Now, please, just go."

With my hat in my hands, I walked to the doorway and turned back to her. "Don't forget to feed the horses."

"Goodbye, Alexander."

I SAT IN FRONT OF THE FIRE IN THE LIBRARY, STILL REELING from my encounter with Rachel. She'd never been what I would describe as a warm person. Yet she was always polite and accepting of my friendship with Samuel. Occasionally, the children had been allowed to play with my brood, but I could tell it made Rachel nervous.

A horrible thought came to me then. What if Rachel had killed him over the school argument? Maybe she was that desperate to keep them safe?

As quickly as it came to me, I dismissed the idea. Rachel loved him. Even if they'd argued bitterly over whether the children should go into town for school, she would never hurt him.

"Lord Barnes?"

I looked over to the doorway to see Miss Cooper. She'd changed from her blue dress into a drab brown. Even an ugly dress couldn't make her look bad.

"Have you seen Jasper?" she asked.

"He went into town," I said. "Do you need something?"

"No, I wanted to thank him. He found a book in your library that I'd asked him about and left it outside my door. So kind of him."

I waved her closer. "Come sit with me. I'm having a drink and nursing my wounds."

"Are you all right?" Her gaze swept over me.

"Yes, these are wounds of the heart from my visit with Rachel."

She sat in the chair next to me, then folded her hands in her lap. "How was the poor woman?"

"Angry." I proceeded to tell her the entirety of our conversation. "I should have known she'd be furious with me. It was the only time Samuel had ever disagreed with what she wanted for the kids. She sees me as a conspirator."

"Will she be all right by herself?"

"She's sending for her brother." I shared with her the details of my arrangement with Samuel about his estate. "As you know, she couldn't own property without him leaving it all to me. This was Samuel's way of making sure they were taken care of in case anything happened."

"How smart." She pinched her lips together using her thumb and finger and stared into the fire. This, I'd learned already, was her thinking face. "Do you think she'd consider sending the kids to school if I talked with her?"

"Not yet. For now, I'm going to leave her alone. Hopefully, at some point, she'll forgive me, and we can resume our friendship."

She cocked her head to the side, watching me. "For your friend to have that much trust in you says a lot about your character."

"I'm not perfect, but I'm honest."

Footsteps on the stairs from the third floor warned me of the impending pack of my children. I'd waited until now to tell them about Samuel. They hadn't known him well but were fond of him. I worried it would be upsetting, given their own mother's death.

They filed in and sat on the couch. "I have bad news," I said. "My friend Samuel has died."

"Those poor kids," Josephine said.

"Did someone kill him?" Flynn asked.

"Why would you ask that?" I asked.

"Because he's married to a brown lady," Flynn said as he glanced at Josephine.

"Someone shot him," I said. "We don't know who or why."

"How will you find out?" Theo asked.

"I'm not certain," I said.

"Can we go now?" Flynn asked. "I want to finish my snow fort."

"You may go."

Flynn tugged on Theo's shirt. "Come on."

Theo nodded and the two jumped up from the couch as if it were on fire.

"Can I come?" Cymbeline asked.

"No. This fort's only for boys," Flynn said.

"That's not fair," Cymbeline said. "Papa, make them take me."

"Stay here with me," Josephine said to her sister. "I'll play checkers with you."

Cymbeline, mollified for the time being, stuck her tongue out at her brothers as they left the room. "And you can't let me win on purpose, Jojo. We have to play for real."

"I didn't let you win last time," Josephine said. "You beat me."

"Are you sure you aren't fibbing?" Cymbeline said.

"Of course not, goose." She patted her sister on the head before she turned to me. "Papa, I'm sorry you lost your friend,"

"Thank you, dearest one," I said, drawing her close. "I'm sad, but I have a lot of happy memories of our time together."

The little girls rushed over and fought for a place on my lap. I settled each on a knee. "We love you, Papa," Cymbeline said.

Fiona snuggled against my chest. "Love my papa."

I kissed them both on top of their sweet-smelling heads as I darted a glance at Miss Cooper. She was looking into the fire with glassy eyes.

Quinn

O n Monday morning, my students appeared bundled in coats, hats, and scarves. They brought the scent of the outdoors and woodsmoke. Most carried their lunch in a bucket or wooden box. I greeted them with a slight smile, too nervous to take in the details of their faces or ages, and gave them specific instructions to hang their coats, put their lunches on the table near the door, and take a seat. "Tallest in the back, please." I used my formal teacher voice and held my head high, as if I were used to positions of authority. Given my age and slight figure, I knew it was important that I present as mature and strict.

My legs wobbled as I took my place in front of the room. I wore my teacher uniform, a black skirt paired with a jacket of the same fabric over a crisp white blouse, sewn by my clever sister. She'd sewn a necktie as well, made of a smart black-and-white-checkered fabric, wide enough to cover my throat and chest.

I did a quick count of pupils. Besides the Barnes children, there were nine others, making a total of thirteen. Wasn't thirteen an unlucky number? I hid behind my desk for a second and scanned the faces until I found Josephine. She gave me an encouraging smile.

No one else moved or made a sound. *Have courage*, I told myself. *Lord Barnes is counting on you.*

I took a deep breath and began.

"We'll start each day promptly at nine. I'll expect the older ones to keep the fire stoked and bring in firewood as needed. The younger of you will take turns cleaning the blackboard and erasers. We'll have two fifteen-minute recesses and one hour for lunch. Those of you who live close enough may walk home for lunch. The rest of you may eat at your desks and then go outside to play if it suits you. You may not speak unless I call your name. If you have a question, you may raise your hand."

I stood in front of the chalkboard and looked out at the innocent faces of the children of Emerson Pass. "I expect obedience and respect while you're here at school. However, there are only three rules that matter most in here and out in the world." I wrote in big letters on the board: BE CURIOUS. BE KIND. PROTECT ONE ANOTHER. "If you conduct yourselves in this manner, we will be worthy of praise in my classroom. If you deport yourselves this way throughout your life, you will have lived a life worthy of the sacrifices your parents have made to get you to this classroom." I glanced around the room. "Is this clear?"

Other than Poppy and Josephine, who nodded, the children stared at me.

"When I ask a question, I would like you to answer with, 'Yes, Miss Cooper.' Shall we try it? One, two, three."

"Yes, Miss Cooper."

I stifled a smile. Their voices sounded good as a unit. "Does anyone have any questions before we begin?" I asked.

Poppy raised her hand.

"Yes, Poppy?"

"Why do we have to protect one another?"

"Because we're a team now," I said. "Teams are a group of

people with a common goal or purpose. Together we are stronger than we are alone."

Flynn raised his hand.

"Flynn?"

"Why should we be curious? I thought we were supposed to learn boring things."

This child was going to give me a permanent sore from having to bite the inside of my mouth to keep from laughing. "Because curiosity leads to questions, which lead to answers, which is what learning is all about."

He tilted his head, as if truly contemplating such an idea. Whatever conclusion he came to, he kept that to himself. *Thank God for small favors*, I thought.

I continued with the business of the day. "I'll have you come up one at a time to my desk so that I might learn a little about your former education and reading levels. While you wait your turn, you will sit quietly and read or look at one of the picture books from the shelf. We're very lucky to have a library, and I'll expect you to treat the books as you would a precious baby."

Cymbeline giggled. Josephine shook her head at her little sister and put her finger against her mouth.

I moved over to the bookshelf and asked them to form a line. For the older children, I gave them chapter books. The younger ones were given ones with pictures. When all had books, I sent them back to their desks.

I asked Martha and Elsa Johnson up first. It was obvious they were sisters, given their matching yellow braids and wide blue eyes. Martha was sixteen and Elsa fourteen.

They could read well, having gone to school in their former town in Minnesota before their parents moved them to Emerson Pass. Second-generation Swedes, they spoke and read English fluently and had a reasonable grasp of arithmetic. Both were tall with good posture and proud, sturdy shoulders. I imagined there wasn't much they couldn't accomplish given the opportunity.

Martha reminded me that her parents owned the dry goods store.

"Do you like it here?" I asked.

She nodded, smiling. "I like wherever my family is."

"And you?" I asked her sister Elsa.

"Me too."

"The only thing we miss from Minnesota are the town dances," Martha said.

"We'd looked forward to dances when we were old enough," Elsa said. "But here, there are none."

I could certainly understand why two young ladies would pine for a dance. "I think if we put our heads together, we might be able to come up with a few ideas for a town dance."

"Really?" Martha asked.

"Give me a little while. If you two study hard and are good girls, I'll speak with Lord Barnes about having one here at the schoolhouse."

Their faces lit up as they nodded enthusiastically. "Yes, Miss Cooper. We'll do our best," Elsa said.

I asked the bigger of the two blond boys to come up next. He approached, looking terrified. Pale blue eyes watched me from under a fringe of hair so fair it was almost white.

"What's your name?" I asked.

"Isak Olofsson," he said in a thick Swedish accent. He pointed toward another of the students. "My brother. Can he come now?"

"Yes."

Isak, in Swedish, asked his brother to join us. The younger of the two ambled up to the desk, looking equally frightened. "This is Viktor." Viktor's hair was the color of dried straw, a little darker than his older brother's. Green eyes peered at me from his square face. I could already see the handsome men they would become.

"We want to learn English," Isak said. "And to read from English books."

Through an awkward exchange, I learned Isak and Viktor were recent immigrants from Sweden. They could not read but seemed to understand English when spoken to and could answer my questions for the most part. It was enough to work with, especially given their obvious keen desire to learn.

Next up were three sisters, who took it upon themselves to come up as a group. I didn't chastise them. We learn from watching others, after all. The Cassidy sisters were Nora, age six; Shannon, age eight; and Alma, age ten. The girls shared the same green eyes and fair skin, but Shannon had dark curls whereas the other two had honey-colored hair as straight as a board.

"Have you been to school before?" I asked.

Alma spoke for them all in a lilting Irish accent. "I went for one year before we moved to America. Since then, no. But our mother taught us to read."

"Not me," Nora said. "Just my letters."

"Letters are a great place to start," I said.

The other two read competently from the first reader but struggled with a few words. They knew almost no arithmetic. I had a feeling they would learn quickly.

The Barnes children filed up one after the other. There wasn't a surprise among them. They all read way beyond their grade level, even Cymbeline, who knew all the words from the early-reader textbook. Josephine read at an adult level, with Theo and Flynn not far behind.

"Are you going to make me read boring stories?" Flynn asked before returning to his desk.

"What kind of stories do you like?"

"Ones about wars and bears and catching fish and boy things."

"If I find you books like that, will you read more?" I asked.

He shrugged and wrinkled his freckled nose. "I could, I guess. Why do you want me to?"

"Because people who read a lot have more to think about."

"I do like thinking," Flynn said. "Mostly about building forts and catching fish."

"While you're doing those things or thinking about them, you can read about them. Won't that be fun?"

"When you put it like that, yeah."

"Yes, not yeah. *Yeah* is not a word."

"But you knew what I meant, so how is it not a word?" He raised one eyebrow and smirked, so much like his father, I had to cover my mouth to hide my smile.

"I expect proper grammar from you, young man. Return to your seat, please."

"Yes, Miss Cooper," he said.

Harley's sister was next. Poppy shared his same sparkle and pretty eyes as well as dark complexion. Skinny and petite for thirteen, she looked much younger than her age. Soft brown curls were pinned back with a bow.

"I've never been to school before," she said before I could ask.

"Have you lived here all your life?" I asked.

"No, before this Harley and me lived in France." She leaned close and talked just above a whisper.

"Harley and I, not me. 'Harley and I.' That's proper grammar."

She blinked. "Yes, Miss Cooper. Before this Harley and I lived in France with my dad and mom, but they died so we came to America to see about some gold or silver. But Harley didn't find any of that because he says the mines are all mined out. He works for Lord Barnes and we moved into a cottage on the property and I keep house. Lord Barnes is very good to us. That's what Harley says. Now I can go to school instead of making deliveries from the drugstore." I might not have noticed the little shudder she made had I not been watching her so closely. I saw it sure enough, and I knew what it meant. My heart nearly stopped. I made a mental note to inquire about this drugstore owner and whether or not he always hired little girls to work for him. For a split second, I thought of my sister. I'd left her all alone in the slums where danger lurked around every corner.

"Miss Cooper, I have a secret." She leaned close and spoke softly in my ear. "No one knows, but I already know how to read English."

"Why doesn't anyone know?"

"Because Harley can only read in French, and I don't want him to feel bad."

"Who taught you?"

"Josephine."

Josephine taught her? When had they found time for that? "That's great news," I said.

"She lends me books, too, but that's also a secret."

"I feel quite sure your brother would be proud of you."

"Josephine said you're going to teach the townsfolk if they come to you."

"That's correct."

"Would you teach Harley?"

"I'll teach any person willing to learn."

She smiled. "I'll have to convince him. He's stubborn as a mule."

"That's all right," I said. "So am I."

The last was nine-year-old Louisa Kellam. Dressed in a thin, frayed dress with holes in the toes of her boots, she was so shy she couldn't look at me when I asked her for her name and age. She could pick out a few words from the primary reader but didn't know any of her numbers.

"Have you ever been to school before?" I asked.

"No, miss. When we lived in Nebraska, Pa says he ain't got time to take me to school and that he needed my help at home."

"What about your mother?"

"She's dead," she said, without emotion.

"How did you get here this morning?" I asked.

"I walked. Our house is just a ways down the road."

I remembered a shack I'd spotted in the woods on the way

into town. I had a feeling she lived there. How could she walk all that way in the snow? She'd freeze to death in that thin coat and those boots with the holes in the toes.

"I really, really want to go to school and Pa don't like it. But if I sneak out before he wakes up, I figure he can't stop me."

Before he woke up? I knew what that meant. Her pa must be a frequent patron at the saloon.

"Do you think your pa would mind if I came out to talk with him about why it's important you be here?"

She shook her head so violently I thought it might fall off her skinny neck. "No, please don't do that."

"Won't he notice when you're not there all day?"

"He sleeps most of the day. I don't figure he'll know."

"All right, then." I'd have to sort through this later. "You can go back to your seat."

I looked down at my class roster. My first class. I hoped I would do them justice.

Martha Johnson, 16
Elsa Johnson, 14
Josephine Barnes, 13
Poppy Depaul, 13
Isak Olofsson, 11
Alma Cassidy, 10
Theo Barnes, 9
Flynn Barnes, 9
Louisa Kellam, 9
Viktor Olofsson, 9
Shannon Cassidy, 8
Nora Cassidy, 6
Cymbeline Barnes, 6

By this time, we'd missed our first recess and gone straight into lunchtime. The children had been remarkably good, even Flynn and Cymbeline, all sitting quietly with their books. Many of whom couldn't read much of them. Life had been hard for them, even the Barnes children who had everything except what mattered most—a mother. Martha and Elsa appeared to be the most fortunate. They had both parents and a father with a good livelihood. I might rely on them to help me with some of the little ones.

"You've been very good, and we worked through our first recess, so you may all have an extra fifteen minutes for lunch."

Flynn's hand popped up.

"Yes, Flynn?"

"Do we have to eat first before we go outside?"

"Yes, please. Now you may all return your books to the shelf, get your lunch, and come back to your seats to eat."

I watched as they put their books away and grabbed their lunch pails and returned to their seats. All but Louisa. She had no lunch. My own stomach, so often empty during my childhood, rumbled in sympathy. Without a word, I fetched mine, intending to give her half. I'd learned to live on little, and I'd had that large breakfast. I halted by the window, watching a pair of winter sparrows flirting on the tree in front of the school. By the time I returned to the front, the situation had been taken care of by the children. Sitting before Louisa were two half sandwiches —not of the same sandwich, as one was on thick brown bread and the other white—an apple, and a boiled egg. I took a look around the room, but everyone's head was down. Josephine only had one half of her sandwich left. Theo was missing an apple. Alma was taking a bite out of one half of a dark bread sandwich. She couldn't have eaten the other half that fast, given the size of the bread. Elsa had an egg on her desk, but Martha did not. It didn't take much sleuthing to figure out Louisa's benefactors.

Louisa looked up at me, the question in her eyes—was she allowed to take the food? I nodded and went back to my desk. Choked up, I kept my head down so the children wouldn't see how moved I was by their kindness. They'd taken my rules seriously, it seemed.

We all ate in silence. Louisa scarfed every morsel of her gifted lunch. The others finished theirs, and I dismissed them to play outside. Everyone bolted from their seats, clearly joyful to get outside for some exercise. They all clambered into their coats and headed outdoors. Shouts of glee followed.

I looked up to see that Louisa remained at her seat. There were dark quarter moons under her eyes.

"Don't you want to play?" I asked.

"Would it be all right if I took a nap over by the stove?"

"Didn't you sleep last night?" I asked.

A look of such misery crossed her face that it chilled me to the core. "Pa had things for me to do the last few nights, so I haven't been able to sleep much."

"You may lie down by the fire," I said as I walked over to the coatrack. "But here, sleep on my coat. The floor's dirty."

She looked down at the front of her dirty dress. "No, Miss Cooper. I'll sleep on the floor."

I nodded and said no more. I knew all about shame.

Alexander

When we came home from our first day of school, the older children tumbled from the sleigh and ran to play in the last few minutes of light. This time of year, the days were short. Miss Cooper, tucked beside me, lifted the blanket from around her lap and allowed me to assist her out of the sleigh. Cymbeline, pretty as a picture in her red coat and matching hat, was fast asleep in the middle seat. With her hat askew and her thick black lashes splayed over her cheekbones, she looked more like the baby she'd once been. Whereas when I'd picked them all up at school, she'd marched right behind the twins looking pleased with herself and quite grown up. My heart ached a little, thinking of her childhood slipping away before my eyes. Soon, my house would be empty of all the noise and chaos. What would I have left then?

"Poor mite," I said. "Tired out from her first day of school."

"She did very well for being so young," Miss Cooper said. "Toward the end of the day, she grew tired and unable to sit still, so I had her clean the erasers and bring in kindling."

I chuckled. "Giving her tasks is a great solution to her naughtiness."

I lifted Cymbeline from the sleigh and carried her toward the door.

Jasper stepped outside to greet us. "Welcome home." He held open the door, and Miss Cooper passed through with me right behind her.

The moment we entered the house, Cymbeline's eyes flew open. "Papa, I was very good at school."

I set her on her feet and knelt on my knees to help her out of her coat and hat. "I'm proud to hear this good report."

Miss Cooper, next to me, unbuttoned her coat and handed it to Jasper, who hung it in the closet.

"It was hard to stay still so long." Cymbeline yawned and rubbed her eyes with the back of her hands in the way that always made me want to hold her close to my chest.

"You did quite well," Miss Cooper said.

Cymbeline beamed. "Miss Cooper said we have to be curious and kind and to take care of our team."

"And did you?" I asked, tweaking her nose.

Cymbeline tugged off her hat. Her curls, happy to be free of their imprisonment, immediately fell over her forehead. "I tried to give someone my sandwich, but Jojo said no."

I looked up at Miss Cooper for an explanation.

"Louisa Kellam came to school without a lunch," she said. "The children took it upon themselves to share theirs."

"But not me," Cymbeline said. "Jojo said I was too little and that I needed all my sandwich."

"Your sister was right to give hers instead," I said, knowing Josephine's heart. She would not want her little sister to be hungry.

"Josephine might need an extra portion at supper tonight," Miss Cooper said as she took out the pins that secured her hat.

Fiona came running into the foyer, calling out her sister's name as if she'd been parted from her for years instead of hours. She threw herself into Cymbeline's arms. "I missed you."

Cymbeline returned the affectionate hug. "Were you bored without me?"

"No. Lizzie let me help her in the kitchen," Fiona said. "We made bread and I got to help churn the butter."

"Lizzie has tea for you in the kitchen," Jasper said. "She made her special raspberry biscuits."

"I love those ones," Cymbeline said.

"Didn't you say that about the oatmeal ones?" I asked.

"Those too," Cymbeline said.

I watched as Fiona and Cymbeline clasped hands and walked toward the door that led down to the kitchen, chattering away about their day. Jasper gestured toward the library. "I've set tea for you and Miss Cooper in the library."

Miss Cooper's eyes widened, obviously delighted. "I'm allowed tea?"

"We all have tea in this house, Miss Cooper," Jasper said, then sniffed.

"Right, of course," Miss Cooper said.

I smiled over at Miss Cooper, hoping to distract her from Jasper's rudeness. "Would you join me?"

"I can't think of anything I'd like more at the moment than one of those raspberry cookies."

"I can assure you—they do not disappoint."

Our eyes locked and we grinned at each other, like children.

Jasper cleared his throat. Out of the corner of my eye, I saw him examine his cuff links.

We walked out of the foyer and through the open doors of the library. A teapot and plates of biscuits and tiny sandwiches waited on the table. Miss Cooper and I took seats opposite each other. Jasper poured tea and then backed away to stand near the doorway. Given my choice of a small staff and Jasper's unwillingness to let go of the past, he was butler, valet, and footman. Unless I specifically asked him to leave, he would stand in wait.

Knowing Jasper would die rather than leave us alone unsupervised, I didn't bother to dismiss him. I wished we could be alone, but my loyal staff saved me from my foibles.

"Tell me about your day," I said. "Were the children what you expected?"

"They were as varied in skills and temperaments as I feared they would be," she said. "I've had to group them by abilities rather than age. They all seemed willing to learn and follow the rules. All in all, it was a most satisfying first day." She leaned over the table to put a few sandwiches and a biscuit on her plate. As she had the other time I'd seen her eat, she dived into the meal with gusto and appreciation.

After her third sandwich, Miss Cooper began to chatter away about her students. I learned more than I wanted to. Louisa Kellam was coming to school without her father's permission or knowledge. I knew Kellam. He was a drunk who did odd jobs around town when he wasn't at the saloon playing cards and drinking. How he kept the poor girl alive was anyone's guess. They lived on my property in an abandoned shack. I looked the other way, even though he didn't pay rent, because of the child.

"I'm worried what will happen if he finds out," Miss Cooper said. "Is he dangerous? Will he hurt her?"

I shared my opinion of John Kellam. Miss Cooper didn't bat an eyelash.

"I thought as such," she said. "I'll have to think about what to do. Louisa didn't want me to talk to her father, but it may come to that."

"If anyone talks to him, it will be me. You're not to go to his place alone."

She waved away my concern with a flutter of her slender hand. "We'll worry about that if it comes."

"Miss Cooper, I realize you're an independent woman, but there are certain situations out here in the West that require a man's help. Preferably a man with a gun."

She raised one eyebrow and popped another cookie in her mouth.

I let it go for now. Miss Cooper's courage both captivated and disarmed me.

According to Miss Cooper, the Johnson girls were smart and a delight. "In fact, they might be a great help to me with the night school students. I could pair them with the women students. If we have any, that is."

She went on to tell me about the Cassidy children—quiet and shy but excited for school. This was good to hear. Mr. and Mrs. Cassidy were good, hardworking immigrants from Ireland. Mr. Cassidy, along with a dozen others, had volunteered his time to help construct the school last summer.

"The two little boys from Sweden, Isak and Viktor, speak almost no English," she said. "They'll be challenging, but nothing we can't conquer."

"Their father owns the tailor shop," I said. "Good people."

Miss Cooper clapped her hands and smiled. Her small white teeth were in such a perfect row in that pink mouth. "I have saved the best for last. You'll never guess. Poppy can read English. And guess who taught her?" She paused dramatically, her eyes sparkling. "Josephine. They did it on the sly."

"She did? But why hide it?" I asked.

"She doesn't want Harley to feel bad."

"How sweet," I said.

"As is your Josephine. I've never heard of such a thing. There's something in the mountain air, Lord Barnes. These are the dearest children I've ever met." She glanced at the ceiling. "I'm blessed to be here. Truly." She looked back at me. "Which brings me to the next subject."

The sound of stomping feet and laughter interrupted us as the children came into the foyer from outside. Merry's voice came next, instructing them to take off their wet coats and boots before they destroyed the floors and caught their deaths.

All five tumbled into the library, looking like the picture of health with red cheeks and noses. "Hello, Papa and Miss Cooper." I swear Jo exchanged a conspiratorial glance with Theo before coming over to kiss me on the cheek.

The boys ran to the fire, warming their hands.

"Are you hungry?" I asked. "Miss Cooper's told me of your generosity toward Louisa."

"My insides are eating themselves." Flynn clutched his stomach.

"I doubt that. Regardless, Lizzie has tea for you downstairs," I said. "Go on now."

After the children left, Miss Cooper returned her attention to me. "I have an idea. I'd like to take the place as your nanny while I'm here at the house as a way to thank you for allowing me to stay here. I'm quite capable of looking after children."

"I'm sorry, no. It's too much."

"It's no trouble. You have to have someone. Merry and Lizzie are obviously busy with their own work."

I considered her offer. As much as I disliked the idea, I was rather desperate. "Just until I can find someone else. And I'll increase your pay. It will give you more to send home."

"Wonderful." She held out her hand. "You have a deal."

I wanted to bring that porcelain hand to my mouth, but I settled for a handshake instead.

Quinn

That night while the children and Lord Barnes ate upstairs in the dining room, I huddled with Lizzie and Merry at the square table in the kitchen. We'd already eaten the most delectable chicken potpie and were now drinking mugs of coffee mixed with thick cream and sugar. I'd never been in a more modern kitchen. They had a boiler and gas range and the largest sink I'd ever seen. Black-and-white-checkered flooring shone under the lights.

"I have to ask. What happened to the children's mother?" I asked, leaning forward conspiratorially.

Lizzie spoke just above a whisper. "She just walked out into the snow in the middle of the night wearing nothing but her nightdress and curled up and froze to death."

"Theo found her," Merry said, tears welling in her eyes.

"He was only six," Lizzie said.

"He's never been the same," Merry said.

"How awful." His sweet little face swam before me.

"She'd always been strange," Lizzie said. "When he brought her here from back east, we had no warning until a few days before they showed up. The Lord and Jasper had gone east for business. One day we got a letter from Jasper that Lord Barnes had married and was bringing his bride home. He was always the spontaneous sort, so we weren't terribly surprised. He makes decisions from his heart, not his head. That's what brought him to America in the first place—this desire for adventure and freedom. He couldn't stomach the idea of doing what his father and father before him had done. He wanted to make his own way. It's highly unusual to give up his rightful inheritance to a younger brother."

"Did you know him then?" I asked.

"Oh yes. Jasper and I worked for the family in England. His family have employed both our families for as long as anyone can remember. He sent for me after the house was built, but Jasper had been with him since he left."

"Were you homesick?" I asked.

"Terrible at first," Lizzie said. "I missed my mum and sister. We all worked together in the big kitchen back home. But Jasper was here, so I wanted to be where he was." She flushed and glanced at Merry. "Oh dear."

Merry leaned closer. "Lizzie loves Jasper."

"Always have," Lizzie said. "Since we were in knickers."

"But he doesn't want to marry," Merry said. "He's old-fashioned and doesn't think he could be married and still be the butler and valet to Lord Barnes."

I nodded. These class distinctions were lost on Americans, but I knew they were very real for our friends overseas.

"At least this way I can be in the same house with him," Lizzie said.

How awful it must be for her to want what she could never have. Would the same thing happen to me if I stayed too long in this house? I'd want to be Lord Barnes's wife and the children's mother. None of whom belonged to me.

"Never mind all that," Lizzie said, obviously wanting to change the subject. "Lady Ida was strange from the start—mood swings and a terrible temper. For weeks she'd be in bed and then up for days at a time, wandering the house. She wanted nothing to do with the children. That's why they're so close to their father. He was mother and father to them. Jasper wanted him to hire more servants, but he wouldn't hear of it. He resented being raised by a team of governesses when he was a child. Children saw their parents only a few minutes each day. He swore to all of us that it would not be that way in his house. His *American* house."

"Which would've been fine except for her," Merry said.

"Then she had Fiona and went completely mad," Lizzie said. "The lord found her with a knife over the baby."

I gasped. "No."

"Yes. He saved the wee one just in time." Lizzie's eyes reddened. "When I think of our little Fiona and what might've happened…" She fanned her eyes with one hand. "May God save her soul. I'm not sure any of us will ever forget that awful night."

"The nanny had to lock herself and the children in the nursery," Lizzie said. "She was so frightened she left the next day for Chicago."

"It's been one nanny after the other since then," Merry said.

"We're sure the children conspire together to run them off," Lizzie said. "They put a frog in the bed of the one we had before Nanny Foster."

"They never confessed," Merry said. "But Lizzie and I are certain it was Flynn's idea."

Lizzie shook her head. "That poor woman. I heard her scream from all the way down in my room off the kitchen here. Lord Barnes took away their books for a week."

They went on to tell me all of the previous antics the children had pulled to get rid of the caregivers, including making ghostlike noises outside her bedroom, hiding shoes, adding vinegar to cups of tea.

"The worst was vodka in lemonade," Lizzie said. "Nanny Miller was drunk as could be in the middle of the afternoon and fell into the creek."

"She came back looking like a drowned cat," Merry said. "An angry cat, sputtering and crying."

"Why don't they want a nanny?" I asked. "Because of rules and such?"

Lizzie and Merry looked at each other before she answered. "They don't want intruders. People who aren't part of the family."

"And they see you two as family?" I asked.

"That's right. And Harley and Poppy," Merry said.

"Because of their mum," Lizzie said. "They don't want to love someone they think might leave them. So they make them leave first."

This theory made perfect sense. "I may as well tell you," I said. "Lord Barnes and I have come to an agreement. Since it's been so hard to find someone, I'm going to take care of the children until spring."

Merry squeezed my hand. "That's awfully kind of you."

"Only until he can find someone appropriate," I said. "However, now I'm wondering if my offer was ill-advised."

"Bless you," Lizzie said. "You're just what the children need."

"I do hope they won't put a frog in my bed," I said.

"Just pull back the covers before you get in at night." Merry grimaced. "That was Nanny Shelby's mistake."

Alexander

The children and I dined on Lizzie's chicken potpie filled with soft chunks of carrots, potatoes, sweet onions. Miss Cooper had agreed to stay downstairs with Lizzie and Merry for the meal, giving me time to talk to the children alone. They all ate with great appetites. They'd had a big day.

"I have something to tell you," I said.

"Is someone else dead?" Flynn asked.

"What? No. Flynn, what would make you say such a thing?"

"You always start out like that when you have bad news," Flynn said.

"This isn't bad news," I said. "In fact, I hope you'll find it good. As you know, we've had a hard time keeping a nanny. You're a rambunctious brood, and this remote place we live in is not for everyone. I suspect, also, that you purposely ran off the last few. And you were terrible to Nanny—" For heaven's sake, I'd already forgotten her name. "The one who left this morning. You know who I mean."

Other than Fiona, no one looked at me. Josephine buttered an additional piece of bread for Fiona. Theo pushed a piece of onion around his plate. Cymbeline stabbed a bit of chicken and held it close to her face, as if examining for mold. Flynn guzzled milk.

"I need someone to look after you," I said.

Theo lifted his head to gaze in my direction. "We have Lizzie and Merry," he said with an unusual amount of firmness in his tone. "They're enough."

"And they love us." Flynn set down his empty milk glass. "Unlike these other people you keep bringing here."

"Lizzie and Merry have too much other work to add you to their burden," I said.

"Are we a burden?" Cymbeline's bottom lip trembled.

I waved my hand dismissively. "Not a burden, no. I simply mean that five children are a lot to look after all at once, and they already have too many responsibilities."

"I can take care of us," Josephine mumbled.

I ignored that for now.

"Anyway, until I can get someone else, Miss Cooper has volunteered to help."

Cymbeline and Flynn frowned. Fiona sucked in her bottom lip. Josephine folded her arms over her chest. Theo slouched over his plate. I thought they liked Miss Cooper.

"What is it?" I asked. "Don't you like Miss Cooper?"

"We like her very much," Josephine said, finally. "But she cannot be our nanny."

"Temporary nanny," I said. "And why not?"

"Because she's supposed to be your wife," Flynn blurted out.

I blinked. "What did you say?"

"Papa, we prayed for her to come, and she finally did," Josephine said.

"She's going to be our mama, not a nanny," Cymbeline said. "We already decided."

I'm not one to lose my sense of direction or find myself without words. This time, however, I sat there utterly flab-bergasted.

"Isn't that why you ordered her?" Theo asked.

"Ordered her?" Had I heard him right?

"Like Mr. Carter did," Flynn said. "From the mail."

"Whatever would give you that idea?" I asked. "How do you know how Mr. Carter got his wife?"

"Papa, everyone knows where these women come from," Josephine said. "They just show up one day on the train with a sad little suitcase and suddenly they're someone's wife. We figured you were so clever that you found us a teacher and a new mother in the same person."

I pushed away my plate and folded my hands together on top of the table. This was not at all how I thought this conversation was going to go. "Let me set you all straight. Miss Cooper came here to be our first teacher. Not my wife."

"Oh, so you don't actually know yet?" Flynn asked. "We thought you knew."

"We didn't know, obviously," Josephine said. "Until we saw her. Until we saw you together."

"I'm sorry to disappoint you," I said. "But you have this all wrong."

Fiona started to cry. "The others said she was going to be our new mama."

"When in heaven's name did you discuss this?" I asked.

"This morning," Josephine said. "During our family meeting."

I dropped my forehead into the palm of my hand. They had family meetings without me? When had that begun? It was like a geographic shift, and I was looking at a world I no longer recognized. Because here was the actual ridiculous truth. I agreed with them. I couldn't say that, of course. We'd known Miss Cooper for two days. This time last week we were eating beef stew and discussing how excited we were for our new teacher to arrive. Two days ago, I'd thought she was a white-haired spinster. We were all acting mad. Romances like this were for books, not real life.

"Listen carefully now. You will not mention any of this nonsense to Miss Cooper. Do you understand?"

"Why?" Cymbeline asked. "How will she know the plan?"

"Because you will scare her away," I said. "She came here to teach, not find a husband. She might not even want a husband." I added the last thought hoping with everything I had that it wasn't true.

Josephine scowled and shook her head as if I'd said we were taking a ride to the moon. "Papa, she wants a husband."

"Especially one like you," Flynn said.

Theo nodded, quite solemn. "Papa, she looks at you with her heart in her eyes."

I glanced around the table at their earnest expressions. They actually believed Miss Cooper was for us. My darling babies were all romantic fools, mirroring my unspoken, irrational daydreams. We wished for love with such fervor that we'd imagined that a wife and mother had fallen suddenly from the sky. Or, in this circumstance, from the train.

I spoke as sternly as possible. "We won't discuss this again. Miss Cooper has been gracious enough to accept the position. If I hear another word, you'll all be punished." With that, I set aside my napkin and rose from the table, acting the part of strict father when, in fact, they'd shaken me. My legs wobbled as I entered the hallway. I heard the familiar creak of the stairs that led to the kitchen. Someone had been standing outside the door, listening. God help me. *Please*, I prayed. *Let it have been Jasper and not Miss Cooper standing in the hallway.*

I jumped when Jasper shuffled out of the library carrying an empty tray. Wonderful. Jasper had not been in the hallway. If Miss Cooper had heard that conversation, she was probably contemplating how to get out of this house and back to the world of rational humans.

"What's the matter?" Jasper asked. "You look a bit undone."

"Let's go into town for a drink. I want to get out of the house." When had it gotten so warm in here? I loosened my tie.

His eyebrows raised. "Town?"

"Yes, town."

"For a drink?"

I rubbed the skin between my eyebrows, irritated. Why did he have to question me? If I wanted to go into the saloon, then I would go to the bloody saloon. "I know, it's unusual, but I feel the urge for some fresh air. Do you have a problem with that?"

He flinched as if I'd smacked him. "Not at all."

"I'm sorry, Jasper." I sighed and ran a hand through my hair. "I had a strange interaction with the children, and I'm rattled."

"No explanation necessary. I'll have Harley prepare the horses."

"First, I need to speak to Miss Cooper. Do you know where she is?"

"Downstairs with Lizzie and Merry." He watched me with wary eyes, as if I were a stranger to him. "Shall I fetch her for you?"

"No, I'll go down myself. I'll be back in a few minutes."

"As you wish."

Quinn

I was at the sink in the kitchen drying a plate when I heard heavy footsteps on the stairs. Lord Barnes burst through the door seconds later. His hair stood up in the front as if he'd been running his hands through it, and his tie was loose about his neck.

"Lord Barnes, may I help you with something?" Lizzie leapt up from the table where she'd been polishing a silver serving tray with a cotton cloth.

"Who was in the hallway just now?" he asked.

"That was me," Merry said. She'd climbed up on the step stool to put a bowl up on the top shelf and stood there now, frozen. "I'd come from the library. I had to put more logs on the fire. Is something the matter?"

"Oh, so you weren't listening to the conversation in the dining room?" he asked.

Merry's knuckles whitened as she pressed the bowl against her chest. "No, Lord Barnes. Was I supposed to?"

"No, no. Of course not." He ran a hand through his hair, proving I'd been correct about the origin of its dishevelment. "And no, nothing's the matter. I just came down to tell you that

I've talked to the children, Miss Cooper." Lord Barnes leaned against the wall, as if he were tired.

My heart sank. His dark expression told me everything I needed to know. "They were upset?"

"What? No, no. They quite like you. Yes, they quite like you."

I studied him. Why was he repeating himself, and why the emphasis on the word *quite*? He picked at the skin around his thumbnail as his gaze darted around the kitchen. "Anyway, they're upstairs in the dining room. Perhaps bring them into the library after you're done here and talk to them about things."

"Things?" I asked.

"You know, how you expect them to behave and such," he said. "Jasper and I are going into town for a drink."

"Lord Barnes?" Lizzie asked. "To the saloon?"

"Yes, we're going to the saloon," he said. "Just this once, so you mustn't worry about my moral corruption, Lizzie." He nodded at us and then practically ran back up the stairs.

"What's gotten into him?" Lizzie asked. "The saloon?"

I folded the damp towel and hung it over the side of the sink. "Perhaps it went poorly with the children and he didn't want to say."

"No, it's something else," Lizzie said. "I think the death of Mr. Cole has him worried and sad." She nodded, as if trying to convince herself. "Yes, that's all it is."

A FEW MINUTES LATER, I HERDED THE CHILDREN INTO THE library and had them sit together on the couch. They obeyed without question, with Cymbeline between the twins and Fiona on Josephine's lap.

"Your father told you I'm going to look after you until he can find a proper replacement, is that right?"

Nods all around. Fiona tracked my every movement with adoring eyes. I had one on my side. Was it four to go?

"We're going to come to a few agreements," I said. "Like school, there are rules."

Five pairs of eyes were fixed on my face.

"I ask that you're respectful and obedient. In exchange, I'll treat you with kindness. If you're well behaved, we can have fun adventures together."

Flynn raised his hand. "Do we have to raise our hands like at school?"

I swallowed a laugh. "Not at home, only at school. Here, you'll wait your turn to speak and be courteous to your family members, but you don't have to raise your hand."

"What's courteous mean exactly?" Cymbeline asked.

"Courteous means polite and thoughtful. It means you *do not* put frogs in beds," I said.

Flynn and Cymbeline giggled.

"That was extremely naughty," I said with a pointed look at Flynn, then Cymbeline.

"You didn't know her." Josephine's eyes shone with a feverish hatred. "She was awful to us."

"What about all the other nannies?" I asked. "Lizzie told me all about your antics."

Theo and Josephine looked into their laps. Flynn and Cymbeline smiled, reminding me of cats after a kill. Fiona seemed oblivious to her siblings' previous misbehaviors as she wrinkled her little brow and looked confused.

"None of them belonged here." Flynn crossed his arms over his chest and jutted out one pointy chin.

"They were scary old ladies," Cymbeline said. "Not pretty like you."

"Pretty is on the inside," I said.

"They weren't pretty in there, either," Josephine said. "You're both."

This clever girl had certainly figured out how to soften me. I must remain stoic and impenetrable to their charms. Falling in love with the Barnes children would do none of us any good. I was not their mother. I wasn't even their real nanny. At some point, I would have to leave them and move on to my own home and life. I was merely an interloper, I reminded myself. Spending time with these precious children was my way of paying back a kind man for his hospitality and employment. Remaining aloof had never been a strength. On the contrary. I fell for any living being who needed and wanted my affection. Stray cats, lame dogs, motherless children. All foils to my resolve. "All right then, can I have your promise that you'll be obedient and respectful to me?" I asked.

More nods and smiles.

"And I do not care for amphibians or reptiles of any kind. If you put one in my bed or anywhere else near me, I'll have to go home to Boston."

All five faces transformed from earnest to sorrowful. They hadn't understood I was only teasing. If they only knew how much more difficult it would be for me to leave them than for them to be left. I suspected Lord Barnes would marry again soon and give them a mother. Probably someone from the east or even England. A blue blood debutante type. Someone of his world.

A spasm of jealousy hit me between my shoulder blades. *That is quite ridiculous*, I told myself. *I barely know him.* Why had God cursed me with such an imagination?

"We don't want you to leave," Cymbeline said.

"We want you to stay forever and ever," Fiona said.

I smiled in a way I hoped was reassuring. "I don't want to go away either, so put that out of your minds. I was only teasing. About going to Boston, that is. Not about the amphibians." I waggled a finger at them.

"It was Flynn who put the frog in her bed," Cymbeline said in a rush of words. "None of the rest of us like frogs either."

I allowed myself a stiff smile, even though inside I wanted to throw my head back and laugh. "I'll hold you to this."

For the first time, Theo spoke. "What do we call you here at the house?"

I hadn't thought about that, but it was a good question. I was Miss Cooper at school. Nanny Cooper didn't sound right somehow.

"You may call me Miss Quinn at home. However, you mustn't share it with the other children. When we're at school, I'll have to treat you like I do all the others."

"Even though we're special?" Cymbeline grinned and swung her legs.

"That's correct." I tented my hands under my chin. "Now let's get ready for bed. If you wash up, clean your teeth, and put on your nightgowns with no fuss, I'll read to you the first chapter of a book before lights out."

All five bounced from the couch as if there were springs under them. Josephine and Flynn both grabbed a lantern, lighting the kerosene wick before heading toward the hallway. I did the same with one more, then picked up the two books I'd already chosen from the shelves earlier and followed them up the stairs to the bedrooms.

As promised, they obeyed my directions. Sharing space in the bathroom, one by one they brushed their teeth and washed their faces. I had to send Flynn back for a second scrubbing, as the dirt under his fingernails appeared to be almost as old as him.

In the hallway, he held out his hands for inspection. "Much better," I said.

"A little dirt never hurt anyone," he said.

"It hurts me," I said.

"Why?" Flynn asked.

"Because it does," I said. "It's a grown-up thing." I patted his back. "Now stop asking questions so we can have our story."

THE TWO LITTLE GIRLS HAD CRAWLED UNDER THE COVERS ON their twin beds. Flynn, Theo, and Josephine sat cross-legged on her bed. I slipped next to Fiona and read the opening passage from *Heidi*. I'd chosen it from the shelves of the library, remembering how much I'd enjoyed it as a child. Like the Barnes children, Heidi was without a mother. As for me, I was like Heidi—a visitor in a remote and beautiful place.

The lamplight flickered as I read. Fiona fell asleep after only a few pages. Her body, warm and heavy beside me, reminded me of my sister, and a pang of homesickness washed through me. I pushed the pain aside. These children needed me present in the here and now. They had a way of making everything immediate. I liked this, as it kept me from thinking too much about the family I'd left behind.

When the first chapter was done, Cymbeline had also fallen asleep. I shooed the boys off to their room.

At the doorway, Flynn stopped. "Miss Quinn, will you tuck us in?"

"I'll be right there," I said, as I pulled Cymbeline's quilt over her shoulders.

While I was adjusting Fiona's blanket around her small, chubby body, now curled into a ball, Josephine pulled back her quilt and slid into bed.

I stood, smoothing my skirts. Josephine lay on her side, watching me.

"How about you, Miss Josephine?" I asked. "Would you like a tuck-in?"

She smiled. "I'm too big, aren't I?"

"I don't think there's an age limit." I crossed over to her bed and sat on the end. With my fingers I traced the stitches of the red-and-white flower pattern on the quilt. "What a pretty quilt."

"My mother brought it with her from New York." She folded her hands under her chin and looked toward the sleeping form of her sisters. "I'm the only one who remembers her."

"The boys don't?" I asked, surprised.

"They remember some things, but not very many. They're bad memories mostly. I remember good things too."

"Like what?"

"There was a time when Mother tucked me in. Before the boys were born, I guess it was. She used to sing to me when I was very little."

"Do you remember any of the songs?"

"Not really. Did your mother sing to you?"

I smiled, thinking of my mother's raspy, off-key voice. "My mother's talents aren't musical, but yes, she sang to us when we were young until we asked her to stop."

Josephine's expression turned wistful. "I can't remember if my mother ever laughed."

"She must have at one time or another," I said.

"What's your mother's laugh sound like?"

I thought for a moment. How could I describe one of the most precious sounds in the world? "Quiet, like she wants the laugh to stay in her throat but can't quite manage."

"Do you miss her?" Josephine asked.

"I'm trying hard to be brave but yes, very much."

"What's your sister like?"

I smoothed the quilt up over her shoulder. "I'll tell you more tomorrow. Right now, you need to go to sleep. The morning will come early." Standing, I took the lantern from the bedside table.

She yawned. "Thanks for reading to us."

I turned to go, but a cold hand reached out to me. "Miss Quinn? I wouldn't mind if you kissed my forehead."

"All right, then." I leaned over and kissed her softly, as I'd done the others. "You have sweet dreams."

"You too."

I left the door open a crack and headed across the hallway to the boys' room. They were in their beds and turned on their sides talking quietly. I wanted to stand in the doorway and eavesdrop, but resisted.

"Gentlemen, are you ready for your tuck-in?" I asked.

They rolled onto their backs in perfect time, as if they'd choreographed the move. I suppose they'd learned to work together for space in their mother's womb.

I stood between their two beds and gazed down at Theo, then Flynn. They wore matching red-and-white plaid pajamas, but even in the muted light I could tell them apart. Not only did the scar give Flynn away; their personalities were in stark contrast, which made them appear to look different even though they were identical. The scholar and the scoundrel, I thought. I adored them equally.

"Miss Quinn?" Theo asked.

I sat on the end of his bed. "Yes?"

"Are you ever afraid of the dark?" Theo wrinkled his nose.

"Not really," I said. "I'm usually so tired at the end of the day, I fall right to sleep. Are you?"

"Not if Flynn's here. But sometimes I can't fall asleep."

I smiled as I smoothed the quilt over his legs. "You're a lucky boy to have a brother to keep you company. Do you know what my sister does when she can't sleep?"

He shook his head.

"She tells herself a story, like the ones she likes to read."

"Mine would have pirates," Flynn said. "And a ship."

"What about you?" I asked Theo.

"I'd tell a story of a happy family at Christmastime," Theo said.

"That sounds like a story I'd like to read." I moved over to Flynn's bed, where he had shifted to his side. His eyes fluttered as he tried to stay awake. This little one played hard and probably slept even harder. I swept a lock of hair from his forehead.

He looked up at me sleepily. "No kisses. Boys don't like them."

"I wouldn't dream of it." I chuckled and fluffed Flynn's hair, then Theo's. "Good night, sweet princes. Sleep well."

With lantern in hand, I left the door slightly ajar as they mumbled their good-nights. In my room, I undressed and readied for bed. After washing and brushing my teeth in the bathroom, I tiptoed back to my room, conscious not to wake the children. The floorboards didn't squeak as they did at my own home. I slipped into the cold sheets and blew out the lantern. It had been a long, stimulating day, and I was weary both mentally and physically, even though it wasn't much past eight. I closed my eyes and curled into a ball, waiting for the bed to warm from my own body heat. The house creaked, as if saying good night to its inhabitants. Soon, I warmed and drifted off to sleep, content with a good day's work done.

Alexander

✿

Around nine that evening Jasper and I nursed whiskeys in the corner of the saloon. Tonight, I'd made an exception to my aversion to public drunkenness and gambling. I wanted to gather as much gossip as I could about Samuel's death. Men in bars talked too much.

A man named Mike Murphy ran the saloon. I leased him the building. Other than that, I stayed out of his way. Every town needed at least one watering hole, whether I approved of what went on here or not.

"Do you ever wish we'd settled in Denver instead?" I asked.

"Never." Jasper gestured toward the window. "A man can breathe here."

When we'd come west, I'd bought up land in Denver. Whole city blocks belonged to me. If my family had taught me anything, it was that land ownership equaled wealth.

The rest of my land holdings were for profit. Emerson Pass was my heart.

I fell in love with this part of the country the moment we arrived that first spring. Meadows of columbine, lilies, and buttercups grew in the valley between mountains that kissed the bluest sky I'd ever seen. Aspens with their light green leaves fluttered in the breeze. The dry air smelled of pine and firs. In the time it took to unhitch our horses, I imagined the town we could build in this valley. I'd decided right then. This was home. I'd rebuild from the ashes.

"Why do you ask?" Jasper finished his whiskey and set the empty glass on the table.

"I don't know. I guess I'm wondering if I've been naive that this town is safer than most places."

"There are bad people everywhere. Here there are fewer of them because there are fewer people than in the city. You're not responsible for Samuel's death."

I traced the rings in the pine table. The first winter I'd spent here, Samuel had taught me that the growth rings in a tree told the history of a place as well as any book. Pale rings were from spring growth, whereas dark ones were from late summer. Skinny rings were indicative of drought or other environmental impacts such as insects or too-densely-populated forests. Fat lines told the tale of an abundant growing season. I'd teased him about his love of trees. "Trees never let you down, unlike people," he'd said.

I wished the trees could tell me the secrets of the night Samuel was murdered. What had they seen? But trees only talked to Samuel, not to me.

"Harley and Merry have asked if they might attend night school," Jasper said, pulling me from my brooding.

"Excellent."

Jasper said nothing.

"Is there a reason they shouldn't?" I asked.

"Their evening duties would fall to someone else twice a week," he said. "And what will the children do without Miss Cooper? Who will put them to bed?"

I studied him for a moment, trying not to laugh. Jasper did not care for change. "I'll put the young ones to bed. Harley's duties can be done before and after school."

"And Merry's?" One eyebrow went up as he tapped his middle finger on the side of his glass.

"Two evenings a week won't cause the house to go into chaos," I said. "This is important for them."

He lifted both brows this time but didn't say anything further. Long-suffering Jasper. My ways continued to scandalize him, even though he would never admit to it. I'd become too American for him.

Still, he was loyal to me. Even during the embattled years with Ida, his dedication never wavered. I believe he would have let someone chop off his hands rather than any harm come to me or the children.

I spotted the Higgins brothers as they came through the door and raised a hand in greeting.

"Come sit with us," I called out. "I'd like to buy you a drink for saving our schoolteacher."

They ambled over as Jasper rose to order the drinks from Mike.

"How is she?" Clive asked.

"Quite well," I said.

They each took a chair as Jasper approached with four glasses of whiskey.

"We heard there's a night school starting," Clive said.

"You interested?" I asked. Neither brother had gone to school, having been born and raised on the prairies with nothing more than a lean-to on their father's claim. Their mother had died giving birth to Clive and left them to grow up without an education or anything much to begin with. They'd come here, hoping for a chance, and they'd gotten it.

"Nah, probably not," Wayne said.

"Why not?" I asked the Higgins brothers. "A few hours a week and you could learn to read."

"I'd feel stupid sitting there in desks made for kids." Wayne slapped his thigh. "Can you imagine these gangly legs in the classroom?" Wayne and Clive were strapping young men, broad-shouldered and tall with light hair bleached even blonder from the Colorado sun.

I chuckled but had no intention of letting him off that easily. I'd have to provide incentive to them in another way. "Are you ever bored during our long winter months? Wouldn't you love to read an adventure story during those evenings when there's nothing else to do?"

Clive straightened slightly and looked over at me with an inquisitive glint in his eyes. "I'd like that, yes."

"I'll make you a deal," I said. "If and when you're ready, you may borrow any book from my library anytime you want."

Clive's eyes narrowed. "Let me get this straight." He gestured with his hand to indicate the patrons in the bar. "You're willing to let any of these men here inside your home, handling your books, simply because you want us all to learn to read."

I rubbed my chin. When he said it out loud, I sounded a bit daft. "That's correct. It's important to me that everyone in our town has access to books. What good are they collecting dust in my library?"

"Books improve lives," Jasper said.

"How exactly?" Wayne asked.

"Let me count the ways," I said, quoting Elizabeth Barrett Browning, then inwardly cringing at my pretentiousness. "Entertainment during long winter months, transportation to other worlds, learning about new subjects. Your life will expand through reading, I can promise you."

"Why do you care about us expanding our lives?" Wayne asked.

"Yeah, what's it to you?" Clive asked, not unkindly but sounding genuinely curious.

I blinked as I tried to form an answer that wouldn't make me sound arrogant and condescending. "Because I care about the people in this community."

The men still seemed unconvinced.

"You give away a lot of meat," I said. "Why do you do that?"

Wayne shrugged but didn't say anything.

"No one goes hungry in our town," Clive said.

"You told us that when we came here," Wayne said. "And we took it to heart. If we have scraps or extra, we give them away."

"This is the same thing," I said. "Miss Cooper is a teacher. I have books."

Clive leaned forward and peered into his whiskey. "If you're willing to have us into your home and share your books, then I suppose we could try school."

"No promises that it'll work," Wayne said. "Higgins men aren't known for our brains."

"Most men aren't," I said.

We all chuckled and sipped from our drinks.

"Lord Barnes, we were sorry to hear about Samuel Cole," Clive said.

"He was a good man," Wayne said.

"You hear anything around town?" I asked quietly.

Wayne glanced nervously around the room before returning his gaze to me. "We have some fresh beef coming in tomorrow. You should stop in and get some."

"I'll do that," I said. "Now, who wants a refill? I'm still buying."

THE STARRY SKY AND FULL MOON SHED LIGHT OVER THE SNOW as I drove us home. Oliver's and Twist's hooves made a pleasant *clip-clop*. The world seemed untouched and perfect under the glow of that yellow moon.

Jasper's shoulders sagged slightly from the whiskey. On the way there, his posture had been upright and stiff, but now he resembled a mere mortal.

"You and Miss Cooper," Jasper said.

"What about us?"

"You fancy her." He paused as he looked up at the sky and let out a long sigh. "She fancies you."

"I'm sure of the first thing, anyway," I said.

He fell silent, adjusting his hat, then buttoning his coat up to his neck.

"It's been three years," Jasper said. "There's no reason why you shouldn't remarry. Not all women are like Lady Ida."

"True. Miss Cooper doesn't seem the type prone to either madness or hatred, regardless of the weather," I said. "Ida was fragile even before she had Josephine."

"Did you know how fragile she was before you married?" he asked.

"No. I was in love. You remember."

"I do. I remember exactly."

"You saw it from the beginning, didn't you?" I asked.

"I hoped I was wrong."

I shuddered as I slipped into the memory of the night I'd found Ida standing over our two-week-old Fiona's crib with a knife.

Ida wore nothing but a thin white nightgown. Her fair hair had been crudely chopped and fallen in tufts around her bare feet. I grabbed her by the waist and tackled her to the floor. She didn't struggle as I pried the knife from her hand and tossed it across the room. Seconds later, she went limp as a rag doll on the braided rug and curled into the fetal position. Fiona had wakened during the commotion and started screaming. Josephine, at age ten, had come running from the room she shared with Cymbeline. She paled and slumped against the doorframe at the sight before her. Her mother on the floor with hair like a baby chick. Me, on my knees, weeping. The knife glittered in the moonlight.

"Papa," she whispered.

"Take the baby," I said. "Get the others and lock yourselves in the nursery."

Two weeks later, Ida had walked into the snow wearing nothing but her dressing gown.

Now, I blinked and looked up at the stars. Those days were gone. We'd come out of that awful time to the present.

My wife had changed dramatically after the birth of the twins. Before them, she'd been prone to sadness and irrational fears, but she'd still been able to participate in life. With Josephine, she'd been trepidatious and overly worried about the baby, yet distant from her. After the boys came, she seemed uninterested in them and preferred to spend her days in her room, painting or drawing. I hired a nanny to help, and we continued to live as we had. At the mercy of Ida's moods. I loved the children enough for both of us. At least, that's what I told myself.

During her energetic cycles, she'd come to my bed. I'm ashamed how weak I was. Even knowing how sick the pregnancies made her, I was unable to fend off her advances. She became pregnant with Cymbeline. When she gave birth, she wouldn't feed or hold her. One night, she said the baby had been sent from the devil to kill her.

I asked Dr. Moore to examine her. He said he'd seen it before. Psychosis after giving birth. He assured me the irrational fears would subside after a few months. He'd asked if she'd demonstrated any unstable symptoms before this. I lied to him. I couldn't tell him of her manic behavior, of the ups and downs I'd endured with her from the very first year of our marriage. The weeks she wouldn't get out of her bed. The many, many nights she couldn't sleep, pacing around the house like a caged tiger. The endless cycle of despondency followed by a clamored elation.

He was right. Three months after Cymbeline came, Ida returned to her usual behavior. The manic cycles continued, but she no longer thought the baby was sent by the devil. In hindsight, I can see that her psychosis grew deeper and more violent, ending finally with her poised over her own baby's crib with a knife.

Even now, after three years, shame flamed inside me. Her poor, tortured mind had finally been given relief as she died in the cold, all alone. I'd grieved for my babies who would never know their mother. Yet, and I'm ashamed of this too, I felt a sense of relief. Living with her had been a daily hell. Without her, I could bring calm and routine into my home.

Bloody hell, this was not doing me any good. Rehashing everything for the thousandth time. Allowing the shame to bubble to the surface and strangle me. Was I deserving of a new love? A second chance for happiness? I had no idea. Was it bold and ridiculous to hope that Miss Cooper would fall in love with me and agree to be my wife? Would that even be the right thing for her? I'd driven one woman to madness already. I'd brought danger into Miss Cooper's life by bringing her out here.

Oh, but she was breathtaking. And intelligent. Graceful, steady, and exceptionally brave to come all the way out west to teach school on the frontier.

"What do you think of Miss Cooper?" I asked. Oliver and Twist both whinnied in response. "I'd say the horses like her."

"She's lively and authoritative. Like a herding dog."

I laughed. "And you disapprove?"

"No, as a matter of fact, I'm rather taken with her myself."

I nudged his shoulder. "Jasper, are you growing soft on me?"

He sniffed. "I'm thinking of the children. What could be better than a herding dog for your brood?"

"What about for me? Do I need a herding dog?"

"I think you know the answer to that."

I laughed again.

"You're interested for real," Jasper asked.

"I'm interested," I said. "Not that I remember how to court someone."

"I'm happy to hear this. Lizzie and I have worried you'd never get over what happened with Lady Ida."

"It's too soon to know if there's anything special between us, of course. The children are keen on the idea." I told him about the strange way they'd reacted to her looking after them. "They were adamant that she would be my wife, not their nanny. I've never known them to do or say anything so outlandish. Then they asked if I'd ordered her, like Carter did with this wife."

I expected Jasper to chuckle over that. Instead, I heard him sniff and looked over to see him dabbing at his eyes.

"Something in your eye?" I asked.

"A fleck of dust," he said.

"You really are getting soft on me."

"I've always been soft when it comes to the children," he said. "It's shameful how they have me wrapped around their fingers."

"You and me both," I said.

We turned into the driveway toward the house. The familiar scent of woodsmoke welcomed us home. "What about you? Do you ever think about marrying?" I asked.

"How could I and continue to work for you? Butlers do not marry."

I turned to look at him. His profile in the light of the moon was as sharp and precise as his statement. "If there was someone you wanted, we could build a cottage for you. There's no reason to keep to those old rules. Not here."

"Lizzie's certainly embraced the new ways. It's that blasted raspberry wine she drinks after supper. Her tongue loosens, and the next thing I know she's telling me she loves me."

"What did you say?" Was he joking? No, his features were arranged in their usual serious position. "I thought you two were mortal enemies."

"How a person could be so irritatingly cheerful is beyond my comprehension. However, I wouldn't describe her as my enemy. I vacillate between wanting to kiss her and send her to her room with no supper."

I chuckled. "Given that she cooks our supper, that would be difficult. I'd go with kissing."

"There's a bothersome and distracting tension between us. Acting upon it could ruin both our lives."

"I'm not sure how taking a woman to bed could ruin your life. Especially if you've married her first."

"I'm not the kind to fall in love."

"You could be happy together. What's wrong with happiness?" I asked. "You want it for me."

"Happiness is for other people. Normal people."

"You're the most stubborn man I've ever known," I said.

"Thank you, lord."

"That was not praise." I slowed the horses as we passed by the house. The horses neighed, happy to see the barn. "Listen to me carefully. If you continue to break both your hearts by being a mulish fool, then I have no choice but to send you home to England."

"You wouldn't."

"I wouldn't. But I can't have you hurting Lizzie."

"You're being ridiculous."

"Let me ask you this," I said. "What would you think if I told you Clive Higgins was asking about her?"

He didn't answer, but his shoulders stiffened.

"Should I tell him she's available for courting?" I asked.

"She wouldn't like him. He's uneducated."

"I believe the ladies find him handsome."

Again, silence, then a sniff.

Forgive me for my white lie, I prayed silently. *But what's a man to do with a mule?*

"If she liked him, it would settle things once and for all," Jasper said.

"Sure thing. I'll throw them a nice wedding reception in the garden next summer. Soon they'll have pretty babies, and you'll still be all alone in your room downstairs."

"Excellent idea."

Despite his words to the contrary, his tight tone betrayed him. I smiled to myself in the darkness. Clive Higgins might need to drop by to borrow some sugar one afternoon. Nothing like a little competition to wake a man to his destiny.

———

AROUND NOON THE NEXT DAY, I HEADED OVER TO TALK TO the Higgins brothers about what they knew. They were both behind the counter, although the shop was empty of customers.

"Good timing, Lord Barnes," Wayne said. "We were about to close up for a short lunch break. Care to join us?"

"I've eaten, but would be happy to sit with you."

"Follow me," Clive said as we walked to the back of the store where the brothers shared a small office.

While Wayne unpacked stacks of sandwiches and set them on the desk, Clive offered me a glass of whiskey. I politely declined. "It's a little early for me."

They didn't waste any time with more niceties and launched into their reason for asking me here. "I don't know if it means anything, but Kellam was in the saloon after Cole was killed. Drunk, as usual," Clive said.

"Running his mouth," Wayne said.

"About?" I asked.

Wayne unwrapped his sandwich as if it were a Christmas present. "He said he overheard Carter and some of those old men that hang around his shop playing checkers all day talking about how they were going to make sure the Cole kids didn't show up at school."

"He said they were getting a group together to go out and talk to Cole," Clive said. "Set him straight that they best keep to themselves or there would be trouble."

"What else did he say?" I asked.

"That was about it," Clive said. "We told him he should go to the sheriff and report what he'd heard. But you know how it is with drunks. You can't reason with them."

"True enough," I said.

"He doesn't look after that daughter of his," Clive said. "Poor little thing's in here all the time begging for scraps."

"She came in last week and asked if we had anything for her," Wayne said. "She was limping and holding herself real careful, like she was hurt. I think that bastard beats her."

Clive swallowed a bite of sandwich before continuing. "I asked if her pa had any luck hunting and she said he tried but never could get anything."

"A drunk fool like that isn't going to be able to hit a jackrabbit," Wayne said.

"Anyway, we told this to the sheriff already," Clive said.

"But we thought we better tell you, too," Wayne said.

"We didn't get the feeling the sheriff cared too much one way or the other," Clive said.

I stood and prepared to go. "Thanks, gentlemen. I appreciate it."

"Let us know if you need anything," Clive said.

"Anything at all," Wayne said. "As long as this stays between us. We don't need any trouble."

"You have my word."

I FOUND SHERIFF LANCASTER PLAYING CARDS AT THE SALOON. We made eye contact, and he gave me a slight nod. "Give me a second, Barnes."

"Sure."

I took a stool at the counter and made small talk with Murphy while I waited.

A few minutes later, Lancaster cursed and threw down his cards. "Too rich for me." He stood and grabbed his cowboy hat from the rack and nodded toward the door. Outside, he tilted his head toward the sky and sniffed, like a dog on a hunt, then walked through the alley to the back of the building. I had no choice but to follow him. Lancaster wasn't one to take direction. He'd made it quite clear my English title meant nothing to him. Nor did the fact that I owned every building in town.

Most likely from years on a horse, the sheriff walked bowlegged. His lanky, skinny frame didn't seem inclined to move fast as he took a cigarette from his denim pants pocket and stuck it in his mouth. I wondered what he'd be like in a shoot-out. Did he draw his gun in the lazy way he walked? If so, I hoped we didn't have any shoot-outs on his watch.

Murphy had shoveled the snow around the back side of the building as well as the front, making it a good place to talk. Lancaster leaned against the brick wall and lowered his hat, shielding his eyes from my view. With a white handlebar mustache and a face with more crevices than the volcanic rock formations I'd seen during my visits south, he was as crusty as they came.

"What do you want?" He struck a match against the brick and lit his cigarette.

I told him what I'd learned from the Higgins boys. "They said they already told you. I wanted to see what you knew."

"Yeah, I talked to them. Those boys at Carter's were just blowing off steam." He took a long drag from his cigarette. "What do you know about Kellam?"

"Not much. I know his daughter's attending school without his knowledge and that Miss Cooper is worried about him coming to her classroom and dragging the poor child out by her hair."

I waited as he let out a long stream of smoke from his lungs. One couldn't be in a hurry with this fellow.

"I went out and talked to Mrs. Cole a few times." He had the raspy timbre of a heavy smoker. I wanted to give him a glass of water. "She told me about the financial arrangement her husband made for her."

I watched him carefully. Where was he going with this? Would I have to fight him for her right to the money? "Yes. What's that have to do with his murder?"

"It puts you as the prime suspect."

My immediate reaction was to lambaste him, but I held my temper and answered calmly. "Samuel Cole was a rich man, true. In comparison to my own wealth, however, it was of no consequence."

"That right?"

"That's right. Anyway, Samuel was my friend."

"What about her? Any motive to get rid of him?" The tip of his skinny, hand-rolled cigarette burned orange as he took another drag.

"They had a good marriage despite the tensions from the outside world."

He tossed the cigarette on the ground and stomped it with the heel of his boot. "Let me know if you hear anything else, but you need to prepare yourself. This murder may never be solved."

"Isn't it your job to do so? The governor sent you out here to keep law."

"Let me put it to you this way. As far as I'm concerned, the guy got what he deserved. He brought a woman like that here and lived with her like man and wife. What did he expect?" Without another word, he sauntered away, disappearing around the corner of the building.

I picked up his cigarette and tossed it in the trash bin Murphy kept near the back door. Then I headed down to the barbershop.

I ENTERED THROUGH THE FRONT DOOR OF CARTER'S barbershop. All heads turned, and the room silenced. Carter was giving the postmaster, Ray Owens, a shave. At a table in the front, two bearded men I didn't know played checkers. Two others I'd seen around town read a newspaper and smoked hand-rolled cigarettes. The room smelled of smoke and shaving cream.

"Looking for a shave, Barnes?" Carter asked.

Matthew Carter was in his fifties with a paunch, a long white beard, and white hair slicked back with thick pomade. He was a good tenant, never late with his rent or outwardly hostile. However, I'd heard from others that he resented my power and money.

"I'm here about Cole's murder," I said. "Wondering if you gentlemen know anything about that." Cigarette smoke hovered near the ceiling like a cloud cover.

"What would we know?" Carter asked.

"You and your friends here have let your opinions be known when it came to the Cole children going to school." I left it at that, hoping to bait someone into talking.

"Like you said, no secret there," Carter said as he scraped the blade across Owen's chin in short, fluid movements.

"Did you dislike it enough to kill a man?" I asked.

Carter didn't bother to look up from his work. "Not sure what you mean." Scrape, scrape, scrape went his blade.

"I heard something about a group of men joining up to go out and talk with Cole. You know anything about that?"

"Can't say as I do," Carter said. "But talking ain't the same as killing."

The rest of them were all back to pretending to play checkers and reading the paper.

"May I ask why you care?" I asked.

Carter lifted his head to look at me. "Listen, Barnes, you may own most of this town, but you don't own our thoughts. This is America. We're free to think however we please. I don't want their kind here. As much money as you have, you can't control our opinions. You don't like it? Too bad."

"I don't like it. My friend's dead because of a bigot. I'll find out the truth. Trust me, whoever was involved will pay."

"You're not going to find answers here," Carter said.

That was clear. I tipped my hat and left. Once outside, I drew in a deep breath.

Knowing I wouldn't be able to concentrate back at my office, I headed toward the park. Often, I'd eat my lunch there and watch the ducks. I trudged with some care through the banks of snow caused by the plow Harley had used earlier to clear the streets. The storefronts had been shoveled but were slick under my feet.

Harley and I had planted grass, laid brick walkways, and built benches around the pond, creating a park for picnics and family gatherings in warm months and ice-skating during the winter. Only a couple feet deep, the water was too shallow for swimming. However, it made for great ice-skating in the winter months. Today, a thick layer of ice covered the pond and was likely to remain until late March. I brushed several inches of new snow from a bench near the water's edge and sat. The sun hung low in the sky and shed a wintry blue light over the landscape.

With great squawking and fluttering of wings, a flock of black-and-white ducks swooped over the pond and onto the ice. Surprised by the slick surface, they slid on their feathered bellies. Affronted by this indignity, they rose on their webbed feet and took tiny steps, then slid a few inches and repeated the cycle, all the while pecking the ice with their bills. Their quacks sounded more like bleats as they complained to one another. Food sources this time of year were at the mercy of the weather.

As I sat there, I thought through my next move. If today had taught me anything, it was that Samuel's death was not going to be solved by the sheriff. I had nothing to go on, other than a suspicion his murder had been caused by bigotry. I had to come to a reconciliation that I might never know who killed my friend. Until Rachel forgave me, I couldn't do much for her, either.

Agitated, I left the ducks to their hopeless search for bugs in the ice and walked back toward the main street. Before I knew it, I found myself in the yard of the schoolhouse. Just to check on Miss Cooper and the children, I told myself as I trudged through the snow to the front steps. I pulled out my pocket watch to check the time. Just after two. They would let out for recess in a few minutes. I peered through the windows. Miss Cooper was at her desk with four of the children. The rest were hunched over their lessons.

Perhaps sensing my presence, she raised her head and spotted me. Embarrassed to be caught, I raised a hand in a wave. She smiled and nodded. That smile. I swear my heart grew larger in my chest.

Quinn

The days rolled by one after the other as we settled into a happy routine. After breakfast, the children, Lord Barnes, and I hustled into the sleigh and Harley took us all into town. Lord Barnes went off to his office while the children and I went inside the warm classroom. The school day flew by for me. I hoped it did for my students. They all seemed content enough and were so well behaved I worried something might be wrong with them. Did the mountain air deprive them of oxygen and make them submissive? When I asked Lord Barnes about this theory, he laughed and said it was my superior discipline skills at work. Like a silly schoolgirl, I basked in the glow of his compliment all day.

In the afternoons, Harley came for all of us and we made our way home, stimulated from the cold, fresh air and hungry for tea. Lizzie and Merry always had refreshments ready for us when we returned. Then, the children could do as they pleased for the hour or so before supper. I took the opportunity to write letters home or to read in the library during this time. Lord Barnes often did the same, sitting at his large desk in the corner, the sound of his pen dipping in and out of his inkwell a comforting sound as I wrote from the smaller desk.

Lord Barnes insisted I eat supper in the dining room with him and the children.

When I asked Lizzie if this was appropriate, she gave me a strange smile and patted me on the shoulder. "Dear, Lord Barnes makes his own rules. If he asked you to sit with the family, then it's perfectly fine. I suspect he's happy for the company."

I was also happy for the company. I'd never met a man as interesting or as curious about such a variety of subjects. Throughout supper, he entertained the children and me with his stories of his travels. He'd been all over Europe and even to the tip of Africa. "Nowhere felt like home," he said one night. "Until I came here."

After supper, I would get the children ready for bed, supervising baths and checking to make sure Flynn had washed behind his ears. When they were ready, I would read to them as I had that first night, all snuggled together in the girls' room.

By the end of the week, I was tired but happy as I closed the flue on the stove in my classroom. The Barnes flock was playing in the snow in the last light of the November afternoon. I'd just pinned my hat to my head when Harley appeared.

"Harley, you didn't have to come for me. I'm on my way out," I said.

"It's not that, Miss Cooper." He took off his newsboy cap and held it in both hands with his gaze directed at the floor. "I had a question for you. About night school."

"Of course." I stuck the last pin in my hat and reached for my coat.

"I've never had any school. Other than knowing how to write my name and a few other words, I can't read any English."

"Not having opportunities is nothing to be ashamed of. There's only shame in not taking them when they're presented to you."

He nodded. "I suppose. I'm worried I'm too stupid to learn."

"I'm a very good teacher," I said. "And you're a bright young man. Lord Barnes wouldn't trust you with his beloved estate if that weren't true."

Harley flashed a sheepish smile and rubbed a wayward curl back into place. "I'll be bringing Miss Merry with me."

"I'm glad." Merry's assessment that Harley didn't know she was alive might not be true, given the way his cheeks bloomed red.

He gestured toward the door. "After you, Miss Cooper."

I locked the schoolhouse door and joined the children in the sleigh.

We were all quiet as we headed down Main Street toward Lord Barnes's office. Even the Barnes children were tired after a long week of school. The Johnson girls were already at work in their father's shop and waved to us as we drove by. I spotted Isak sweeping the floor of the tailor shop. His father was bent over his work, sewing something by hand. We passed by the apothecary and the Higgins Brothers Butcher. A few men in the barbershop were playing checkers while Mr. Carter gave a man a shave.

The cloud cover was close and gray. By the time we pulled up in front of Lord Barnes's office, large, fat flakes fell from the sky.

He must have been waiting for us because the moment we stopped, he came out the side door of the building looking dashing in his black coat and fedora. "Hello, family," he said.

The children all called out to him as he climbed in next to me.

"Miss Cooper, how was your day?"

"Quite fine, thank you. And yours?"

"Better now." Lord Barnes winked at me as he tucked the blankets around my lap. "What more could a man ask for than this?"

I brushed a snowflake from my cheek, unsure what he meant.

He leaned close and whispered in my ear. "A sleigh ride home next to the prettiest woman in town."

"Lord Barnes!" I whispered back, pretending to be horrified by his boldness.

"All I do is speak the truth, Miss Cooper."

Flustered, I turned away to watch the flakes of snow dance in the frosty air and smiled to myself. If he only knew how my heart raced in his presence or how I longed for a kiss. What was happening to me?

———

WHEN I WOKE THE NEXT MORNING, THE SKY WAS A VIBRANT blue. Two new feet of snow sparkled like tiny crystals under the sun. Hearing the voices of children, I washed and dressed quickly and went to round them up for breakfast. Flynn and Cymbeline were already up and gone outside to play, Josephine informed me when I entered the girls' bedroom. "On Saturdays, the staff has the day off, which means we take care of the animals and our own meals." She sat sideways on the window seat behind Fiona. They wore plain gray dresses with drop waists. Josephine used a soft-bristled brush to comb out tangles in her little sister's hair. A white bow lay in wait.

"You're both such big girls to get yourselves dressed and ready for the day," I said.

"Jojo helps me," Fiona said, then winced as a particularly stubborn tangle met the brush.

"Sorry, pet," Josephine said. "You must have been wild in your sleep last night."

Fiona grinned. "Miss Quinn, one time I fell out of the bed."

"She was lucky not to break something." The knot out, Josephine tied the bow around Fiona's curls.

"Papa said I bounce," Fiona said.

Josephine popped from the window seat and smoothed her skirts. "We're ready now."

"Would you like to meet our pigs?" Fiona asked.

"You have pigs?" I lifted Fiona off the window seat and gave her a kiss on top of her head before setting her on her feet.

"Baby ones." Fiona's voice wobbled. "They'll get killed after they're fat."

"Fiona likes bacon but doesn't care to think where it comes from." Josephine gave her sister an indulgent smile.

"I understand completely," I said.

"They have curly tails," Fiona said. "And pink noses that make funny sniffing noises."

Fiona kept hold of my hand as we went down the stairs to the main floor. Ironically, the scent of bacon greeted us the moment we stepped into the dining room. Lord Barnes and Theo were already seated at the table. The elder Barnes read from a newspaper and Theo from a book. They both looked up and said good morning. Jasper stood watch.

"I let the other two eat and go out," Lord Barnes said. "I hoped just this once we could skip the prayer."

"It's your conscience." I winked at Josephine.

"I'll say my prayer silently," Josephine said. "Fiona, you should do the same."

"Yes, Jojo." Fiona kept hold of my hand as we contemplated what to choose for breakfast.

I added a blob of eggs to Fiona's plate in addition to the two pieces of bacon she asked for. Once we were seated, Lord Barnes set aside his *Denver Post*.

"Any news from the world?" I asked.

"Not anything worth repeating," Lord Barnes said. "Would you like it? The news is a week old by the time I get it, but at least I can keep somewhat abreast of the world's events."

I declined his offer, saying I might read it later if I had a quiet moment.

"And what do we plan to do with our day?" he asked the girls.

"We're showing Miss Quinn our pigs," Fiona said.

"And the rest of the barn," Josephine said. "We have chickens and Buttercream."

"What's a Buttercream?" I asked.

"Our cow," Fiona said.

"Because she makes us butter and cream," Josephine said, sounding like a weary old woman.

"Cymbeline named her," Lord Barnes said. "She's rather fond of both."

"I couldn't agree more," I said as I slathered butter on the sourdough bread Lizzie had made so expertly. "I'm not sure there's anything better than butter."

Fiona giggled.

"You'll need to borrow a pair of my rubber boots," Lord Barnes said, "if you're going out to the barn. Yours won't do. I'll accompany you. I wouldn't want you to slip and hit your head again."

I laughed and let my eyes twinkle back at him. "Lord Barnes, I'm perfectly capable of walking out to the barn without supervision."

"Yes, but where's the fun in that?" he asked.

Aware that we'd been lost in each other's gazes, I looked away. Josephine and Fiona both beamed at me.

"This is going to be a great day," Josephine said as she let out a happy sigh. "All of us together."

"Like if you were our mama, Miss Quinn," Fiona said.

I flushed from head to toe. Was my crush on Lord Barnes this obvious that even a three-year-old could see it? Or did they want a mother so badly they'd projected that role onto me?

I stole a glance at the object of my affection. He grinned at me, then winked.

I gulped and looked down at my plate, overcome with sudden emotion. Could it be possible that Lord Barnes saw a future between us that involved more than employer and nanny? If so, was that what I wanted?

Of course it is, you ninny. Pretending otherwise is ridiculous. Who wouldn't want Alexander Barnes and his brood of sweet angels?

AFTER BREAKFAST LORD BARNES CONVINCED ME TO PULL ON A pair of long, unattractive farmer boots as well as a manly jacket made of coarse canvas material. Lined with flannel and stuffed with down feathers, I was too warm standing in the foyer. They placed a gray knit cap on my head. I was about to pull on my gloves when Lizzie appeared with a pair made from a gray cashmere yarn.

"I made them for you," Lizzie said. "These are your Colorado gloves. They'll keep you warm on your rides to and from school and if you want to go out for a walk with Lord Barnes. For example."

"Thank you, Lizzie." I smiled, admiring the perfect stitches. "How did you find time for this?"

"I like to keep my hands busy," she said.

Lord Barnes had taken another jacket from the closet and was now putting it on over his brown coat and trousers.

Fiona jumped up and down, clapping her gloved hands. "Hurry, Papa and Miss Quinn. I want to find Cymbeline."

Josephine and Fiona wore matching thick red coats, white hats, and scarves.

"You two are pretty as a postcard," I said.

They smiled. "You are too," Josephine said.

"What's a postcard?" Fiona asked.

"I'll explain later," Josephine said.

"Ah yes, one last thing." Lord Barnes reached up to the top shelf of the closet and pulled down a scarf. "You'll want this too, Miss Cooper."

I reached for it, but he ignored me, wrapping it around my neck. His mouth turned upward in a slight smile as he looked down at me. "Now you're ready."

I had to tear my gaze from his beautiful eyes for fear I might fall into them and never escape their green pools. "Thank you," I said. "And now we must go out before I roast."

I squinted into the bright light. My eyes watered from the shock of the cold. Still, the fresh air invigorated me. A new layer of dry snow made the world quiet and without scars. The air crackled with energy. I had an urge to flop down and make an angel as I had as a child.

Josephine smiled up at me. "Do you see it? How perfect it is after new snow?"

"Yes, very much so."

Fiona had hold of Lord Barnes's hand. "Come see our swing, Miss Quinn."

Josephine linked her arm in mine as we walked in the fallen snow, following behind Lord Barnes and Fiona. I bunched my skirt into one hand. Despite the awkwardness of my overly large boots and cumbersome dress, we moved easily through the powdery snow until we reached a large oak. A primitive wooden swing hung from a thick branch.

"Look up," Josephine said.

I did so. A square wooden structure perched in the branches above. Snow covered its flat roof, and a rope ladder dangled from an open doorway.

"Papa built it," Fiona said.

"Really?" I looked over at him.

He chuckled as he took a tobacco pipe from his jacket pocket. "Don't look shocked, Miss Cooper. I'm not only a useless lord."

"Would you like to swing?" Josephine asked.

"Oh no. I'm too big," I said.

"Nonsense," Lord Barnes said as he lit his pipe with a match. "This swing holds me."

Before I could protest, Josephine dragged me over to the swing. Someone must have used it already this morning, because the wood had been cleared of snow and ice. However, the seat hung about six inches over the snow. I'd have to keep my legs straight if I were to move at all. "How will I pump my legs?" I asked.

"Papa will push you," Fiona said.

"It's the only way in the snow." Josephine tilted her head, as if this were a most serious matter.

I sat gingerly and stretched my legs out into a straight position. Holding tightly to the handles, I waited as Lord Barnes, with his pipe in one corner of his mouth, walked around to the back of the swing. The scent of the pipe tobacco came with him.

His first push on the small of my back was no more than a nudge. I could feel the gentleness of his hands even through my layer of clothing. The second, however, was more powerful, lifting me high into the air. Skirts flying around me I swooped up and back, each time flying higher. I laughed like a child. Fiona squealed with delight, obviously thrilled that I was having such fun. Josephine's expression, on the other hand, was one of longing. Did she miss her mother? Had Lord Barnes pushed her on the swing like this?

"All right, that's quite enough swinging for one day," I said.

Lord Barnes wrapped his arms around my waist to stop me. For a split second he held me tightly against his broad chest. I drew in a sharp breath and smelled his shaving cream mixed with tobacco smoke. His physical nearness evoked something carnal. A stirring of my blood. Heat and desire and the wish that I could know all of him. I longed to be swept into his arms and taken to his bed. Never in my life had I imagined such things.

He loosened his grip. I tried to jump gracefully from the swing. Instead, I fell into the snow face-first. Sputtering, I shook the snow from my head and face. Fiona bounded toward me, laughing. She launched herself into my arms and we both fell backward in the snow. We giggled as we tried to untangle from each other and the snow. Lord Barnes set his pipe on the abandoned swing and dropped down next to us. With one hand he lifted Fiona to her feet. He offered both his hands and helped me upright.

Josephine and Fiona were now lying on the snow and fluttering their arms and legs, making angels.

He kept hold of my hands and looked into my eyes. "Do you know how to make a snow angel?"

"I know exactly how to make a snow angel," I said, sassy.

His gaze shifted downward and seemed to fix on my mouth. "Shall we have a competition?" he asked, low and husky.

"What's the prize?" I asked, matching his tone.

He blinked three times, clearly surprised at my flirtatiousness. "You're a lady. Which means you get to decide. If it were up to me, I'd ask for a kiss."

"A kiss?" I whispered. "In front of the children?"

"I'd wait until later if you wanted me to." His eyes glittered under the sunshine as he leaned close to my ear. "I'd wait a lifetime if I knew at the end, I could have a taste of your mouth."

I stared at him, mesmerized by his proximity and boldness, and whispered into his ear. "Lord Barnes, I thought you were a gentleman."

"You make me lose my head. I'm powerless when I'm near you and unapologetic for my adoration."

This, after two weeks? Oh well, I thought to myself. If he insisted on being unapologetic, why couldn't I?

Without another word, I shuffled through the snow next to the girls. Lord Barnes followed me into the snow and like the children, we moved the snow with our arms and legs into a pattern of an angel.

"I'm making another one," Fiona said, shouting as she flung herself backward into the snow next to me.

I turned my head to look at Lord Barnes and caught him watching me, his eyes startling green in all that white. "I guess you do know how, Miss Cooper. But mine's still better."

I laughed. "Let's ask Josephine to judge."

Lord Barnes got to his feet first and lent a hand to me, pulling me up, then brushing the snow from my jacket and cap.

"Which is better, Josephine?" he asked.

She looked from his to mine. "Well, Papa's wins for size but

Miss Quinn's is more even. See there, Papa, one of your angel's wings is bigger than the other."

"Jojo, look," Fiona said. "Do you see the bird?"

A winter sparrow hopped from one bare branch of an aspen to the next. The girls headed that direction, temporarily distracted from their father and me.

He drew close. "I'm devastated to lose. I had my heart set on that prize."

I blushed, laughing. "I'll have to think about what I want, then."

He gave me a wolfish grin. "Don't think too long or I might forget all about it."

"You could forget me so easily?" I asked, teasing.

"A thousand years could pass and you'd still be on my mind, Miss Cooper."

"You're much too charming for your own good," I said.

"Let's go, Papa. Chase me, Papa," Fiona shouted as she ran toward us.

"Saved by the baby," he yelled back to me as he set out after Fiona. "Or I might have gotten a prize after all."

"Don't you wish," I said.

Fiona ran toward the barn with her father on her heels.

Josephine hung behind with me. She offered her arm. "You best hold on to me. Those boots are much too big for you."

There was a quiet energy in her as we walked arm in arm toward the barn.

"What are you thinking about so intently?" I asked.

She tilted her head toward me until it almost touched my shoulder. "I was just thinking how happy Papa's seemed since you came here. And the kids too."

"Does that make you sad?" My heart was in my throat suddenly. Did she not want me here?

"Quite the opposite. We've been waiting for you for such a long time."

I swallowed. What did one say to that?

Josephine pressed my arm against her side. "I knew you'd change everything."

"For the better, I hope?" I kept my voice light.

"Yes, Miss Quinn, for the better. You'll see in time I'm right," Josephine said. "You're meant to be here with us."

"Has it been hard to look after the younger ones?" I asked as we made our careful way toward the barn.

"I don't know any other way, so I can't say for sure. Papa's needed me, and I've done so because I love them. Anyway, I'm happy when I'm helping others."

"I love the sentiment, but you mustn't forget about yourself. You're still a child, after all. You should be having fun, not worrying so much."

"That changed the moment my mother walked into a blizzard."

Her raw honesty made my legs and arms tingle. "Oh, Josephine, that must have been awful."

"It was a bad time, but we made it through. That's what people do, you know?" Her voice was as brittle and fragile as a piece of crystal. I wondered how much her stoicism cost my little Josephine, this grown woman in a child's body. Would it make her into a bitter woman? One who wished she'd had the gift of innocence for longer?

By now, we were at the barn. I caught the scent of hay and horse stalls. "This is like a barn from a picture book," I said.

"Really?" Josephine said. "To me, it's just a barn."

"It's much more than that." Painted red, with white-trimmed doors, the handsome barn added to its idyllic surroundings instead of taking from them. A wooden fence made an area for the animals to roam free in warmer weather. How I wished my mother and sister were here. "This barn is like art."

"Come on, then. If you like this, wait until you see the piglets," Josephine said, giggling.

We entered through one of the enormous double doors. Built of round-cut and crosscut timber, there were at least a dozen small windows that let in the wintry light. Bales of hay were stacked in the rafters. Pitchforks, shovels, and various other tools hung neatly in a tack room. The floor was made of wide, rustic planks and was surprisingly clean. Stalls for the four horses, the milking cow, and the pigs occupied one side of the barn. Poultry took up the rest of the space.

A dozen laying hens in various colors of red, white, and speckled scratched and pecked greedily from the cracked corn scattered on the floor. Twelve-inch nest boxes with beds of straw were built upon a three-foot platform.

Fiona ran between the chickens with her arms spread out like wings and made squawking noises. They must be accustomed to her, because the hens appeared undisturbed as they pecked at the floor.

Cymbeline ran toward us and tugged on my jacket. "Miss Quinn, do you want to meet everyone?"

"These are our chickens." Josephine rattled off their names. Most were clearly chosen for their coloring: Cinnamon, Salt, Pepper, Chili, Clove, Cocoa, Ginger, Mustard, Nutmeg, Vanilla. Having run out of spices, Josephine explained, they went with beverages. "Coffee and Tea were all we could think of. You'd be surprised how hard it is to come up with so many names. And then in the spring, we get fryer chicks. They don't get names because we kill those for food."

"No, we don't." Cymbeline shook her curls and crossed her arms over her chest. "We get those from the butcher shop."

Josephine shot me a look that told me the chickens for eating were not all from the butcher shop. "We can't name anything we're going to eat," Josephine said. "That's Papa's rule."

"Good rule," I said.

Four turkeys, with their ugly red wattles like neck scarves, swaggered about in a group and glared at us from beady eyes. Did they know Christmas was coming soon?

"Do the turkeys have names?" I asked, feeling guilty that the thought of a crispy brown turkey right out of the oven made my mouth water.

Josephine gave a covert shake of her head, clearly not wanting to bring up a sore subject in front of Cymbeline.

Cymbeline pulled me over to the water trough. Two white ducks lifted their heads. At the sight of Cymbeline, they let out a friendly, somewhat foolish quack from their orange bills.

"This is Gin and Tonic," Josephine said. "Papa named them. They aren't the cleverest animals. But they're funny."

"What's their purpose?" Given their names, I knew they would not be for dinner. Thank goodness. They were too cute to be eaten.

"Sometimes they make fat eggs," Cymbeline said. "Lizzie uses them for omelets."

The twins called us over to look at the pigs. Josephine led me by the hand, and the boys parted to give me prime viewing. A long, plump pig lay on her side as eight piglets suckled. Mama didn't raise her bristled pink head to greet me as the ducks had. I didn't take offense. She was probably tired.

"Her name's Sweetpea." Theo had climbed up to sit on the four-foot wall that enclosed the stall. "She's very smart. Pigs are intelligent animals. Did you know that, Miss Quinn?"

I smiled over at him, charmed by the earnest expression on his freckled face. "I've read about it in books, but having never met a live pig, I couldn't say for certain."

"Spend any time with a pig and you'd know," Flynn said.

"Do you see their tails?" Cymbeline asked. "Aren't they too perfect?"

"Perfect indeed." The pink darlings with their swirled tails and pink tummies were much too adorable to think of them as bacon. I understood Cymbeline's dilemma. I wondered how the sow had become pregnant, as I saw no other pig. I decided to keep that question to myself.

"Did you see our rooster?" Flynn asked, pointing to the red

rooster. "We call him King." The way he strutted about the barn as if he were in charge had certainly earned him his name.

"He crows very loud," Fiona said.

"King's rather obnoxious," Josephine said. "But without him, we wouldn't have fertilized eggs."

Cymbeline's eyes flashed with annoyance in the way my sister's did when I told her something she already knew.

"Miss Quinn, come with me." Cymbeline dragged me over to the stall where a fawn-colored cow with large brown eyes chewed her cud. "This is Buttercream." Buttercream looked unbothered by my presence, busy as she was with the cud.

"She's a Jersey," Flynn said as he sidled up next to me and petted Buttercream's head. "This old girl makes the best cream." He rubbed his stomach. "Lizzie churns it into butter."

"We have cream with the wild berries in the summer," Josephine said from behind me.

"Harley grows raspberries." I turned to see that Poppy had joined us. She wore a pair of overalls made of denim and a knit cap over her two braids. How freeing it must be to wear any form of trousers. I wished the other girls could dress the same, while tramping around in the barn anyway. As for me, I would have been delighted to be out of a corset and a dress.

I walked over to the stalls where Lord Barnes shoveled horse dung. I'd thought Lord Barnes would look out of place with a shovel in his hand, given his pedigree and that crisp British accent. Wearing long rubber boots over his wool trousers, and an old tweed coat, he looked as if he belonged here. If anything, he looked even better out here than inside, which I hadn't anticipated possible. Perhaps feeling my gaze, he looked up from his work. "Hello there. What do you think about our little farm?"

"I like it quite well."

"We don't bother with beef," Lord Barnes said. "We buy our meat from the Cassidy farm."

"What about the pigs? Do we eat them?" I asked.

"We slaughter a few for us and sell the others to the Higgins boys," he said.

Why? I wondered. Didn't Lord Barnes have enough money without raising pigs?

"I wanted the children to have some experience with real work," Lord Barnes said, as if I'd asked my question out loud. He leaned against his shovel. "The pigs are their responsibility. They raise and sell them for profit, which then goes into funds for their future. The rest of the farm is for our consumption."

"The lessons they learn from their enterprise will be invaluable to them," I said.

"It's my hope," he said before going back to his shoveling.

"Miss Quinn, do you want to help us gather the eggs?" Cymbeline asked.

I most certainly did not want to help gather eggs. Chickens scared me. What if they didn't want to give up their eggs? However, I knew it wasn't a good example for our human chicks to see my fear, so I agreed.

"How do I do it?" I asked as we stood in front of the nest boxes. Each box had a brown egg tangled in straw.

"First, we'll scatter some feed for them in there." Cymbeline pointed to a small area closer to the front of the barn. She called for Fiona.

Fiona came running over. "Is it time?"

Josephine reached into a bin from the shelf hanging on the wall and scooped a handful of corn and grain into a small tin bucket. She handed it to Fiona. "Here you are."

Fiona, bucket swinging in her pudgy hand, walked to the feeding area. The hens gathered around. For a moment I was worried they were going to peck at the small girl, but the moment Fiona tossed the first handful, they focused on their breakfast.

"Now we collect the eggs while they eat," Cymbeline said as she handed me another bucket. "Once we have them all, we take them to Lizzie. She washes them in her big sink."

"Lizzie won't allow anyone else to wash the eggs. She's afraid we'll get sick if they're not washed properly," Josephine said.

I leaned closer to inspect the egg in the first box. It wasn't terribly dirty, but I was certain the brown spot on part of the shell was dried chicken manure. Grateful for my new gloves while simultaneously hoping they were washable, I reached in and grabbed the egg, then set my prize gently at the bottom of the pail. I glanced behind me to see if any of the hens were ready to claw my eyes out for stealing their eggs. They were all too busy with their corn to notice me. "Does Harley do all these chores while you're at school?" How did he do all of this alone?

"No, Merry gets to collect eggs during the week," Cymbeline said, bitterly. "She's lucky. Saturdays and Sundays are the best days."

I gathered a few more eggs, as did the girls. Soon, the nests were empty. Cymbeline and I then took out any soiled straw and replaced it with new. Josephine swept the floor of scraps of straw and other debris. Flynn was over with Buttercream doing the milking while Theo fed Sweetpea. Lord Barnes continued his hard work in the stalls.

All in all, I had to agree with Cymbeline. Saturday was a good day.

LATER, I WAS COMING OUT OF THE NURSERY AFTER PUTTING Fiona down for a nap when I ran into Lord Barnes.

"Miss Cooper, how did you enjoy your first day as a farmer?" he asked.

"This has been the best time of my life." I smiled up at him. "Everything. The school, your children. Even the pigs."

"Is this only a position to you?" he asked softly as he looked down at me with vulnerability in his eyes. For a man rich and powerful, he appeared no older than Theo.

"I'm fond of the children, thus it doesn't feel like work." I stared at the tips of my boots, shy but unable to depart. The hallway, dim and narrow, made it impossible to ignore how his presence made my skin tingle and my pulse race.

He inched closer. I caught the pleasant scent of his shaving soap. He lifted my chin and looked into my eyes. "Is it only the children you care for, or is there room in your heart for me?"

My stomach turned over. "There's room for you. A lot of room."

He grazed my cheek with the backs of his fingers, his eyes pools of sincerity. "I'll fill every empty spot of your heart if you'll allow me to."

"Lord Barnes, you're bold and terribly inappropriate." I cocked my head to the side and gave him a sassy, flirtatious smile. This was a dangerous game to play with my employer. Somehow, I didn't care. I was as reckless and wild as the animals that roamed outside these walls.

"Do you think I'm playing with you?" he asked, smiling down at me.

"I think you're a lord and I'm a schoolteacher. Is this a game to you?"

"I don't play games. Titles mean nothing when it comes to the heart. I'm a man who knows what he wants."

I swallowed. "Good, because I've never cared for games." I turned away, feeling his gaze on my backside as I walked on shaky legs toward my room. Once inside, I plopped on my bed, dizzy from the interaction. A craving as I'd never experienced had taken hold of me. I wanted Lord Alexander Barnes in my bed. What kind of wanton woman was I? But again, I couldn't seem to muster any shame.

Alexander

That evening, after bathing and replacing my work clothes with dinner attire, I passed by the closed door of the girls' room. From inside came the high-pitched voices of Fiona and Cymbeline, then Miss Cooper's lower one. The boys were not in their room, so I assumed they must be bathing. Since she had everything under control, I headed downstairs to my library to spend a few minutes reading by the fire.

I sat in my favorite leather chair. My muscles were pleasantly tired from the day's work. I was looking forward to a warm supper and more time with my kids and the beautiful woman who had appeared out of nowhere in my house and life. Miss Cooper had offered to put together a hearty soup. Usually on Saturdays, Lizzie left us slices of cold ham and a German-style potato salad.

I vacillated between euphoria and utter mortification at the way Miss Cooper's eyes had shone when I'd so brazenly spoken my thoughts out loud. I was so preoccupied by my juvenile misstep and the periodic images of her flushed skin and lips the color of ripe raspberries that it was impossible to concentrate on the book in my lap.

After a few minutes of blissful quiet where I contemplated all things Miss Cooper instead of reading, Jasper announced the arrival of Mrs. Cole.

"Shall I send her in?" he asked.

I rubbed my eyes and set aside my book. "Yes, please." Weary, I rose from the chair and prepared myself for the inevitable onslaught of her rage. I must remember what I promised Samuel. I was to look after her. If that meant I had to take the brunt of her anger, then so be it. Seconds later, she burst into the room. "Thank you for seeing me," Rachel said.

"Please, have a seat. Jasper can bring tea."

"No, I can't stay. I've come to say I'm sorry for acting like a spoiled child."

"You didn't," I said. "There's no need."

She bounced around my library like a coiled spring, all the while working a lace handkerchief between her long fingers. "I'm angry and took it out on you, which wasn't fair. You've been nothing but good to me. To us. Did you know you're the only one who stood by Samuel when he came back with me?"

Standing near the fire, I gripped my hands together behind my back. "Grief makes us say strange things. You mustn't think about it another moment."

"Wilber, my brother, has come. I feel safer with him at the house." She sank into the couch, as if suddenly exhausted. "He's ashamed of me—keeping us all hidden like mole rats. He thinks the children should go to school. He said my fear shouldn't keep them from opportunity."

"What do you think?" I asked quietly as I sat across from her.

"I think what I've always thought. It's best to stay away from trouble." She spread the handkerchief over her lap. "That said, I've decided to send them to school. Wilber will drive them." With her head tilted downward, she spoke so softly I leant forward to hear her better. "I should never have come here in the first place. Shouldn't have let myself fall in love with Samuel."

"In the history of humankind, I don't think we've ever been successful in denying the heart's desires."

She looked up at me. "What about you? Do you ever curse yourself for falling in love with Ida?"

I wanted to say yes. I wanted to say how I'd cursed God and my own foolish heart. How could this be the woman I'd pledged my life to? I didn't say any of those things, of course. What good would it have done Rachel to hear how broken our union had been? "She gave me five wonderful children. For this I'm grateful."

"When does the gratitude come back? Right now, I'm just so mad at him."

"I'm not sure it's the same for everyone," I said. "My feelings for Ida were complicated. By the end, I was so twisted up in guilt and contempt and fear that I couldn't even recall my early feelings of love for her. Now, though, I remember the few good times we had." I smiled at the memory of the first time I'd been introduced to Ida at her father's apartment in Manhattan. She'd looked lovely and pristine in a white dress, and yet her eyes had portrayed a wild recklessness I'd been drawn to. "The initial qualities that attracted me to her were the ones that inevitably broke me."

Rachel's brown eyes had softened. "We were never sure exactly what went on over here."

"She was very sick for a long time." I kept it at that. The secrets of Ida's troubles would remain within this house. I had a strange sensation sometimes that if I spoke about them, even here with my trusted staff and the children, it would make the terror of those times remain within these walls and taint any future in which there was more laughter than tears. "There was nothing I could do to help her."

"We suspected as much," Rachel said. "Samuel was never one to ask."

"No, most men don't. Although we know anyway."

"I'm sorry we weren't better friends to you."

"You were. Samuel was always there when I needed to go fishing or be outside. Seeing him happy with you gave me a great deal of joy."

She twisted her handkerchief around one finger like a bandage as she spoke. "Between Samuel and me, it was good. We didn't always agree, but we respected each other. From the beginning, it was as if we'd always been together, and then those babies came, and I had everything I could ever want. I've always been strong. A person like me had to be, God knows, in this world that's been set up to bring me down on my knees at every turn. But this. Going on. Living. I can't imagine how I will."

"You will." I'd wondered the same after Ida's death. I could remember wanting nothing more than to sleep. To shut away everything. But I had to continue on for the children. I had to make sure their childhood wasn't only about their mother's illness and death. I'd wondered how the children would ever be happy again. Theo's pinched, drawn face the night after he'd found her lying dead in the snow hovered before me. I blinked to get rid of the picture. "I thought the same, but somehow you do."

Footsteps down the stairs, followed by voices and laughter, interrupted our conversation. Rachel startled at the noise. "Are those the children? What's happened to the terrifying nanny?"

"She left. We have Miss Cooper now."

"The schoolteacher is here? Living with you?"

I waited until I heard them all head downstairs to the kitchen before I explained, rather awkwardly, how Miss Cooper had come to stay with us and her subsequent offer to take the place of the nanny. "The staff is off today. She and the kids are going to the kitchen to make something for supper."

"I haven't heard them sound like that—happy and gay—I don't think ever," Rachel said. "This Miss Cooper must be special."

"The kids fell for her rather quickly." As had I. The fire had died down and the chill crept in like a thief. I tossed in a few more logs. "All in all, yes, she's quite remarkable."

Rachel's quick mind was already way ahead of me. Not surprising. Women were always smarter than men about matters of the heart. "Alexander?" That's all. Just my name, yet I knew exactly what she was asking.

"I can't seem to help myself." I gave her a reluctant smile.

"Don't. It's no crime to be happy. This is a lonely country all alone. The winters are long without someone to warm your toes."

I returned to the fireplace and retrieved the poker. "She's young. Only twenty-two." I prodded the logs into a better position before returning to my chair. "I'm not sure she'd be interested in an old man like me."

"Love knows no age or color." She smiled in a way that didn't reach her eyes. "Anyway, if you have a chance for love, you best take it. You never know how long you'll get."

I fought the lump in my throat. "It's still hard for me to understand he's gone."

"Yes." She stuck her handkerchief into the sleeve of her dress and scooted to the edge of the couch cushion. "I should go. I left the kids with Wilber. They may have tied him up by now."

I stood when she did. "Before you go, we should talk about what I've learned."

She went still. "What you learned?" The words were like a dry creek bed, desperate for rain.

"It's nothing, really." I summarized what the Higgins brothers had told me and followed up with my conversation with the sheriff.

"What you're telling me is that we'll never find out who did this," she said.

I nodded. "I respect you too much to lie to you. But I've come to a similar conclusion."

She touched her fingertips to her forehead. "I should get back. Thank you, Alexander."

"You're welcome."

I watched her leave, her posture ramrod straight, as if she were holding herself together by sheer will.

Quinn

❧

On Tuesday evening, Harley drove Merry and me into town thirty minutes before our first night class so we could stoke the fire I'd left that afternoon. As I wrote the lesson on the blackboard, I feared no one would show. It had dumped snow for hours. Although clear now, the temperatures had dropped into the teens. Until the heater warmed the room, it was too cold to take off coats. I kept mine on as I wrote a lesson on the board. Merry stoked the dying embers back to life with a couple pieces of kindling. Harley shoveled a walkway in front of the porch.

I turned from the board as a woman walked through the door. There was no mistaking who she was. Dark-skinned with enormous brown eyes and a long, graceful neck, Rachel Cole wore a fashionable and expensive-looking coat over the latest style boots.

"I'm Mrs. Cole."

"It's a pleasure to meet you." I held out my hand and we shook. Her gloves were made of fine black leather. I was self-conscious of my rough nails and calluses. "What can I do for you?"

"I wanted to get a look at you," she said.

"A look at me?" I swallowed as my stomach twitched from within. Her hat was the most beautiful I'd ever seen other than in *Vogue*, where they displayed all the Paris fashions. The closest I came to those were the clothes my sister made from the pictures.

"You can't know a person without looking into their eyes," she said.

I smiled and widened my eyes. "What do you see?"

"Someone either naïve or brave." Her mouth twitched into a ghost of a smile.

"I suppose I could be both. Maybe one naturally goes with the other?"

"I'll just say straight out, Miss Cooper. My children look like me, not their father. This means they're not welcome here in town. When Alexander came to talk to me after Samuel died, I sent him away. I couldn't bear the thought of them coming here and being hurt. They're all I have." Her voice caught. She dropped her gaze to her hands. "Alexander spoke highly of you. He seems to think you'll treat my babies like you do the others."

"You have my word." I stared back at this formidable woman, trying not to let my intimidation show. She was exceptionally pretty. Tall in stature, and eyes that seemed to peer right into my mind. I felt a fraud under her scrutiny. And even shorter and scrawnier than usual.

"Will you teach them the same as you do the others or will you make them learn on the porch?"

I crossed my arms over my chest and answered with the confidence I didn't feel. "This is my school. I make the rules. All children will have a desk in this classroom. All children will be treated with respect."

She tugged off her gloves without taking her eyes from me. "What makes you different?"

I fingered the edges of my necktie. "I'm a teacher, Mrs. Cole. Anyone who wants to learn is welcome in my school."

"There's another family like us," she said.

"Pardon me?"

"The Chinese family who live down at the old mill by the river."

I stared at her. "Alexander hasn't mentioned them."

"They're kin of the original miners who came here in the sixties. I don't know much about them, other than they're a woman and two children. They've been ostracized from the rest of the community. Samuel told me they stay away from town."

Why hadn't Alexander told me of them?

"My husband used to take them wild game he trapped or killed. Without him, I don't know what they'll eat this winter." She looked toward the window, as if she were expecting some-one. "I've been preoccupied with my grief and forgot about them. I woke in the middle of the night and remembered they're all alone out there."

I nodded as my mind whirled with this new information. "Does Lord Barnes know about them?"

"I'm not sure. If he did, Samuel never mentioned it."

Harley was outside the door stomping snow from his boots. He stepped inside and flashed a smile at Mrs. Cole. "Good evening, Mrs. Cole."

"Harley." She nodded at him. I couldn't be certain, but I thought she softened slightly. "Thank you for your help with the animals."

"My pleasure," he said. "Let me know if you need anything."

"Wilber's here now. We'll be fine," she said. "I've decided to send my children to school."

"Between Lord Barnes and me, we keep close watch on Miss Cooper and the students," Harley said. "We'll be sure to keep watch for yours."

"Thank you, Harley." She turned back to me. "Will there be a desk for them? There are three. Two sons and a daughter." She went on to tell me their names and ages: Noah, age eight; Roman, age seven; and Willa, age six.

I gestured toward the desks. "There is room for all, Mrs. Cole. I assure you."

"Very well." She nodded and turned to leave, her long skirts swishing around her legs. As the door opened and closed, I caught a glimpse of a gentleman in a tall hat sitting at the helm of a small sled. He must be the brother who had come from Chicago to look after them. He leapt from the driver's side to help Mrs. Cole onto the seat, then joined her. I watched as they drove away, bells on their sleigh ringing in the cold night air.

I turned to Harley and Merry, who were huddled near the stove. "Will we have trouble over this, do you think?"

Harley rubbed the palm of his hand against his chin. "I'm not sure."

"But you'll still let them come, won't you?" Merry asked. "Even if you're scared?"

The trust on her face was such that even if I'd wanted to, I could not disappoint her. She believed me to be honorable, and I would be, even if it caused difficulty. My father had said no one ever made a difference in the world unless they were willing to face controversy. "I'm terrified, but I'll risk my life for their right to come to school." I walked over to the window and stared out into the blackness. Was there danger lurking out there?

"Is she right about the others?" I asked.

Merry nodded. "We see glimpses from time to time. It's only women and children down there from what I know. They have no one to turn to if they're without a man."

"Even if they would come to town, could they?" I asked. "I mean, how would they get here?"

"I could bring them," Harley said. "If Lord Barnes agreed to it."

"I'll talk to him," I said. "For now, we're focused on this evening. If anyone shows."

"We're here," Harley said.

"If it's only you two, we could have stayed home and been warm," I said, smiling as I walked over to stand by the heater.

Merry took my place by the windows. "Here comes some-one," she said. "Two actually. The Higgins brothers." She pressed her nose closer to the glass. "Oh no, I think they're leaving. They turned around and are headed the other way."

I rushed over to stand by Merry. She was correct. They each carried a lantern. In that dim light I saw fear on their faces. These giant men had risked the wilderness to come west but were too intimidated to come inside a schoolhouse?

"I'll change their minds," Harley said. He threw open the door and called out a hearty greeting. "Hey there, Wayne and Clive. You're going the wrong direction."

They stopped and slowly turned toward us. Clive raised his arm. "Evening."

"Come on in," Harley said. "Miss Cooper won't bite."

Wayne nodded and tugged his brother's arm. "Right, yeah. We can't stay the whole time, most likely."

"No problem," Harley said, and held the door open wider, which was making it even colder.

"Tell them to get in here before we all freeze to death," Merry said. Always practical, I thought. And she was right. The stove was no good in this kind of cold.

The Higgins brothers stomped onto the porch. I went to the doorway to greet them. "Come in, come in."

"Miss Cooper," Wayne said, tipping his hat.

"Thanks for having us," Clive said.

The two men plucked their hats from their heads and held them to their chests as they wiped their boots on the rug.

I told them to keep their coats on for now. "You'll learn faster if you're warm."

They shuffled to the middle of the room and lowered them-selves into the desks. "Told you we'd look ridiculous," Clive muttered to his brother.

I bit back a smile. They *were* awfully large for the desks.

The next arrival was Mrs. Cassidy, a pretty woman with light red hair and a narrow face. Like me, she wore a threadbare coat and boots that had obviously been polished in an attempt to hide their age.

I welcomed her with a smile that I hoped conveyed warmth. "Keep your coat on," I said. "We'll need to stay warm."

Mrs. Cassidy took off her hat and hung it on the rack, then took a seat with the gentlemen. Merry and Harley took their seats as well, and I went to the front of the classroom. "And so we begin."

HARLEY MADE SURE MERRY AND I WERE SAFELY INSIDE BEFORE driving to the barn to put away the horses. What a long day the young man had, I thought as I followed Merry into the house. The ride home had chilled me to the bone. If I'd been willing to spend money on myself instead of sending it all home, I would have bought myself a new wool coat and a pair of boots that hadn't worn thin.

Oh well, I was home now. The day was almost done. Lord Barnes would be waiting up for me. It was nearing nine, so the children would be in bed already. As much as I enjoyed our nighttime routine, I was grateful to have no one but myself to put to bed. Mostly, I would be glad to spend time with Lord Barnes.

He appeared in the foyer. "Good evening, ladies. How was it?" He helped me off with my coat and hung it in the closet. I inwardly cringed when his fingers lingered on the threadbare fabric of my coat's elbows.

I busied myself unpinning my hat. Why was it that poverty made one ashamed? It wasn't that I hadn't worked hard during my adult life and even before then. I put that thought aside as Merry answered Lord Barnes's question.

Her eyes shone as she took the pins from her hat. "It was just as I imagined. The desks and books and the smell of chalk."

"Did you have a good showing?" Lord Barnes asked.

"Besides Harley and Merry, there were three others." I told him about the Higgins brothers and Mrs. Cassidy.

Lord Barnes nodded, obviously delighted. "Clive and Wayne showed? I wasn't sure they would."

"They almost ran away." Merry giggled. "But Harley convinced them to come inside."

She spoke Harley's name as one would describe their favorite meal. They'd been sweet tonight, huddled together over the same textbook.

"You've earned the rest of the night off," Lord Barnes said to Merry. "Lizzie made a fire in both our rooms."

Her eyes glistened. "Thank you, Lord Barnes. For everything."

"Off with you now," he said.

"Good night, Merry," I said. "I'm proud of you. It's not easy to do something new."

She flushed. "I'm proud of *you*, Miss Cooper. Oh, Lord Barnes, you should have seen her up there. The way she made it all seem so easy. Even for slower people like me."

"You're not slow," I said firmly. "You're as quick as they come. One can't be expected to know academics if one's never had the opportunity for school. You remember that."

"Yes, Miss Cooper." Merry ducked her chin, shy, but I knew my words pleased her by the slight upturn of the corner of her mouth. She would come to learn her value at some point. These transformations didn't happen overnight. My job as her teacher was to keep reminding her. She was the type of student who thrived under praise. "Well, good night then." She scuttled away, still smiling.

"Are you cold?" Lord Barnes asked. "Lizzie left a pot of hot tea for you."

"I'd love tea." I rubbed my gloved hands together. "The night is frigid."

"There are biscuits too," he said, gesturing toward the library.

Lizzie's cookies, which Lord Barnes and all the children called biscuits, were already etched into my consciousness as the epitome of comfort. "Sounds heavenly. Teaching works up an appetite." I moved past him toward the library. What did he see when he watched me from behind? Did he see anything he liked, despite my lack of curves?

"I sent Jasper to bed early, so we're all alone," Lord Barnes said as we reached the library.

I hesitated at the doorway. It wasn't appropriate for us to be alone without Jasper to supervise. Yet I wanted desperately to spend time with him.

He laughed as he sat in his usual chair by the fire and picked up a glass of whiskey. "Come on, now. I won't eat you up."

"You know it's not proper." A trail of fire raced up my back and flooded my face. I sounded ridiculous. There was something about this uninhabited land that made the rules from home seem outdated.

"What's the worst that could happen?" he asked.

The worst? An image of him grabbing me in his arms and kissing me flashed before me. That would be bad. And very good. I didn't think it was possible, but I flamed hotter.

I clutched the tie around my neck and shook my head to dispel my traitorous thoughts.

"Miss Cooper?" Lord Barnes asked, with a teasing lilt to his voice. "Are you all right? You've flushed quite pink. Are you ill?"

"No, I'm fine."

"Does that mean you'll come in and have tea?" His eyes danced with amusement.

"Yes, I suppose it's all right just this once," I said.

I sat in the chair closest to the fire and allowed him to pour the tea. My mother had taught me that tea was a woman's task, but Lord Barnes didn't seem to know that convention. Or perhaps, like so many things, he didn't care. After taking a sip, I directed my gaze at him, then lost nerve. Was letting my mind wander to the idea of us foolish? He was an aristocrat, rich and unbothered by such petty details as to where or even *if* the next meal would come. This library with its shelves of books and posh furnishings and expensive liquor was the world of Lord Barnes.

"What is it?" His eyebrows raised and he grinned, looking very much like Flynn. "Am I in trouble?"

"Should you be?"

He looked over the rim of his glass as he took a sip of his whiskey. "Not at the moment, no."

"Sometimes it seems like you're silently laughing at me. Why am I so amusing?"

He grinned as he crossed one leg over the other. "You amuse me for several reasons."

"And what are those?" I asked, grinning back at him despite my best efforts to remain aloof.

"You've got spunk. And you know how to laugh at yourself, which I think is a wonderful quality. Watching you struggle to be proper makes me laugh, because inside that perfect little shell of yours is the heart of a rebel. And by shell, I mean your outer beauty, which in my opinion is unparalleled."

"Lord Barnes, you are full of nonsense." My heart raced at such a speed I was afraid it might explode from the exertion.

He pressed his hand to his chest. "I speak the truth."

I smoothed my skirt and drank from my cup. The warmth of Lizzie's expertly brewed tea traveled down my throat and into my stomach.

"You won't fall in love with one of those handsome chaps, will you? If you fall in love with one of them and not me, you'll break my heart."

My hand trembled as I set the cup back in its saucer. "Lord Barnes, be serious."

"I'm quite serious." His eyes no longer sparkled with amusement. In fact, they glittered with a raw intensity that made my stomach bubble like champagne in a crystal flute. "Your presence here has brightened our lives. My life."

I must change the subject, I thought. *Get us back to the task at hand.* "Rachel Cole came to see me tonight. She's changed her mind about school."

He rose from his chair and crossed over to the liquor cabinet. "She came to see me the other day and said as much. I wasn't sure she wouldn't change her mind." He returned with a glass of whiskey and sank heavily into the chair. I'd reminded him of his burden and loss by mentioning her. For a moment, I wished I'd kept it to myself for a few more minutes and enjoyed basking in his smile.

"She said she wanted to look me in the eye and decide for herself what kind of person I was."

"That sounds like her." He smiled as he drank from his glass. I watched, temporarily distracted by the way his lips puckered when he swallowed. "She must have liked what she saw in those eyes of yours."

I chuckled. "She said I was either naïve or brave."

He rose from the chair and ambled to the fire, then poked the logs with the iron rod. The flames rose high, warming the half of my body that faced the fireplace. He placed his forehead against the mantel. "God, I hope this is the right thing to do. I promised Samuel I'd keep them all safe." He turned away from the fire to face me. "Not to mention your safety and that of the other children. How far will these men go?"

"We can't back away from what's right, even if we're frightened."

"I don't want you to be scared," he said softly. "In fact, I deplore it."

"A man's dead because someone didn't want the Cole children in school. I'm frightened, yes. But the test of courage is to do that which we know is right even if there are consequences." I looked at my hands, knowing I needed to broach the subject of the Wu family. If he knew about them and had made a conscious choice to exclude them from the community, I would be crushed. Women and children should not live in shacks without food or warmth. Not in the society Lord Barnes said he believed in and was actively building. Not in any community. I didn't care about the color of their skin or whether their ancestors were buried in these parts or in another land across the sea. Would he agree with me? Was it only because of his alliance with Cole that he'd been willing to include children of a different color?

I elongated my neck, hoping to portray confidence. The palms of my hands were damp with perspiration, and the pulse at my neck quickened. "Did you know there's a Chinese family living in the old mining camp?"

"What did you say?" His voice sounded dry and strange.

"Mrs. Cole said there's a Chinese family living down by the old mining site—a woman with children. *School-aged* children. Samuel took them fresh meat on a regular basis. They're afraid to come to town. Did you know about them?"

He rocked back on his heels, silent. The click of the second hand on the grandfather clock marked time as I waited for his answer. "I'd heard rumors. Samuel never said anything to me. I'm not sure why that would be." He said the last part under his breath.

"Maybe he thought you wouldn't share his sympathies."

A muscle above his right eye twitched. "Did he think so little of me? Do you?"

"Shouldn't a rumor of this kind be investigated?" A swift anger rushed through me. "I'd have thought your ideals would have encouraged you to look in the shadows."

His face reddened. "Isn't that a little quick to judgment? You've no idea what I've done or not done for the poor in this community."

"What have you done?"

"I've given them work," he said. "They've earned their own way instead of accepting charity."

"Charity?" I was hot as the fire poker now. "If they're ostracized from the community, how are they supposed to get work? The kindness of community is all that will separate them from either freezing to death or going hungry."

"Why are you angry with me? I can't give someone work I didn't know existed. I'm not clairvoyant."

"They might starve if we don't do something," I said. "Do you understand that?"

"I'm quite aware of the winters here," he said.

We glared at each other for a good five seconds before he broke the tension with a low chuckle. "Listen, tiger, we're in agreement. If anyone in this community needs help, I'm willing to provide it. However, I need to understand the situation better first."

"What's there to know? There are children who need help. And stop laughing at me. None of this is funny."

"I'm not laughing."

"You are. Inside. I can see it in your eyes," I said, still furious. "I don't appreciate being dismissed."

"I've done nothing of the kind." He held up both hands. "Before you lambaste me further, did she give you any other details?"

"No, only that they live in the abandoned shack."

"I haven't been down there for a long time," he said, much too lackadaisically for my liking.

"This isn't like contemplating whether or not we should have a picnic by the river. What are we going to do? We need a plan. When I think of those hungry children... We can't wait. We have to go there and see what they need."

He crossed around the coffee table to where I sat on the couch. "May I sit?"

I nodded, holding my breath to steady my nerves.

He draped one arm over the back of the couch. "I like the word *we*, Miss Cooper, but I'll take care of this. You have enough to do. Jasper and I will drive out in the morning and see what they need. Will that satisfy you?"

"I guess so."

"You don't have to be mad at me." He brushed his finger across my cheek. "We're on the same side."

A flash of desire shook me to my very core. I couldn't look away, captivated by the low timbre of his voice and the way his eyes went all soft when they looked at me.

Finally, I shifted my gaze to my lap. The fire crackled as a log shifted. Several sparks flew against the grate.

He lifted my chin with his finger, forcing me to look into his eyes. "Your wish is my bidding. I'd do anything to win your affection."

"You'd do this for me, even if you didn't want to?"

"Let me put it to you this way," he said. "I'm a man smart enough to know when to listen to a woman wiser than I. So, yes, I'd do it for you, even if I didn't agree, which I do. My ideals are not simply pulled out when convenient."

I let out a deep breath. How could I remain angry when he spoke to me this way? "I'm glad we're in agreement."

He picked up the plate of cookies and held it out to me. "Now, have a biscuit. The nights are long and cold here. It's best to have a full stomach before retiring."

"I've been here long enough to know how long and cold the nights are." I gave him a sideways glance. "Furthermore, in America, we call them cookies."

A hearty laugh came from deep inside his chest. "Have a *cookie*, Miss Cooper, and forgive my imperfections."

"I'll sleep on the last part," I said as I snatched the largest cookie. "Don't hold your breath."

Alexander

❦

I rose the next morning filled with dread. I'd slept terribly,
plagued by nightmares about Samuel. He'd come to me in a
dream, chastising me for my ignorance. *You only see what you
want*, he'd said to me.

The Samuel of my dreams was right, as was Miss Cooper. I
hadn't considered the children in the shadows. White men had
forced Native Americans out of the area decades before I came,
their fate sealed by the discovery of gold, then silver in these
mountains. I liked to pretend none of the atrocities had
happened and that God had made this land just for white
settlers, but it was simply untrue. Long after the gold rush was
over, many immigrants from China had come to seek their
fortune and found nothing but sand. Too poor to go home,
they'd ended up trapped in a country that didn't want them.
Over the years, I'd convinced myself that the tragedies of the
Native American and Chinese people were before my time and
had nothing to do with me. Although that might have been true,
I couldn't hide behind that excuse when faced with the current
reality. A Chinese family had been forced out of our society
because of their ethnicity. Rachel Cole's children were not safe
in town. This was not the community I'd dreamed of.

Miss Cooper was right. How could those forced into the shadows survive, let alone thrive? What were they supposed to do if they weren't welcome?

I was a young man when I first came to America. So young, in fact, that I hadn't yet considered the consequences of my choices. I wanted only to have adventures. The idea of doing what was expected of me seemed like a death sentence. I'd read of the western frontier and the men and women who had braved rough terrain and wild animals to better their circumstances. This idea was so very American to me and stirred my blood. I gave up the inheritance and the title, leaving it all to my younger brother who was so much better suited for it all. I was free and that's all I wanted. Now, all these years later, I understood what a romantic fantasy the wild west had been. In those tales of conquering heroes, there was no mention of the American government's manipulation of white settlers or the atrocities done to tribal nations. The government had promised rich, fertile soil in Indian Territory to anyone willing to bet on a homestead. They'd lured them out west with outright lies for the sole purpose of expansion and destroyed Native American life.

All this said, I had no regrets. I'd made the life for myself that I'd dream of as a boy. All on my own terms and in my own ways.

Jasper and I set out after breakfast with a basket of food put together by Lizzie. Visibility was good, and temperatures had risen into the twenties. When we were out of town proper, I let Oliver and Twist run. Their muscles rippled as they galloped through freshly fallen snow. The fierce wind chilled my cheeks.

Emerson Pass was built in the valley between the sister mountains. A river ran along the base of the southern mountain. During the late sixties, gold had been found in its banks. Word spread, as it does, and hordes of men flocked to the area. At one time there had been five hundred residents. After it became clear in the late eighties that whatever gold or silver was here had already been mined, the town's population shrank to less than fifty. Then a fire burned every structure to the ground. When I got here, there were only a handful of people left, one of whom was Samuel. He'd been friendly but made it clear he wanted nothing to do with my plans. "Build your town," he'd said. "And leave me be."

What he'd been doing for the shadow people was not in the narrative of the story I'd believed about Samuel. I'd seen him as an isolationist. He meant no harm, expecting nothing from others, and expected the same in return. The only exception had been his plea to me.

We came upon the old building where business was conducted back in the mining days. Clearly, it hadn't been built with much thought to the future, as it was nothing more than a shanty with one sloped roof. Twenty yards from the structure, swift river water tumbled over rocks.

The hint of human inhabitants was limited to a trail of smoke out of the tin stovepipe that stuck out of the roof like a groundhog popping up from its hole.

We tied the horses to a tree and ambled up to the shack. I rapped my knuckles on the door. There were no windows, but I detected the murmurings of people inside. Finally, the door opened a crack. A boy with black eyes peered at me.

"Hello." He was around the twins' age, wearing a tattered plaid shirt that seemed sized for an adult, as it came to his knees. His shoes were made of faded black cloth.

"Is your mother here?" I asked.

He shook his head, watching me as a wary animal would a predator. "No, my grandmother. She doesn't speak English."

"I'm Alexander Barnes," I said. "And this is Jasper."

The boy nodded and opened the door a few more inches to get a look at Jasper.

"What's your name?" I asked.

"I am Li Wu."

"If I talked to your grandmother, would you translate for me?" I asked.

Li's gaze darted from me to Jasper and back again. I imagined a thousand questions ran through his mind. Who were we? What did we want?

"We mean no harm," I said. "I just want to talk to her and tell her about the new school that opened in town."

"School?"

"Yes. Would you like to go to school?"

Li shrugged. "I don't know."

"Will you ask your grandmother to come to the door?" I asked.

After another moment of indecision, he nodded his head in agreement. "Wait here." He closed the door. A few minutes later, he returned with an elderly woman. She was not much bigger than her grandson. Wrinkles lined her hazel skin.

"I've come from town. My name is Alexander Barnes, and this is Jasper."

"She is called Jun," Li said.

"Jun, we're friends of Samuel Cole's." I waited for Li to translate.

She listened to Li, then said something in Chinese to him.

"She says Samuel is our friend," Li said.

"I'm sorry to have to tell you this, but he was killed," I said.

Again, Li translated. The old woman flinched and put her hand on her chest.

"She wants to know what happened to him," Li said.

"He was shot. Murdered."

She clutched the collar of her threadbare dress and asked Li another question.

"Was it because of his wife?" Li asked.

"We don't know," I said. "I learned he looked after you and wanted to see if you were doing all right out here."

"He brought us food," Li said, translating for his grandmother. "And now we have none."

"We understand," I said. "We're here to offer our help."

From behind me, Jasper presented the basket of food. "We brought this," he said.

A flicker of a smile crossed Jun's face.

"She says thank you," Li said.

"May we come inside?" I asked.

Jun nodded and motioned for us to enter.

The interior was clean but bare, consisting of a woodstove, two rickety chairs, a crude table made from faded boards, and a stool that looked left over from an early saloon. Bedding consisted of blankets on a mat near the stove. Several pots were stored on a shelf, as well as a tin bowl and a few plates. A broom was propped up by the doorway.

A little girl of about three sat in the middle of the bedding. She watched us with a mixture of curiosity and fear. She called out to her brother, who went to sit next to her.

Jun fluttered her hands toward the chairs and spoke to us in Chinese.

"She wants you to sit," Li said.

I caught Jasper's eye. He clearly felt as awkward as I.

"Can you ask her to sit instead?" I asked.

"She won't," Li said.

So we took the chairs and Jun sat on the lone stool.

Li told us their story. His grandparents had come for the gold but like so many were too late. They'd stayed anyway, living in a shanty not far from the mining site and surviving by fishing from the river and collecting nuts and berries, as well as growing a vegetable garden.

"No one bothered us in those days," Li translated. "All the white people had gone away."

Jun's husband had died just before the fire burned the town, leaving her alone with her teenage son, Quon. She and Quon moved to Denver, hoping to find work. After a few years, Quon met Ting, and they were married. As a family they decided to return to this place by the river where they had been happy.

"We met Samuel then," Li said, continuing to translate his

grandmother's story. "He taught Quon to hunt and fish. His wife gave us seeds for our garden. Samuel brought us supplies from town."

First, Li had been born, then five years later, baby Fai.

"We were happy. But then the sickness came, and both Quon and Ting died," Li said. "And we had no one to hunt for us."

Jun cried as she told us this last part of their sad tale.

"Samuel came and told us not to worry. He would look after us."

For several years now, they'd relied on Samuel for fresh meat and supplies from town. He chopped wood for their stove so they would not freeze. Rachel had sewn clothes or sent ones her children had outgrown. "We would have died without him. Then he stopped coming. For days and days, we waited but he didn't come. We've eaten the last of the beans. The baby cries and cries from hunger."

Jasper, clearly beside himself, stood and began unpacking the basket. A hunk of Lizzie's homemade cheese, a bottle of creamy milk, a loaf of fresh sourdough bread, several apples, and slices of ham were soon spread out on the table.

"Come eat," Jasper said to the children.

They jumped from the floor and ran to the table. The little one squealed as her brother lifted her onto the chair Jasper had occupied. I rose from mine and told Li to sit.

Jasper sliced bread and made sandwiches from the cheese and ham for all three of them. He found two tin cups on the shelves and poured them each a glass of milk. We gave them time to eat before asking further questions. I paced by the door, wondering what in the bloody hell I was to do now.

When they'd had their fill, Fai jumped from the chair and twirled in a circle. With her shiny black hair and round face, she was absolutely precious.

And Jun, raising them all alone without money. Relying on the kindness of a man who could provide food but no real life outside of this shack.

I knew this was arrogant of me, but I wanted to save them. I had no right to project my English ways onto them, but they could not live this way. It wasn't right.

"Mrs. Wu, I have a position in my kitchen. My cook needs someone to help her. We have a large garden in the summer that also needs attending. Would you be willing to work for me?"

Li told her what I'd said.

Jun shook her head.

"I don't know English cooking," Li translated. "And how would I get to your house?"

"You and the children would live in the staff quarters downstairs," I said. "I'll pay you a salary, plus offer room and board. Li could go to school with my children. Fai can stay with you. I have a three-year-old daughter, too. They can play together."

The stunned expression on Jasper's face was almost laughable. I was sure to catch hell on the way home. Lizzie wouldn't be able to resist offering help to the Wus. I could count on her to find lighter-weight tasks for the old woman. We had one spare room downstairs. It was small but certainly better than this.

"I am old and not much use," Li translated. "And the other children are all white. How could Li go with them?"

"All children are welcome at our school," I said.

"I'm afraid to leave," Li translated. "What if we need to come back and someone else is living here?"

"You won't need to come back," I said. "We'll make sure of it."

If only I were as certain as I sounded.

"We will come," Li translated.

Quinn

The morning of the Coles' first day of school, they had not shown when I rang the school bell. Most of my students were already inside, huddled around the stove, other than Flynn and Cymbeline, who were in a heated snowball fight. As they set down their weapons and bounded toward the steps, a sleigh pulled up outside the schoolhouse. Three children bundled in green coats and hats jumped out and shuffled toward me. I gestured for them to come inside, then waved to their uncle. Wilber tipped his hat.

I showed the Cole children where to leave their coats, hats, and lunch pails as the others took their seats.

I knelt to their level and looked them each in the eyes. "I'm Miss Cooper. Can you tell me your names and ages?"

They answered, one after the other, never taking their gaze from me, as if they were afraid to look anywhere else. Noah was eight. Roman was seven, and their little sister, Willa, was six. They were lighter-skinned than their mother but had inherited her high cheekbones and large brown eyes. "I'm going to introduce you to the others."

A fat tear caught in Willa's bottom lashes, and her lips quivered.

"There's nothing to be afraid of," I said. "You're going to make friends and learn so much."

Willa nodded and sucked in her bottom lip.

"Did you know we have two recesses?" I asked.

"Is that where we get to play with the others?" Noah asked.

"And get fresh air and exercise. In between that time, we have lessons. Now come with me." I straightened and offered my hand to Willa. "We're going to tell everyone your names." Together, we walked to the front of the classroom.

"Children, we have three new students joining us today." I looked around at the faces of these young people I'd grown so fond of. *Please, God, don't let them disappoint me today.* If I caught a hint of cruelty, I would put a stop to it immediately. However, as my gaze flickered about the room, the children seemed oblivious. No one flinched or gave me any indication that they saw anything but another child.

I introduced them by name. "Who can tell them what our class rules are?

Josephine raised her hand. "Be curious. Be kind. Protect one another," she said.

"Excellent. Thank you, Josephine. Also, when you wish to ask a question or speak, you must raise your hand. Understood?"

The Cole siblings nodded. I pointed to two empty desks next to the twins. "Those are for you, Noah and Roman." I escorted Willa to a desk between Cymbeline and Nora Cassidy. "Cymbeline, I'd like you to be Willa's buddy for the day. If she has any questions, you will answer them, all right?"

Cymbeline gave me a radiant smile, all sunshine and innocence. At the moment, anyway.

Next I asked if anyone had any questions for our new students.

Flynn raised his hand. "Do you like games? Or snowball fights or racing?"

Noah and Roman nodded.

"That's great, because I do too," Flynn said.

Willa raised her hand and waited until I called on her. "I don't like snowball fights."

"Did you all hear that? At recess, Willa would like to exercise her right to abstain from snowball fights."

Shannon raised her hand. "What does abstain mean?"

"Who would like to look it up?" I asked.

Elsa's hand shot up. She always volunteered to find the word in the dictionary when we had a new one to learn. She'd told me that just looking at all those words on the page made her happy. "Yes, Elsa, you may look it up."

Elsa bounded from her desk to open the dictionary I kept on my desk. We waited as she flipped pages.

"Here it is. Abstain is a verb," Elsa said. "To hold oneself back voluntarily, especially from something regarded as improper or unhealthy."

Flynn raised his hand. "Does Willa think snowball fights are unhealthy?"

I gave him a stern stare. "Are you using the rules?"

"I'm curious," he said.

"But was that kind?" I asked.

"Is being funny the same as being kind?" he asked.

"Not usually," I said.

"That's too bad," Flynn said.

"Willa, tell us why you don't like them," I said.

"I don't like them because they hurt," Willa said. "My brothers throw too hard. One time they gave me a bloody nose and then Mama sent them to bed with no supper."

Noah groaned quietly. Flynn leaned over and patted his shoulder. "Sisters."

They exchanged grins in a moment of obvious solidarity. A new friendship formed right before my eyes.

The rest of the morning went by without incident. By lunchtime, it was as if the Cole children had always been with us. The sky was clear, and a fresh layer of powdery snow had fallen overnight. I sent them all out to play after everyone had finished their lunch. Willa hung behind, looking out the window. I was about to encourage her to join the others when Nora came rushing back inside. "Willa, want to play hopscotch with us?" Nora said.

Cymbeline was outside making a stack of snowballs that she would surely use for an evil attack against her brother. There would be no hopscotch for that one. I should have paired Willa with one of the sweet Cassidy girls instead, I thought.

"How do you play?" Willa asked.

"It's easy. We'll show you," Nora said as she held out her hand. Willa took it and the little girls walked out to the porch together.

Offering friendship came naturally to innocent children, who saw only another child and not a skin color or social status. *May they always remain thus*, I prayed. *Don't let the world change them.*

I added the Cole siblings to my class roster and stood gazing at it for a few minutes. These young souls had been entrusted to me. I could only hope to do them all justice.

———

THAT EVENING, I SAT WITH LORD BARNES IN THE LIBRARY AS he told me about his morning visit to the Wus. He described their living situation and how they'd come to Emerson Pass. "Mrs. Wu's been living out there alone with two small children. It was heartbreaking to see."

"And Samuel helped them all these years?"

"Yes, it seems so."

"What do we do now?" I asked.

"I've invited her to come work with Lizzie in the kitchen. She and the young ones will take the spare room down there."

I couldn't believe what he was saying. "You asked them to live here?"

"Yes. I know it's rather unorthodox."

"Unorthodox? Is that the word?" My eyes filled with tears.

"Miss Cooper, what's the matter?" He leapt from his leather chair and thrust a handkerchief onto my lap. "What did I do wrong?"

"Nothing. I've never heard of anything so outrageously kind." I dabbed at my eyes with the handkerchief as tears continued to leak from my eyes.

"I thought you'd be happy with me." He knelt on the floor next to my chair and looked up at me with such a bewildered expression that I laughed through my tears.

"I am." I wiped my eyes and took a long breath, in and out, before speaking. "Lord Barnes, I'm quite undone. I've never known anyone like you in my life."

"It was the baby," he said. "She looked at me with that face, and I could see how hungry and cold she was. I couldn't walk away."

I love him, I thought. *With all my heart.* It was all over for me. This was the man I wanted.

"What is it?" he asked. "You're looking at me strangely."

"I have all these feelings." I stopped, not trusting myself to speak further for fear of everything in my heart spilling out onto his lap.

"What kind of feelings?" His eyes, glossy as green silk, held my gaze.

My mother's voice came to me then, reminding me that Lord Barnes was my employer, not a man. An employer with a *Lord* before his name. I had no title—nothing in front of my name but *Miss*, and it was likely to remain thus.

"Feelings for me?" he asked.

My stomach was filled with sparrows, fluttering their wings. "Yes. For you. Ones I don't know what to do with. There are so many differences between us."

"Differences?" he asked.

"You're a lord and I'm a schoolmistress." I folded and unfolded the hankie. "You're rich and I'm poor."

"I don't care anything about titles or circumstances. You're beautiful and good and full of life. How could I not fall in love with you?"

I wiped my cheeks. "It seems to me, Lord Barnes, that this wild country has made you wild."

"The country hasn't made me wild. I was born this way." The corners of his mouth lifted into a brief smile. "This place is like me, wild and free. I listen to my own instincts, not those deemed proper by a society I don't even believe in." He brushed his thumb across my jawline. My breath caught. "Do you know what my instincts are telling me to do right now?"

I shook my head as the muscles in my thighs tightened.

"They're telling me to kiss you."

I couldn't look away, drawn as I was to him as if an invisible force cleaved us together. I was an innocent when it came to men, but I knew the look of hunger when I saw it. This was not the appetite of an empty stomach but rather a craving only a man and woman could feel for each other. One for which there was only one single remedy.

"Have you ever been kissed?" he asked.

I nodded, dizzy. "Once." And then he'd married my best friend and broken my heart.

"What happened to this fool who kissed you?"

"He married my friend the very next week." Even after two years, my body remembered the shock when I'd heard the news. A vast emptiness had crashed through me, leaving me in a tunnel of black from which there was no return.

"Why would he do such a thing?" Lord Barnes asked, his voice incredulous now.

"For the same reason you would," I said. "He married someone with money. Someone from an important family."

"I can marry whomever I please." Lord Barnes's eyes flashed with arrogance but also rebellion. "I have no one to answer to but God and my children. I'll marry for love with no regard for anything else. What about you? Would you marry for love or money?"

"Love. Always love," I said. "Even though I have only love to offer in return."

"And what would make you love a man?" His eyes twinkled at me. "If not money?"

"Kindness. Compassion. A curious mind."

"What about a man with children?"

"I suppose it would depend on the children," I said. "I'm particularly fond of the ones in this house."

"Could you live in Emerson Pass and be happy?"

"That would depend on the man."

He smiled and ran the back of his finger over my cheek. "Two things to know, Miss Quinn Cooper. I care only about you, not convention. And I would never pursue you without the hope that you'll soon agree to be my wife. I've no interest in toying with you. My flirtations are not mere trivial fun. May I have permission to court you?" His words sounded strangely intimate, as if we were embarking on a journey where we were the only travelers.

I stared at him, probably looking like a hooked fish with my mouth hanging open. Hands shaking, I clasped them together and held on for dear life as the room seemed to tip. The world had changed in an instant. My world had changed. *Permission to court you. Agree to be my wife.*

"I've never been courted before. My plan was to be a spinster."

He laughed. "Respectfully, Miss Cooper, there's no way you're ending up a spinster. If I'm not to your liking, there will be men lined up at your door."

"You're to my liking," I said, quietly. "You may court me."

He placed his hand over his chest. "Would you dine with me this evening? The children can eat downstairs with Lizzie."

"Just the two of us?"

"That's the idea, yes."

"Yes, I would like to dine with you." Was this courting? If so, I liked it.

"Supper at seven, then?"

"Supper at seven."

A sigh seemed to come from deep inside him. He picked up my hand and caressed it with his thumb. "May I call you Quinn? I want to court the woman, not the schoolmistress."

Desire, hot and swift, swept over me. "You may call me Quinn."

"And you may call me Alexander."

I looked down at the hankie in my lap, suddenly shy. "I should probably check on the children."

He rose from the floor and offered me his hand. "As you wish."

I allowed him to help me to my feet, then scurried away like a frightened bunny. As I came to the doorway, I glanced back, expecting him to send me off with a benign wave. Instead, he said two words. "Quinn, wait."

My breath hitched at the sound of my name coming from his mouth.

With long strides, he quickly ate up the distance between us. "You're not leaving here until I kiss you for the first time." He pulled me to him with one arm around my waist. I gasped as he captured my mouth with his in a hard kiss. This was not like the chaste peck I'd had before. Lord Barnes was masterful—rough yet tender and tasting of whiskey. When he withdrew, I fought the urge to pull him back.

"What do you think of kissing?" He brushed a loose strand of hair away from my neck, and I shivered.

"I think I'd like to try it again."

Always the gentleman, he obliged. This time the kiss was tender and restrained. "That'll have to sustain us for now," he said when he withdrew his mouth from mine. "I'd rather spend the rest of my life kissing you and never accomplish another thing, but we have work to do."

"If I were never to be kissed again, I'd die happy, knowing I was kissed by you."

He tightened his grip around my waist, drawing me close. The muscles in his chest and arms made my petite frame seem even smaller. "You will be kissed again. Hopefully by me and only me." To prove himself, he kissed me again, this time teasing me with his tongue.

A soft moan came from deep inside me. I pressed my chest against him, wishing there were fewer clothes between us. I wanted to see all of him, touch all of him. "I've...I've never felt anything like this," I said, breathless.

"You have no idea of the delights to come," he whispered in my ear. "Now off you go before I kiss you again."

"I'll see you later." I pecked him on the cheek, then slipped from the room and took the stairs two at a time to the third floor with my pounding heart and dampened skin. I shut the door and stood against it, reliving every moment. Pure joy flooded me. I twirled in a circle and wanted to sing and dance and tell my mother and sister and anyone who would listen. *I'm in love with Alexander Barnes. And he loves me.*

Alexander

✦

S till stirred from the taste of Quinn's kisses, I headed
downstairs to talk with Lizzie. The moment I entered
the kitchen, a glorious scent of yeast and butter assaulted
my senses. Lizzie kneaded dough at the kitchen island, humming
to herself. Steam from a large pot on the stove fogged up the
windows. Such a contrast to the hovel I'd seen earlier.

"Lizzie, may I have a word?"

She whirled around, still holding the lump of dough in her
floury hands. "Lord Barnes, you scared me to death. What are
you doing down here?"

"I'm sorry. I didn't mean to startle you," I said as I came to
stand at the island. "I have a favor."

"You know I'd do anything for you."

"This is a rather large favor." I laid out the situation with the
Wus. By the end, Lizzie's eyes were practically bugging out of
their sockets.

"Am I hearing you correctly? You invited them to live
with us?"

"Yes. Or, rather, work for us. For you, that is," I said.

"But I don't need any help. And what about the baby? I
already have little Fiona. Who will look after them?"

I scratched my head. I hadn't actually thought that part through.

"Just like a man, Lord Barnes. Not looking at all the angles." She punched her dough one last time, then put the mass in a buttered bowl. "I don't want some old lady in my kitchen. What we should do is have her look after the little ones while the rest of them are at school. We're short a nanny, after all."

"Lizzie, you're so smart."

"I have my moments."

"Will you mind if they're in the spare room down here?" I asked.

"It'll be tight, but I can manage." She spread a cloth over her bread bowl and placed it nearer the stove. "Speaking of which, I have a favor to ask you."

"Ask away."

"I'd like to have my own cottage on the property."

"You would?" I was amazed by this request. When I'd offered before, she always said she would be too scared to live alone. She liked the main house and her cozy kitchen and bedroom.

"Yes. I'd like to get married and have a few children of my own," she said. "I'd like to do so in my own home. Nothing fancy. A cottage will do, like the one Harley and Poppy have."

"Do you have your eye on a fellow?"

"I did. For too long I've had my eye on the wrong one. I'm off that now. Do you have any suggestions?"

"The Higgins brothers are single. Nice-looking, too." My suggestion was evil, but this was a dire circumstance. Jasper was going to lose his chance.

"A cook marrying a butcher. How perfect," she said, laughing.

"Well, you work on finding the right husband and the moment the winter's over, we'll start building."

"With my luck, the cottage will be quicker than the husband."

I sat on a stool and rested my elbows on the wood-block island. "Lizzie, what do you think of Miss Quinn?"

"It doesn't matter too much what I think, given the way you two were kissing earlier."

I covered my eyes with my hand and looked at her through my fingers. "You saw us?"

"I'd come up to bring tea but decided you two were otherwise occupied." Lizzie disappeared in the pantry for a moment and came back with a bowl of raw potatoes.

"I hope the children didn't see us," I said, worried.

"No, they were all downstairs in the kitchen at the time." She wagged a finger at me. "You two should be more discreet unless you want them to think you're getting married. They adore her."

"Do you know what they said when I told them Quinn was going to be their nanny?"

"That she couldn't be the nanny because she was supposed to be your wife?" Lizzie sliced a potato into perfect rounds.

"How did you know?" I asked.

"Lord Barnes, the person who spends the most time in the kitchen of any house knows more about the people in it than anyone else. Everything's discussed in a kitchen."

"I see."

"And you *are* going to marry the lovely Miss Cooper, are you not?"

"If she'll have me, yes."

"It would be splendid to have a mother for the band of rascals. I'd like to see you happy."

"I'd like to see you happy, Lizzie. You're right to give up on Jasper."

Her mouth puckered as if she'd tasted a lemon. "You knew about that?"

"Lizzie, Jasper and I have been together a long time. There are no secrets between us." I lowered my voice. "Not that I'm the expert when it comes to matters of the heart, but I have advice for you. Let one of the Higgins brothers or anyone respectable in town take you out for a drive or skating. I think that might just knock some sense into him."

"That's not right to do to the man who takes me out, though."

"What if he's in on it? Clive and Wayne are good people. They'd be willing pawns in our jealousy game."

She stopped slicing and looked over at me while shaking her head. "I had no idea you were so devious."

"Wear your Christmas dress. The blue one you had on last year at Christmas dinner. I'll have Clive call on you here at the house."

"I'm seeing a new side of you," Lizzie said, laughing. "A clever, wicked side."

"In the name of love, anything's possible." I straightened, wiping a dusting of flour from my elbows. "Now, I have one last request. Would you feed the children down here tonight? Miss Quinn and I have a dinner date upstairs."

"Consider it done. And when will Mrs. Wu arrive?"

"Harley's picking them up on Saturday. He'll help them get settled."

"There are three narrow beds in that room," Lizzie said. "I hope they're not the type to toss and turn at night, or they'll fall right out of the bed."

"You should see what they're sleeping on now," I said.

"Lord Barnes, you're a fine man," Lizzie said. "Don't ever forget that."

"Thank you, Lizzie." Touched, I ducked out of the room before she could say anything further.

THE JOHNSONS' DRY GOODS STORE SMELLED OF SUGAR, wool, and leather. Shelves held copious items, including shoes, work boots, overalls, stationery, soaps, polish, and home items such as kitchenware and lanterns. Wooden barrels were filled with taffy, salt crackers, rice, and anything else one could need. In the corner nearest the counter, a shiny black Singer sewing machine was on display.

Mrs. Johnson was with a customer, so I occupied myself by scanning the rolls of fabric on the shelf behind her. There were several different heavy wools: a forest green, dark blue, charcoal gray, and black.

After the man left, Mrs. Johnson gave me one of her sweet smiles and asked what she could do for me.

"I'd like to purchase some wool for a woman's coat," I said. "But I don't know what color." The state of Quinn's coat and boots had been weighing on me for weeks. She wouldn't get through the rest of the winter with those boots. Her threadbare coat was simply not warm enough for our winters.

"What colors does she like?" she asked. "Who is it for?"

I laughed under my breath. If I told Mrs. Johnson who it was for, the news would have reached the entire town by nightfall. "My sister back home in England," I said. Strange how easily that lie rolled from my tongue.

"And what's her coloring?"

"She's fair with blond hair and brown eyes." I reached into a bowl on the counter containing buttons and picked up a brown button. "This color."

"Interesting," Mrs. Johnson said. "She must look a lot like Miss Cooper."

I laughed. That didn't take long. "Mrs. Johnson, what a strange thing for you to say."

Her amber eyes sparkled at me. "I would suggest the dark green. It'll contrast nicely with her skin." She moved the ladder stored behind the counter over to the spot where the green wool was stacked on a top shelf. "She'll need a liner, though. Otherwise the wool will scratch."

"Fine, whatever you think is best," I said as I wandered over to a glass shelf displaying various styles of gloves.

Martha came in from the back room. "Mother, do you need help?"

Mrs. Johnson said yes, and would she please measure out five yards of the green wool as well as the liner fabric.

"I'll take a pair of these as well." I tapped the glass shelf displaying a pair of long white gloves. "And do you have any wool stockings?"

"It must be very cold in England," Mrs. Johnson said from behind me.

"Frigid. Like this," I said.

"I'd always heard England was rainy but mild." Mrs. Johnson opened the display case for the gloves.

"Can be," I said.

With a knowing smile planted on her face, she pulled out a pad and started to write up a receipt for my items. Next to her, Martha had measured and cut the wool and was now rolling it into a cylinder.

"Don't go to too much trouble," I said to Martha. "I'm taking it straight over to the tailor's shop."

"He's having a coat made for his sister," Mrs. Johnson said. "Isn't that sweet?"

Martha clearly wasn't as savvy as her mother when it came to matters of the heart. She simply gave me the bland, benign smile young people gave their elders and went back to measuring the lining.

"Martha and Elsa are skating this afternoon," Mrs. Johnson said.

"Will Josephine and Poppy be able to come?" Martha asked.

Over the last few years, skating parties on Saturday afternoons had become a tradition. If the weather permitted, families and young people alike came out to skate. The town's fiddler provided music, and Mrs. Johnson made and sold popcorn for a penny a bag.

"I'll bring them all in later," I said.

Mrs. Johnson pointed to a shelf where shiny new Barney & Berry clamp-on skates were displayed. "It would be a shame if our new teacher had to watch while the rest of you skate."

I chuckled. She was right. We couldn't leave Quinn out of the fun. "I'm not sure she knows how."

"She'll have to learn then," Martha said. "Skating parties are the best part of winter, other than Christmas."

"I don't know her size, though."

Mrs. Johnson came out from behind her counter to join me. She picked a pair from the middle of the shelf. "I'd say these should do."

"How do you know?" I asked.

"We sell a lot of boots and shoes," Mrs. Johnson said. "I can judge the size in my sleep."

Mrs. Johnson, with her uncanny sales ability, must have sensed my next request. "Does your sister need a pair of boots?" she asked.

"Mrs. Johnson, it's no wonder your husband's such a successful businessman."

Her expression remained merry. She wasn't serious like her daughter Martha, who appeared to take after the stoic Mr. Johnson. "I have no idea what you mean, Lord Barnes."

"I'll take a pair in the same size as the skates. My sister and Miss Cooper have a lot in common."

"Indeed." Mrs. Johnson's skirts made a swishing sound as she crossed over to the boot shelf. "We've just gotten these in from back east. Practical yet pretty."

The boots were black patent leather with dainty buttons up the side. I held one in my hand, inspecting the quality of the leather and sturdiness of the one-inch heel. We couldn't have Miss Cooper slipping and hurting herself.

"They'll withstand our winters," Mrs. Johnson said. "Or the English one, that is."

"I'll take them, please. And throw in a pound of candies for our skating party, Miss Martha."

"Yes, Lord Barnes." Martha smiled politely before scurrying over to the candy bin.

When everything was packaged up, I bade them good day

and walked over to the Olofssons' tailor shop. I removed my hat while stomping the snow from my boots onto the small rug they kept at the entrance so as not to track any mud or water into the tidy, dry shop.

Near the front window, Mr. Olofsson hunched over his sewing machine working on a pair of trousers. The top of his balding head shone in the sunlight that filtered through the glass. Mrs. Olofsson cut a piece of fabric behind the counter.

I said hello as they looked up from their work. "Good morning," Mr. Olofsson said in this thick Swedish accent. He was a slight man with sleepy blue eyes and a gentle smile, and his profession had given him stooped shoulders.

"Have you been busy?" I asked.

"Yes, yes." Mrs. Olofsson placed her hands over her plump pink cheeks. "We are happy." She was as round as her husband was thin. They shared the same thick accent and sweet disposition.

"I'd like you to make a woman's coat," I said. "But I don't have the measurements because it's a surprise."

"Who is it for?" Mr. Olofsson asked. "If I know them, I can figure size."

"Miss Cooper," I said, mumbling.

"Did you say Miss Cooper? The teacher?" Mrs. Olofsson asked.

"Yes. Her coat's too thin and worn for this climate," I said as my neck went hot.

"Say no more," Mrs. Olofsson said with a knowing wink.

This would be out by lunchtime. *Lord Barnes was ordering a coat for the lovely Miss Cooper. Did you know she's living at the house?*

"Give me a few days," Mr. Olofsson said. "I'll make it beautiful for our pretty teacher."

I escaped finally to the crisp, cold afternoon with the distinct feeling that the whole town would know my heart by nightfall.

WHEN I WALKED IN THE HOUSE, IT WAS QUIET. TOO QUIET. I wondered what everyone was up to and hoped they hadn't caused Miss Cooper too much trouble. To my surprise, they were all in the library. Miss Cooper sat on one end of the couch reading out loud from a novel. Josephine was in her favorite chair knitting something out of a bright blue yarn. Cymbeline and Flynn were sprawled out on the floor in front of the fireplace playing checkers. Theo and Fiona snuggled in my leather chair. I paused in the doorway, taking in the scene. How could one man be so blessed?

I set my packages on one of the tables. Fiona caught sight of me and wriggled off the chair to hurl herself into my arms. Miss Cooper ceased reading and set the book aside as the other children called out to me.

"What did you bring, Papa?" Cymbeline asked. "Is it for me?"

"No, you wicked girl," I said. "They're for Miss Quinn."

"For me?" she asked. "What have I done to deserve gifts?"

I set the two boxes containing the skates, boots, gloves, and stockings expertly tied with bows by Mrs. Johnson into Fiona's arms. "Take them to Miss Quinn, please."

"Yes, Papa. I love packages." Fiona walked with the boxes held out in front of her as if presenting the crown to the king of England, then placed them on Miss Cooper's lap.

"Open them, open them, Miss Quinn," Cymbeline said as she rose from the floor to go sit next to her on the couch.

Miss Cooper untied the string of the box containing the new boots, gloves, and stockings. She gasped as she lifted the lid. "What have you done? These are too much."

"You'll need sturdier boots for the rest of this winter. The almanac says we're in for more blizzards."

"These are so pretty, though. I won't be able to wear them for fear of ruining them."

"You'll wear them," I said. "Or risk my wrath."

"I wouldn't want your wrath." Her brown eyes were as shiny and happy as a child's at Christmas. She fingered the stockings, then rubbed the gloves against her cheek. "I've never felt anything so soft before."

"Open the other one," Fiona shouted as she jumped up and down.

"Inside voice, please," Quinn said.

"Yes, Miss Quinn," Fiona said. "I forgot."

"It's all right. Would you like to pull the string?" she asked.

"Yes, please." Fiona's chubby fingers untied the bow. Quinn lifted the lid of the box. "Skates?"

"Yes, skates. Now that you're a resident of Emerson Pass, you must have skates," I said. "There's a skating party this afternoon. Shall we all go?"

The children all shouted enthusiastic agreements with this idea. I turned back to Quinn. To my alarm, tears had formed in her pretty eyes.

"What is it?" I asked, coming closer. "Do you not like skating?"

"I've never skated before," Quinn said.

"We can teach you," Flynn said. "There's nothing to it."

Quinn wiped her eyes. "That's not it. I'm embarrassed to admit how much I longed for a pair when I was a child. In Boston, skating is quite popular. I was never able to join any of my friends."

"Even though you wanted to?" Cymbeline asked.

"That's right. I asked Santa for skates every year for a long time," Quinn said.

"And they never came?" Fiona asked, tears in her eyes.

Quinn held out her arms to Fiona, who went into them. "Don't be sad. This is such a happy day for me."

"Papa, this was thoughtful of you," Josephine said in her grown-up voice. "We couldn't have possibly gone skating without Miss Quinn."

"We *might* have gone anyway," Cymbeline said, looking doubtful that she would have been able to make a sacrifice for Quinn. The child knew herself well.

"But now we don't have to," Flynn said.

"I would've gone with you and watched," Quinn said. "Which I might have to do today, since I've never been on ice other than the kind you walk on because you have to get somewhere."

"We'll teach you," Flynn said. "But you might slip a little at first."

"Don't be scared to fall," Theo said.

"That's what Papa always says," Fiona said, gravely. "Because that's the way you learn."

"Very wise words." Quinn smiled at me, making my heart race. "For skating and the rest of life as well."

"I'm not afraid of anything," Cymbeline said as if anyone had asked. "Including falling."

"Me either," Flynn said. "Not that I ever fall. I'm the fastest in the whole town."

Quinn and Theo exchanged a glance and a smile. For the second time in a half dozen minutes, I filled with gratitude that someone was managing to reach inside the heart of my sweet boy.

Quinn

✦✦✦

The twins each took one of my hands and led me onto the ice. For a split second I hovered on the thin blades of my new skates before my legs went out from under me and I fell hard on my bottom. The twins tumbled after me, all of us ending up together in a laughing heap.

The boys leapt up, as if springs were tied to their feet instead of skates. They attempted to help me, but it was no use. Every time I put my feet on the ice, I fell, leaving us all in a fit of laughter.

Alexander, with Fiona on his shoulders, skated up to us.

"Papa, she can't stand up," Flynn said.

"Boys, leave this to me." Alexander lifted Fiona over his head and set her on the ice. She sped away, her little feet sure on the slippery surface.

"Papa, Miss Quinn's heavier than she looks," Flynn said.

"Flynn, we never talk about a woman's weight," Josephine said as she came to a stop in front of us. *What a sight I must be*, I thought. A grown woman sprawled on the ice.

Alexander held out his hand and I took it, holding my breath as he attempted to help me to my feet. The skates slid out from under me, and I fell once more on my bottom. My backside was starting to hurt. "It's no use. I can't get up."

He knelt over me. "I'll have to lift you by the waist. It's the only way."

His rich, low voice made my insides do funny flips. "Do what must be done," I said.

With one knee on the ice and the other leg bent, he reached for me, lifting me easily and then holding me tight against him. My legs wobbled, and I thought I was going down again. I clung to him with my arms around his neck, so close I could see the flecks of yellow in his green eyes. "Falling hurts," I said, laughing. "Don't let me go."

He slipped both arms around my waist and held me upright with the force of his strong frame. "You'll have to stay this way, it appears, if you're going to remain on your feet."

"You shouldn't tease me," I said. "It's terrible manners."

"Slip your arm around my back." He shifted so that only one arm encircled my waist. "And let's see if we can take a turn around the pond. All you have to do is slide one skate forward, then the other."

Feeling ridiculous, I lifted a foot, then the other. I did this for six or so steps. "It's working. I'm skating," I said.

His entire body shook with laughter. "Usually, we glide a little. You're more stomping than skating. Are you mad at the ice?"

"I would poke you in the ribs with my elbow, but I'm at your mercy," I said.

The pond was about the width of ten skaters standing side by side and thirty lengthwise. We inched toward the other end as one body. As I felt more secure next to my strong companion, I relaxed and took in my surroundings.

All of my students, other than Louisa and the Cole family, were out on the ice. The Johnson sisters skated by arm in arm, striking in their red coats and hats. Josephine wore a pale green that matched her eyes. She and Fiona skated together with their hands intertwined. Cymbeline had challenged Viktor Olofsson to a race from one end of the pond to the other. Cymbeline's brown eyes were furious as she chased behind him. If one were to win on will alone, it would be Cymbeline. However, a nine-year-old boy and a small girl of six were no match. Viktor won by at least two feet. Cymbeline fell on her knees and pounded the ice.

"She's mad at the ice," I said to Alexander.

"What will we do with our sassy one?" he asked. "She has to learn about defeat."

Flynn coasted by with his red scarf flying behind him and shouted words of encouragement. "You're doing great, Miss Quinn." I laughed and raised a hand toward him, then almost lost my balance. My partner steadied me with a firmer grip around my middle.

As we neared the tip of the pond, the three Cassidy girls stepped onto the ice and immediately started twirling like ballerinas. They were all small in stature but strong as little oxen. Alma had told me they'd been expected to help at the family dairy farm from the time they could walk.

"How sweet they all are," I said.

"Little beasts," he said. "Every one of them."

The sky was the brilliant blue I'd already grown accustomed to, and the sun warmed my back despite the chill. The mountains loomed above like magnificent white giants. With each passing day in this fresh air and Lizzie's nourishing meals, I was growing strong and sure of my destiny. I was the schoolmistress of Emerson Pass. The first teacher in a town made from the grit and courage of men and women who'd come in search of a better life. Yes, I was here in the modern age with bathrooms and a luxurious home to stay in, so it wasn't as if I had anything to do with what had made this place special. But I was here now. I would shape the future through my influence on the young people who twirled about me now. I had the chance for love and family.

"What's my favorite teacher thinking about?" Alexander asked.

I looked up at him. "I was thinking how happy I am here. The hue of the sky." I gestured toward the sound of a winter sparrow's song. "That, there. Do you hear him singing?"

"Yes, he's giving us a concert."

"Back home, I spent so much energy simply surviving," I said.

"You did survive. That's the notable part."

At the tip of the pond now, I held on to him even more tightly as we rounded the corner. My gaze went to Cymbeline, who was now demanding a rematch with Viktor. He had his cap in his hands and was shaking his head.

He touched his free hand to the lapel of his jacket. "Of all my children, she reminds me the most of myself."

"Were you like that—challenging boys much older and bigger than you?" I tried to conjure an image of a young Alexander wearing knickers and a cap, with freckles on his nose like his sons.

"Yes, I'm afraid so. There was never a race or game I wasn't keen to win. That's what drove me to America, I suppose. I wanted to conquer the world in my own way"

"Do you ever regret coming here?" I asked. We continued to move along the ice at a snail's pace, but the skates were starting to feel more like extensions of my feet instead of a weapon meant for my demise.

He made a sound in his chest as if he were carefully contemplating his answer. "As a young man, I didn't think beyond proving myself and craving adventure. Looking back, I can see it was my destiny to come to this place. The questions I had were all answered when I stepped off the train that first day."

"Questions?"

"About who I was. What I wanted. How I might matter. There's something about the way the mountains loomed so dramatically that seemed to speak to me."

"Would you believe me if I told you I was having similar thoughts just now?" I asked.

He stopped us and turned toward me, taking my hands to keep me steady. "You feel it too?"

"It's as if they're challenging me to live as large as they do." I wobbled without the strength of his arm around me but clenched my stomach muscles and managed to remain standing. "When I say it out loud, I feel foolish."

"No. Not foolish at all. You simply feel what I do. Not everyone can." His eyes lifted upward toward the sky, and a flash of pain crossed his face. "In my experience, there are two kinds of people deeply moved by this place. There are those like you and me who are encouraged and inspired here, and those who are driven mad by it. No one can hide from themselves here." The corners of his eyes crinkled. "Do *I* sound foolish? My mother said I was prone to the dramatic."

I laughed. "Let's agree that when we're together we never have to feel foolish for speaking what's on our minds."

"Agreed." He cocked his head, smiling down at me. "We have our own club, don't we? A club of two in perfect harmony together?"

"I think a club has to have at least three members. We're more of a partnership." My pulse quickened as he stared into my eyes. I didn't look away as I might have if it were any other man but Alexander staring at me this way. He was familiar to me, like a home I'd lived in all my life.

A fiddler at the pond's edge began to play a jolly, raucous song. The skaters cheered. Mrs. Johnson appeared with a box of freshly popped corn.

"Shall we skate?" he asked.

"If we have to."

He tucked my arm against his side. "Don't despair. It gets easier."

"Do you ever miss your family? Or the way of life?"

"My family, yes. Not the way of life."

"No regrets, then?"

His torso expanded under my arm as he took in a deep breath. "I have but one."

I tilted my face upward to get a good look at him. His thick lashes over lidded eyes kept me from seeing into the sea of green I'd grown so fond of watching. "What is it?" I asked softly.

"Ida."

Flynn sped by us again, so fast I felt a breeze from his momentum. *Ida.* There were many layers of meaning in those three simple letters that made a name.

"She was my mistake but also my salvation. Without the children, life would have no meaning or purpose. Living with her was like living in a war zone. When she died it was as if ceasefire had been called and I could finally breathe without fear."

"I'm sorry," I said. What else could I say?

"I stayed hopeful right up to the end that she would get better." He spoke lightly, but I could imagine the pain he must feel. "The lives that end after so much suffering—those deaths are the hardest to accept, don't you think?"

"Yes," I said, thinking of my father.

We continued shuffling along the edge of the pond as the children whirled and dashed around us.

I smiled, remembering Father's reaction when I'd shown him the acceptance letter from teacher college. "My father was the happiest I'd ever seen him when I was admitted into the teaching program. We didn't think I'd be able to go because of the tuition. Even so, he told everyone he knew that his daughter was smart enough to get into college."

"How did you manage the fees?" he asked.

"Someone in our church paid everything. We've never known who. He or she was a person like you."

"You think too much of me," he said.

"When I heard what this person had done, I vowed to give back by teaching as many children as I could, especially the ones whom the world had already thrown away."

"Did your father live to see you graduate?"

"No, he died my first quarter." My voice cracked. I'd come home to find my sister and mother huddled together in our cold front room. He'd died in his sleep. His tired heart, having fought so hard, had simply stopped beating. "My mother took it hard. Before we lost him, she always had this optimism that everything would work out."

Fiona and Josephine skated up to us, still hand in hand. "Papa. Miss Quinn. Skate with me," Fiona said.

"I'll fall down without your papa holding me up," I said.

"I'll hold your other hand," Josephine said. "Fiona can hold Papa's hand."

As was usually the case, practical Josephine had it all figured out before the rest of us. The girls parted and each took one of our hands.

"Hold tight," I told Josephine. "Or you'll be without a teacher on Monday morning."

Josephine giggled. "Don't worry, Miss Quinn. I'll never let go."

Together, the four of us inched across the ice laughing, our breath coming out in clouds in the cold air. When we reached the other end of the pond, Cymbeline stood on the ice with her hands on her hips, challenging Isak to a race. Undaunted by losing twice to Viktor, she thought it was a good idea to race his older brother? Our Cymbeline wasn't one to back away from a competition, even if a fool's errand.

Isak, cap in hand, politely declined the invitation. "Cymbeline, you're too little to race me."

She tore off her hat and stomped her skate on the ice. "That's stupid."

"Don't you see what happened with my brother? You have to race people of your same size."

"There's no one my size other than Nora, and she's a girl." Cymbeline pointed at Nora, who was skating peacefully with her sisters. "Look at her twirling around like a dancing doll." They indeed looked like pretty pink-cheeked dolls.

"Cymbie, come skate with us," Josephine shouted out to her.

For a second, I thought she might refuse. Instead, she grinned and stuck her hat over her curls. "Fine, but I'll be back," she said to Isak.

Thank goodness, I thought. Another second and she might have harangued sweet Isak to the point of surrender.

Isak, with an expression of a lamb who avoided slaughter, skated away.

We did one lap all together. The twins joined us, circling around and back.

Poppy shouted out to us as she entered the ice. "I'm here now. Harley and Merry brought me."

I looked over to see Harley in the process of attaching skates to the bottom of his boots. Merry had already made it to the middle.

Josephine broke away to skate with Poppy.

"Do we need a break?" Alexander asked. "How about a bag of popcorn, Fiona?"

"Yes, yes, please, Papa."

We made our way to a bench. Grateful for the rest, I waited while Alexander and Fiona fetched the popcorn from Mrs. Johnson. Soon, they were back with three bags. With Fiona between us, we sat and munched on the salty treat and watched the skaters. The fiddle player continued his merry music. Harley and Merry skated by us, holding hands.

Fiona yawned. "Are you sleepy?" I asked her.

"No, Miss Quinn."

It was a fib, of course. No three-year-old ever wanted to admit to needing a nap.

"I'm tired too," I said. "Perhaps your papa would take us both home? We can have a snuggle and a book."

Fiona brightened. "Just you and me and Papa?"

"Won't that be lovely?" I asked.

After arranging with Harley to bring the others later, Alexander helped Fiona and me into the smaller sleigh. Oliver and Twist nuzzled noses before we set out toward home at a leisurely pace. Alexander seemed in no hurry. Fiona fell asleep against me.

My eyelids grew heavy. I was drifting off to sleep when I saw a small figure walking just inside the drifts of packed snow that defined the road. I instantly recognized the patchwork coat. "It's Louisa," I said.

Alexander slowed the horses. She carried a package wrapped in butcher paper and walked with her head down. Only when we had come parallel to us did she look over at us. Lord Barnes pulled the reins, stopping the horses.

"Louisa," I said. "Would you care for a ride home?"

Her wan face under the bright sunlight seemed constructed of delicate bird bones. She wore her usual ragged knit hat that smashed her dirty hair against the sides of her neck. Her teeth chattered from cold. I silently cursed her father.

"No, thank you, Miss Cooper." She held up the package in her bare hands. "This here's fish heads, and I don't want to smell up your sleigh."

"They won't smell up my sleigh," Alexander said. "This is a magic sleigh."

She squinted up at him, then at the warm blankets. I could see in her eyes the struggle to decide. Instinctively, I knew it was fear of her father that kept her from climbing inside. He would question how she knew us, and then her precious secret would be known.

"We'll take you as far as your driveway," I said. "It's on our way. You can jump out and walk the rest of the way to your house."

She clutched her package to her chest. "Yes, all right. Just to the driveway."

Alexander had already hopped down to help her. He lifted her into the seat next to Fiona and tucked a blanket around her shoulders. In comparison to my little sweetheart, Fiona, Louisa smelled of woodsmoke, lard, and dirty hair. The fish were the least of it.

"Lord Barnes," I said as we set out. "Did you have any of that popcorn left?"

"Why yes, I do." He reached into his coat pocket and brought out the paper bag. "Louisa, would you like some?"

Her eyes grew wide. "You don't want it?" I could practically sense her mouth start to water. I remembered the sensation only too well from my own childhood.

"Yes, Miss Louisa, it's for you," Alexander said as he handed it to her. "I'm getting quite fat, if you want to know the truth. You'll be saving me from eating the rest."

She giggled. "You're not fat, Lord Barnes."

For a second, she stared at the popcorn bag as if she distrusted the contents. Her forehead creased. "Maybe I should save it for Pa. He sent me to town because his stomach was empty and causing him pain."

"I think it'd be best you eat it before we drop you," I said, thinking quickly. "Otherwise, he'll wonder where you got it."

"Yes, Miss Cooper." She opened the bag and reached inside, pulling out a handful and stuffing it in her mouth. I decided against the lesson on manners. When a child was as hungry as Louisa, the last thing she needed was me lecturing her about how a young lady should eat popped corn.

I exchanged a look with Alexander before he clicked the reins and the horses began to trot. After a moment, I turned to Louisa. A path of tears had streaked her dirty face. She'd been crying.

She'd been in town to beg for fish heads from the Higgins brothers and had seen us all skating. I remembered the pang of jealousy; the awful sour feeling in the pit of my stomach; the sensation of acceptance that everyone in the world had more than I and always would. Their laughter and bright coats were swords that had slashed through me and cut away any hope that

I belonged. I was on the outside of a world where there were such luxuries as a full stomach and ice-skating.

I kept all this to myself. But for all that was holy, this child would have a pair of skates before next Saturday, even if I had to beg Alexander to return mine and get her a pair instead.

"What will you make with the fish?" I asked.

"Soup. I got some turnips down in the cellar." She flashed her shy smile. "I grew them all by myself."

"How clever of you," I said. "Did you keep the seeds and starters from the year before?"

Her expression darkened. She looked away and dug into the popped corn bag with new vigor. I couldn't be certain, but I suspected she'd stolen the turnip starters from Alexander's garden. If only he'd known, I'm sure he would have gladly shared. Regardless, this child was a survivor. If she had to steal from a neighbor's barn, then she would do it to stay alive.

Again, I silently cursed Kellam. What kind of man made his child steal for food so he could fritter away any of his wages at the saloon?

We were at the entrance to the driveway now. A puff of smoke above the tree line hinted at the house where Louisa lived with her father. She'd managed to empty the bag of popcorn, which had dimmed the glint of hunger in her eyes. I took the bag from her. If she took the evidence into the house, who knows what could happen?

Louisa jumped from the sleigh before Alexander could get out to help her. "Thank you for the ride." And with that, she began her trudge through the snow toward the thicket of trees that hid their shack from the road.

FIONA DIDN'T WAKE WHEN ALEXANDER CARRIED HER INTO the house and up the stairs to the girls' room. It was nearly three by then, and she usually took an hour and a half nap. I watched from the doorway as he took off her boots and covered her with a blanket. Moved by how gentle his large hands were as they brushed her curls away from her cheeks, I had to fight the lump in my throat.

When she was settled, Alexander nudged me into the hallway and shut the door behind us.

"Harley brought the Wu family over this morning," he said. "Should we go down and say hello?"

I tugged at the collar of his jacket. "Maybe a kiss first? We're all alone for once."

He pulled me close. "I can't think of a better idea."

After a long kiss that left us both breathless, we headed downstairs. Before we took the stairs down to the kitchen, Alexander stopped me for another kiss.

Alexander introduced me to Mrs. Wu and Li as the school-teacher, Miss Cooper. All very proper, which made me want to giggle after our kisses.

Mrs. Wu and Lizzie were at the island rolling out some kind of dough. Apparently, Lizzie had changed her mind about Mrs. Wu only looking after the girls. Given the delicious smell of the dumpling filling, I was pleased she'd done so.

"We're making dumplings," Lizzie said. "Mrs. Wu is teaching me her old family recipe." Cooking didn't require a shared language, I thought, as the two women seemed in perfect communication.

Li and Fai were at the table eating from steaming bowls of chicken soup. Despite their frayed clothing, the children's hair was neatly combed and their faces clean. I sat next to them at the table. "I'm glad to meet you. Are you looking forward to school?"

"I'm not sure," Li said. "I've never been, so I don't know what to expect."

"Do you like to learn and meet other kids?" I asked.

"I think so."

"Then you'll love school." I turned to his little sister. "Did you know you're going to have a friend to play with here at the house?"

She nodded as she scooped broth into her spoon.

"Lizzie told us," Li said. "Grandmother was happy."

Alexander joined us at the table, taking the chair next to me. "Li, please let me know if your grandmother needs anything."

"Do we have to sleep on the beds?" Li asked quietly as he looked into his now-empty soup bowl.

"You don't want to?" Alexander asked.

"At home we sleep on mats," Li said.

"Whatever your grandmother tells you to do is fine with me," Alexander said. "But I think you might like a bed."

The kitchen door flew open and Flynn, Theo, and Cymbeline piled into the room, breathless and arguing over who was the fastest skater. They stopped in their tracks at the sight of Mrs. Wu.

"Good, you're back," Alexander said. "This is Mrs. Wu. She's going to be working here with Lizzie. And these are Li and Fai."

The Wu children looked at the Barnes siblings with fear in their eyes. Who wouldn't? They were so robust and loud.

Cymbeline bounced over to get a better look. She pointed at Fai's hair. "Shiny and smooth."

Fai watched her but didn't reply.

"I like it," Cymbeline said as she ruffled her curls with her fingers to make it stand up. "My hair's curly and I hate it."

Fai let out a squeaky giggle. "No, pretty hair."

Flynn sidled up next. "So you're going to live here with us?" he asked Li.

"Yes." Li pointed to the door that led to the bedrooms. "In there."

"Do you like baby pigs?" Cymbeline asked. "Because we have some."

Li shrugged. "I don't know."

Flynn flopped into the chair next to Li. "Do you want to see them?" His voice was too loud, I thought. He's going to frighten this poor child.

"I don't know." Li's shoulders slumped as he looked around the table.

Theo had joined us by then. "We have a cow and chickens, too." He spoke softly, as if he knew Flynn was a little too much.

"Cow," Fai said with much enthusiasm. "I go."

Poppy and Josephine came through the door next, carrying all the skates. "You all forgot your skates in the sleigh," Josephine said before stopping to stare at Mrs. Wu.

Li looked at me as if to say, "How many are there?"

"There's a lot of them," I said to Li. "You'll grow accustomed to their noise."

Alexander introduced the Wus to Josephine and Poppy. They smiled politely at Mrs. Wu, then came to the table to inspect the children.

"Poppy and I will take the little ones out to the barn if it's okay with Mrs. Wu."

Li spoke to Mrs. Wu in Chinese. She responded back, nodding her head. "She says we can go look at the pigs."

"Great. Daylight's burning. We need to go now, or it'll be too dark to see anything." Flynn bounced up from the table.

"Put the skates in the mudroom," I said. "All of you, Flynn, not just the girls."

"Give them here," Flynn said to his sister.

They all left in a mad rush, Flynn and Cymbeline fighting about who could show Li what first and Josephine holding tight to Fai's hand.

"I think I'll stay inside." Theo slumped against the back of a chair.

"Do you feel all right, Theo?" I asked.

"My throat hurts," he said.

I motioned for him to come closer and then felt his forehead. "He's warm," I said to Alexander.

Alexander went to him and placed his hand on the boy's forehead. "She's right. Let's get you to bed, young man."

I expected him to protest, but instead he went limp against his father, who lifted him in his arms.

"Lizzie, will you make him some tea with honey?" I asked.

"Yes, yes. I'll bring it up," Lizzie said.

As I followed Alexander up the stairs, I heard Mrs. Wu speaking in rapid Chinese.

Alexander

I gazed at Quinn across a candlelit table. We'd started the meal with a few of Mrs. Wu's sausage-stuffed dumplings and were now enjoying roast chicken. I'd had Jasper bring up a good bottle of wine from the cellar, which he'd decanted and poured before disappearing to check on Theo. He'd been sound asleep when I came down for dinner.

Quinn ate heartily and drank often from her glass. For such a sliver of a thing, the woman had quite an appetite.

She caught me staring at her. "What?"

"I enjoy your enthusiasm for a meal."

She set down her fork. "It's embarrassing how much I love Lizzie's food. And those dumplings were the best thing I've ever eaten. Don't tell Lizzie."

"She would never forgive you," I said.

"I'm feeling rather guilty about leaving her with all of the kids tonight, plus two more with the Wus," she said. "And we took away her day off."

"She offered," I said. "Knowing the Wus would need her." I'd promised to make it up to her next week with an extra day.

"Christmas is coming soon. We'll kill one of the turkeys to eat for supper."

"I hate thinking of the poor dears as supper," Quinn said.

"They're delicious dears. And anyway, that's what they're born for."

"They live only to be slaughtered. How sad."

I laughed. "It's best to know one's purpose."

"I suppose." She dipped her chin before tucking back into her piece of chicken.

When we'd finished, Jasper swept in to take our main course plates and replace them with a dessert of pound cake.

"What are your traditions at Christmas?" she asked after a scoop of cake.

"We attend church on Christmas Eve," I said. "And then wake up in the morning to open gifts. In the afternoon Harley and Poppy join us for a meal. It's the one day of the year I've convinced Jasper to allow the staff and the family to eat together. You?"

Tears moistened her eyes as she glanced toward the windows. "We also go to church and then home to a meal. Nothing like the feasts Lizzie makes, I can assure you. But a special day, none-theless."

"You miss them?" I asked, knowing the answer.

"Yes. Every day. Christmas will be strange without them."

"I understand," I said. Someday, when I'd gotten her to agree to be my wife, I would bring them here. All in good time, I told myself.

Quinn

✦❦✦

I woke with a start. Something was wrong. I bolted upright and swung my legs to the floor, the space between my ears thudding with my heartbeat. The sound of a child's cry pierced the silence. Theo. I must have heard it in my sleep.

The room was mostly dark, without even an ember in the fireplace to help. However, a sliver of moonshine made it possible to see objects in the room. I reached with my fingers over to the bedside table to find the matchbox and pulled one out, then struck it against the rough side of the table. It lit, thankfully, and I used it on the lantern.

The clock read just after midnight. I ran out to the hallway, my nightgown swirling about my legs. Toes numb from the cold floors, I rushed to the boys' room. Theo thrashed around on his bed, moaning. A quick glance toward Flynn told me that he was sound asleep.

I went to the side of Theo's bed. His eyes sprang open, wide and scared. Damp curls clung to his forehead. Sweat soaked the collar of his pajamas.

I placed my cool hand on his forehead. His fever was much hotter than it had been that afternoon.

"Miss Quinn. I don't feel well."

"I know, sweet prince." I ran out of the room and down the hallway to Alexander's room, then pounded on the door. "It's Theo. He's worse."

Seconds later, Alexander appeared, wearing pajamas.

"He's burning up," I said.

We rushed to Theo's bed. His ragged breathing and glazed eyes turned me cold with fear. "Alexander," I said, more of a croak than words. "What do we do?"

Alexander picked him up, his face pinched with worry. "Let's take him into the library." We rushed down the stairs. I almost slipped in my socks but grabbed the railing just in time. In the library, Alexander placed the little boy on the settee.

"Let's give him more aspirin," Alexander said. "There's some in my desk."

I rushed over to the table where the liquor was kept and poured a glass of water. Alexander dumped a teaspoon into the glass, and I stirred to dissolve the powder. He lifted the boy against his chest and pressed the glass to his mouth. "Please, Theo, swallow. This will make you better."

Theo's eyes remained closed, but he opened his mouth like a baby bird and drank.

"We need cold compresses," I said. "I'll get them from the kitchen."

As I ran out of the library and down the stairs, it occurred to me for the first time that I was wearing my dressing gown. My toes were completely numb and my breasts, for what they were, completely bare under the thin flannel fabric. This thing was nearly as old as I, too short, with a frayed hem.

Lizzie came out from the door that led to the bedrooms at the same time I entered in the kitchen. She was dressed in a thick robe and wool socks. "Is it Theo?" she asked.

"Yes. He's taken a turn for the worse. How did you know?"

"I heard your footsteps on the stairs and figured." Lizzie pulled two white cloths from a stack by the sink and ran them under cold water. "Take these up. I'll make tea."

I flew up the stairs. By the time I returned, Alexander had Theo out of his soaked pajamas and covered with just a light blanket. Theo shook so violently that his teeth chattered.

"He's always been prone to terrible chest colds," Alexander said. "He was small when he was born."

I knelt on the floor next to them, my embarrassment over my attire long since forgotten, and placed the cold compress on his forehead. Theo groaned and shuddered.

I continued with the cold compresses against his forehead and chest, hoping it would cool him. The room was so cold, we could see our breath.

"How did you know he was sick?" Alexander asked.

"I heard him cry out." I pushed aside his damp hair, which stuck to his flaming pink cheeks.

Lizzie came up with a sweater that she insisted I put on. She also brought a pot of regular tea. "Thank you, Lizzie," I said, and squeezed her hand.

"Whatever I can do to help," she said. "Call for me and I'll come."

For an hour, Alexander and I alternated between the cold compresses and medicinal tea. The aspirin seemed to have no effect, so we gave him a little more. Another hour passed with no improvement.

"Should we send for the doctor?" I asked as I dabbed a clean, dry cloth over his sweaty skin.

"He won't do anything," Alexander said. "Other than look at him and declare him feverish. The man's a quack."

I didn't argue. Most doctors were. Selling their wares and miracle cures to the hopeful and desperate. I'd spent hard-earned money just last year for my mother's breathing problems. None of the powders did any good.

I was growing desperate when Lizzie returned. This time she brought a strange-smelling tea with her. "It's from Mrs. Wu," Lizzie said. "She says it's an ancient Chinese cure for fevers."

"What is it?" I asked.

"No idea," Lizzie said. "Some kind of herb mix that she added to hot water and stirred."

"Should we try it?" I asked Alexander.

"Nothing else is working. Some herbs can't hurt him." Alexander helped to get Theo upright. He took the cup from Lizzie's outstretched hand and lifted it to Theo's mouth. "Take a few sips. It'll soothe your throat."

"Here, let me try," I said, taking the cup.

Theo opened his mouth, obedient even while incoherent with a fever. I tilted the cup just enough that he was able to take a small amount. After the third sip, Theo shook his head and collapsed against his father's arms. Alexander guided him gently back onto the pillow.

"She said he has to drink all of it," Lizzie said. "Use this." She handed me a spoon.

"You sit him up and I'll feed it to him," I said.

Spoonful by spoonful, I fed him the strange-smelling concoction. Finally, the cup was empty, and Theo collapsed back onto the pillow.

After a few minutes, he calmed somewhat and stopped thrashing about. He curled on his side, moaning softly in his sleep. We continued with the cold compresses. I winced over the way they made him shiver.

Finally, around three in the morning, his fever broke. We wrapped him in warm blankets and took him upstairs to his bed. Lizzie had changed his sheets while we were downstairs. Once Alexander had him settled, he sat on the edge of the bed and caressed the boy's cheek. I sat on the other side of him, watching the man and his son, both of whom had captured my heart the very first moment I met them. If I'd only known what was waiting for me here. All this love.

Theo opened his eyes. "Hi, Papa." He turned to me. "Miss Quinn? Why are you both here?"

"You had a high fever," Alexander said. "But you're better now."

"I kind of remember some bad soup," Theo said. "Did you feed me bad soup?"

"A special tea made by Mrs. Wu," I said. "I think it cured you."

Theo closed his eyes and turned onto his side. "I don't want to miss school."

"Go to sleep, little man," Alexander said as his shoulders sagged with obvious exhaustion.

"Yes, Papa."

We gave Theo one more look and added another blanket over his quilt.

We fetched our lanterns and walked into the hallway. He rubbed one hand over the stubble on his face as we made our way down the hallway to my room. The shadow of whiskers made him seem older and dangerous. At my door, we halted. He turned me toward him and splayed his fingers in my loose hair. "I've never seen you with your hair down."

"I'd forgotten it was down," I said. "This was a tumultuous night."

He gave me a tired smile. "I couldn't have made it through without you."

"You could. You did before I came."

"I can't remember before you." He kissed my cheek, then lightly on the mouth.

I smiled up at him, my chest all achy and soft. "Get some sleep." When I turned toward the door, I slid slightly in my stocking feet.

Alexander wrapped an arm around my waist. His eyes locked with mine. For a second, we froze, our lanterns hung at our sides with his one arm around my waist. "You must be careful not to fall." His voice sounded low and throaty and made the spot between my legs quiver.

"It's too late," I said. "I've already fallen."

He trailed a finger down the length of my neck and slipped under the collar of my nightdress. Under the soft fabric of my gown, my nipples hardened and ached for his touch. "Do you know how badly I want you in my bed?"

"I won't know what to do," I whispered. "I'm afraid I'll disappoint you. I know nothing."

"I'll teach you." He pulled me closer. The hard muscles of his chest and thighs pressed into me. The sweater Lizzie had given me seemed suddenly hot and cloying. "The things I'll do to you will make you forget your fear." He kissed my neck, then nibbled my ear. I shuddered and let out a soft moan.

I might burst into flames, I thought. Right here in the hallway.

He kissed my mouth, penetrating with his tongue. His stubble scuffed my sensitive skin, but I didn't care. I arched my back and clung to him with my free arm. When he lifted his mouth from mine, I saw the question in his eyes. Would I let him inside my room?

It took every ounce of strength to say what I said next. "Alexander, not yet. Not until we're married."

"I know, my love. I know you're right." He placed one finger over my mouth. "You're all I think about. Do you know that? I'm consumed with your beauty and goodness. Every night before I fall asleep, I imagine you next to me when I wake up in the morning. Tell me you'll marry me soon before I die of thirst."

I held his scruffy chin in my hand and pecked his lips with mine. "I'll quench your thirst, Alexander Barnes. Soon."

He dropped his arm from my waist, and I escaped with my virginity barely intact. Once inside, I stood against the hard, cold wood as my heart thudded in my chest. I held my breath and listened for footsteps. Finally, I heard him walk away from the door toward his room. Only then could I breathe.

Alexander

✣

When I reached my room, I undressed and crawled into bed. The clock said it was almost 4:00 a.m. I closed my eyes and thanked God for sparing my boy, then, despite how I wished Quinn were next to me, fell into a deep sleep.

I overslept the next morning. Still weary, I sat up and rubbed my eyes. It was after ten. Was Theo all right? What kind of father was I? Sleeping when he might have taken another turn for the worse. I threw on my dressing gown and rushed down the hall to the boys' room. Theo was asleep in his bed. I sat on the edge and gazed down at him. His cheeks were no longer bright red but a cheery pink instead. I brushed hair from his forehead.

His eyes fluttered open. "Hello, Papa. May I have a drink of water?"

"Yes, yes." I went to the dresser and poured him a glass from the pitcher. There was a note propped up against the mirror addressed to me in Miss Cooper's handwriting. I grabbed it as well as the glass of water.

Theo had risen slightly, his eyes fixed on the glass.

"Can you hold it?" I asked.

"Yes, Papa. I'm feeling much better." Theo took the glass and sipped tentatively at first, then downed the entire glass.

"Do you remember much from last night?" I asked.

He wrinkled his forehead, obviously searching his memory but coming up with nothing. "The last thing I remember is riding home from skating and feeling very cold."

"You gave me quite a scare."

"I'm sorry, Papa."

This boy and his earnest expressions, I thought. "Nothing to be sorry for. Sickness can get all of us at one time or another."

"Not you, Papa. You're strong." With a tired sigh, he settled back against the pillow. Despite his improvement, a spasm of fear jerked through me. He'd been so ill. I had no idea how close we'd come to losing him. "Or Flynn. My sisters. Everyone's strong but me."

"You're quite strong," I said. "When you were first born, the midwife told me you might not live. But you fought. Sometimes it's the smallest amongst us who have the most grit."

His nose crinkled as he turned onto his side. "Mother told me I was weak."

I drew back in surprise. "When did she tell you that?"

"Do you remember that time I had a bloody nose from wrestling with Flynn?" he asked.

I vaguely recalled the incident. If memory served, Ida had been about six months pregnant with Fiona.

"She said Flynn was the strong one. That he'd taken all the strength and that I'll die young."

I couldn't believe what I was hearing. How could she have said such a thing to a wee boy? "Theo, this is quite simply not true."

His round eyes watched me, world-weary and resigned. "How do you know?"

"Because I'm your father. I know everything about you." I smoothed the bedcovers over his thin legs. "There are all different kinds of strengths."

"Like what?"

"Flynn and your little sisters are made of solid stock, no question. Your and Josephine's strengths are more of the kind that come from in here." I tapped my chest. "You have strong hearts that make you kind and compassionate and so very generous. Did you know that it's harder to be kind than physically strong?"

"Are you sure?"

"Physical strength is good, too, of course. But as you grow older and become less agile and strong, what remains untouched is what's inside you. Your kind of strength never goes away. In fact, a kind heart continues to grow larger the longer you live. Kindness takes practice, after all."

"It does?"

"Absolutely." I placed my hand on his shoulder. "The way you see the suffering in others and try to help is a great gift to the world. When you become a man, you'll be a force of good."

"Why did Mother tell me I was weak? Could she not see what you see?"

I hesitated before answering. Since Ida's death, I'd struggled to keep my bitterness toward her inside. She was the children's mother. They deserved to remember the good parts of her. "Theo, your mother was not well. She couldn't see anything clearly."

"Like a blind person?"

"No, not like that. Even if a person's eyes don't work properly doesn't mean they can't see with their other senses. Your mother's illness made it so her brain saw everything the wrong way. She could only see darkness. No light at all, do you see?"

"Miss Quinn said it wasn't my fault that Mother went into the snow."

"Did you think it was your fault?" I stared at him, incredulous and horrified. Had he thought this all along?

"Yes," he whispered. "I thought it was because I was..." He trailed off. His eyelashes fluttered as he blinked several times.

"Because of what?"

"Being here. Being the weakest." Tears leaked from his eyes.

I reached into my robe for a handkerchief and used it to soak the dampness from his perfect cheek. "Darling boy. None of your mother's troubles were because of you."

"I heard you and the doctor talking about how Mother got sick after we were born."

"That is true. But it's not because of anything either of you did, but that there was something in her brain that wasn't right."

"Miss Quinn told me that too."

"And do you believe her?" I asked.

His gaze lifted upward. "I want to."

In the seconds it took before I answered my little boy, a myriad of thoughts crossed through my mind. Like me, Theo blamed himself for Ida's death. How many times had I thought if only I hadn't made her pregnant a third and fourth time? I'd blamed my lust for her troubles. However, if what I was telling my little boy was true, then wasn't it the same for me? What was wrong with Ida was no one's fault. Not even hers. I'd blamed her for what was out of her control. She hadn't wanted to be sick. She'd wanted to live before the mental illness had pushed her into darkness.

"Papa, what is it?" Theo reached from under the covers to grasp my hand. "What's made you sad?"

"What happened to your mother was no one's fault. We have to forgive ourselves and her for what happened and move forward."

His dark brows came together. "Papa, do you love Miss Quinn?"

I blinked, then laughed. "How did you know?"

"Josephine told us. She knows these things because of the books she reads. At least that's what she said."

"Well, she's right."

"She never tries to make me be anything but myself," Theo said.

"How would you feel if I married Miss Quinn?"

"I'd feel happy. Have you asked her?"

"Not properly. But I plan to."

Theo smiled. "She has to say yes, Papa. There's no one else in the whole world as good as you."

I kissed his forehead to hide the tears that sprang to my eyes. "You're pretty good yourself."

LIZZIE AND MRS. WU WERE IN THE KITCHEN FEEDING FIONA, Li, and Fai a lunch of potato soup and bread.

"Hi, Papa," Fiona said from the table. "I'm having lunch with my new friends."

"I can see that." I kissed the top of her head.

"After this Lizzie said we could go out and see Harley in the barn."

"I can help with the chores, Lord Barnes," Li said.

"Thank you, young man," I said. "But when you're feeling well enough, I'd like you to go to school with the others."

Li looked at his bowl of soup. "I won't know anything."

"Miss Cooper will teach you what you need to know."

"Will they call me bad names?" Li asked.

"No. Miss Cooper would never allow that."

"Calling someone a mean name is mean," Fiona said.

I chuckled and rumpled her hair. "Yes, it is.

"Now I have to go into town. I'm picking up a present."

"For me?" Fiona asked.

"No, pet. For Miss Quinn. I've had a new coat made for her and it's ready."

From the island where she smashed cloves of garlic, Lizzie twittered. "There's no saving you now."

"That, Lizzie, is the absolute truth."

Quinn

T he Monday afternoon after our scare with Theo, I came home from school weary and in need of a long winter's nap. When we came into the house, Alexander met us at the door.

He whispered in my ear as he helped me out of my coat. "My love, are you exhausted?"

"I am." *My love.* I'd never tire of hearing those words out of his mouth.

"How's Theo?" Flynn asked.

"Much better," Alexander said. "He slept a lot today, but he ate some of Lizzie's soup."

Flynn's pinched face relaxed. "I'm going to see him. Just to make sure."

All day at school, Flynn had fretted silently over his twin. At lunch he hadn't even wanted to go outside, staying instead to clean the blackboard. When I'd asked him why he would miss the chance to be outside, he'd shrugged and said, "Without Theo, it doesn't seem right to have fun."

The children all scurried off to find out what Lizzie had for them in the kitchen.

"I'll look after things this afternoon," he said. "You rest. I have something special for you later."

I reluctantly agreed, my fatigue winning against any other argument.

He kissed me lightly and pointed toward the stairs. "Off with you."

I trudged up the stairs and down the hall, stopping at the boys' room first. They were both on their beds facing each other. From what I could tell, Flynn was in the middle of telling Theo the details of the day. "Then, Miss Quinn told us about the time the Americans dumped all this tea into the Boston Harbor. It was a band of resistant fighters and they went in the middle of the night and threw it all off the sides of ships. I wish I'd have been there."

Theo, hanging on every word, nodded. "Did they get in trouble?"

Flynn noticed me then. "Miss Quinn, tell him what happened next."

"I'm tired from talking all day," I said. "But later, I'll tell you about it."

"Thanks, Miss Quinn."

"I'm off to rest," I said. "I'll see you at dinner."

"Miss Quinn," Flynn said. "Are we bad because we're part English?"

"No, of course not. That was all a long time ago. England and America are great friends now."

"But how can that be?" Theo asked. "If they were enemies before?"

"Politics is complicated," I said. "The best thing to remember is that it's not people but governments who create wars."

They both stared at me with blank expressions.

"By government, I mean men in power. They want something the other country has and decide sacrificing young men's lives is the way to get it."

"Will we ever have to be soldiers?" Theo asked.

I put my hand over my chest. "I'll pray you won't. I hope we'll never have another war where we have to send our sons off to fight."

"I'd want to fight," Flynn said. "If we had a war, that is."

"Miss Quinn, you said mothers send sons off to war," Theo said. "What happens if you don't have a mother?"

I fought tears and examined my fingernails until I could think of a sensitive response. "Young men are sent off to war by the women and girls who love them but also by fathers and uncles and even grandfathers. While they're gone, those who wait at home pray for their safe return and never ever stop loving them. It doesn't have to be a mother."

"What if you were our mother?" Flynn asked. "Then we'd have someone to send us off and wait for us to come back."

Tears spilled from my eyes. I brushed them away as quickly as I could. "It would be my great honor to be your mother. If I were, there is no place you could go that I wouldn't be waiting here when you return. There's nothing I wouldn't do to keep you well and safe."

"Just like last night when I was sick?" Theo asked.

"Yes. Exactly like that."

AFTER SUPPER AND BEDTIME, ALEXANDER AND I MET IN THE library. He had me sit and set a package on my lap. "Open it," he said.

"What have you done now?" I untied the string and tore away the brown paper. A note card lay on top of tissue. In perfectly even handwriting, it read: "For my lovely Quinn. To keep you warm when I cannot. All my love, Alexander." I lifted the tissue and pulled out a forest-green wool coat. "Alexander, it's beautiful." I stood, and he helped me into the heavy overcoat. Lace trim and a smart belt, with a hem that reached just above my ankle, it was as nice as anything I'd seen on the finest ladies of Boston.

He led me over to the mirror in the foyer. "Olofsson made it especially for you. Anna helped me pick out the material."

I stared at my reflection in the looking glass. "I feel posh and fancy. And warm."

From behind me, Alexander smoothed the sleeves with his hands. "The dark green suits you. Anna thought it would."

"She knew it was for me?" I flushed. "Everyone in town knows about us?"

"They know only that I'm in love with you," he said.

My eyes flew wide open. "You're in love with me?"

"My love, isn't it obvious by now?"

THE WU FAMILY HAD BEEN WITH US A WEEK WHEN LI ASKED if he could come to school with us. Dressed in clothes from the twins' outgrown closet and buoyed from a week of Lizzie's meals, he looked like a different boy. I tested his reading and arithmetic abilities first thing that morning. Oddly enough, given his limited resources, he could read at the same level as my youngest students. When I asked him how he'd learned to read, he explained that his mother had taught him the basics before she died. "Mr. Cole brought me books when he came," Li said.

"I'm pleased for you," I said. "And this is only the beginning."

Around noon, the sky darkened and began to dump snow. A howling wind shook the schoolhouse. Unable to focus, I paced at the back of the classroom watching the sideways snow. At one, Harley showed up and suggested I cancel school for the rest of the day. I agreed without hesitation. He offered to take the Cole and Cassidy children home and come back for the Barnes brood, Poppy, Li, and me. Louisa had not come to school that morning, or I would have asked Harley to take her along with the others. I hoped she was home, warm and fed, but I feared the worst.

Theo, too, was out that day, not well enough yet to venture out into the cold.

I peered through the glass window. Snow fell so thickly it was as if there were a gauze in front of my eyes. The Johnson and Olofsson kids usually walked the few blocks to their parents' shops. I decided right then that it wasn't safe for them to try to find their way alone. If they lost one another and became disoriented, they might freeze to death. There wouldn't be room in the sleigh for all of us. Harley would have to take two trips, delaying our trip home. More importantly, the Johnsons and Olofssons would worry if they saw Harley head out of town with some of the students and their own didn't come home. They might try to come for them, which could lead to disaster.

They were all in their coats and hats and about to head for the door. "Wait. I'm going with you." I grabbed the rope from my desk. "Josephine, you stay here with the others. When Harley comes, have him pick me up at the Johnsons' store."

"What're you doing?" Flynn asked.

"I'm going to walk them to their parents' shops. We're all going to hold on to this rope," I said to the others as I put on my new coat. "So that no one gets lost."

I took the lead, with Martha at the back. "Keep a tight grip and put one foot in front of the other."

The moment we were outside, the wind nearly knocked me over. Hard snow stung our faces as we tromped across the schoolyard. "Keep holding tight," I yelled. The wind made it impossible to know if they heard me or not. We trudged along this way, one foot after the other. Thank goodness for my new coat and boots. The buildings in town were bulky white blocks, but at least they were visible. After what seemed like hours but was only a few minutes, we reached the tailor's shop. Mrs. Olofsson was at the window, white as a sheet.

She flung open the door, motioning for the boys to come inside. "Thank goodness. We saw Harley drive by with the others, so I knew you'd closed school early. I was afraid."

The boys scurried into the shop and past their mother, chattering excitedly about what a grand adventure we'd had.

Mr. Olofsson appeared next to his wife. "You're a smart girl," he said to me. "With the rope."

"I'm headed to the Johnsons' next." We didn't stay for further talk. The girls and I continued our slow pace. My feet had numbed, and my cheeks throbbed from the cold. A few minutes later, we came upon the shop. Mr. Johnson, dressed in his hat and coat, had his hand on the doorknob.

"Come in, come in," he said as the girls and I stumbled into the warm room. "I was about to head out to find you."

Both Martha and Elsa burst into tears. "We were scared," Elsa said. "But Miss Cooper said to just hold tight and put one foot in front of the other."

Anna Johnson rushed toward us, embracing both her daughters and then me. "You're so brave, Miss Cooper. Thank you."

I hadn't felt brave, but we were safe, and that was all that mattered now. "I'm going to wait here for Harley." I explained that he'd taken the farm kids home first and would return for us. "I didn't want to wait for his return for fear you'd worry and try to come for them."

"We saw them drive past, so we knew," Anna said. "Sven was about to leave. If you hadn't been so smart with the rope, who knows what would've happened."

Sven patted me on the arm. "Thank you for keeping my girls safe."

"It's my duty to protect them," I said. "I'd never put them in harm's way if I could possibly help it."

WHEN HARLEY PULLED UP IN FRONT OF THE STORE, Alexander was with him. I waved goodbye to the Johnsons and ran out the door. Alexander met me halfway and scooped me into his arms and carried me to the sleigh. "I was worried sick. What made you do such a foolish thing?"

"I couldn't risk the parents coming for them," I said.

"You foolish, courageous woman." He tucked me into the seat and slid in next to me.

As we set out, I looked back at the children. With the snow and the dim light, it was hard to make out their faces. Theo had stayed home, so Li sat next to Flynn in the back seat. He stared at me with his dark eyes and smiled. "Is school always like this?" he asked.

"No, this was unusual," I said.

Cymbeline sniffed.

"Cym and Jo were crying," Alexander said in my ear. "Worried for you."

"No more tears," I said. "I'm perfectly fine, and now we'll go home and have tea with Lizzie and tell her all about our adventure."

"We were scared you were dead," Cymbeline said. "In the snow like our mama."

My poor babies, I thought. Of course that's what they feared. "I had the rope and no intention of dying," I said. "Do you know why? Because I can't stand the thought of not coming home to you."

Flynn shouted from the back. "I told them all you'd make it just fine. No one's as tough or clever as you, Miss Quinn."

Touched by his belief in me, I had to swallow a lump in my throat before I thanked him.

"Next time I want to come with you," Flynn shouted.

We turned left out of town and had just rounded a thicket of trees when I saw a small figure slumped over a snowdrift. A cold shot of fear coursed through me. The motionless body was a little girl in a patchwork coat. Louisa. She'd been there a while, given the inches of snow that covered her. I yelled for Harley to stop.

"Look there. In the snow." I pointed toward the unmoving

body. "It's Louisa." Without thinking, I jumped from the sleigh and ran to her with Alexander on my heels.

I fell to my knees beside her. Curled in a ball with her hands under her cheeks, she looked peaceful and dreadfully still. *Please God, let her still be alive.* I lifted her arm and felt for a pulse at her wrist. Faint but there. "She has a pulse." Her arms were as skinny as young birch tree limbs. Even in the dim light I could see the blue veins under her white skin.

"We'll take her to our house," Alexander said as he lifted her from the icy snowdrift. By this time, Harley had joined us, having asked Flynn to take his place in the driver's seat. There was no need, however. Louisa couldn't have weighed more than fifty pounds. She hung as limply as a rag doll in Alexander's arms.

He positioned her inside, brushing snow from her coat and ratty knit cap. I tucked blankets around her. What had she been doing out in the snowstorm?

We sat on either side of her. Our warmth would help, I thought, as Harley took the reins from Flynn. "What was she doing out here?" I asked as Flynn settled back next to Li.

"She might've been going to town for food," Alexander said.

The children were deathly quiet. Even Flynn looked scared. I wanted to reassure them that everything would be all right, but I wasn't at all certain that was true.

WE TOOK LOUISA UPSTAIRS TO THE SPARE BEDROOM ACROSS from mine. I asked Alexander to send Merry up to help. "I want to get her into some warm clothes and into this bed."

"I'll ask Josephine for a dressing gown for her," Alexander said.

Merry came, and between the two of us we were able to get her out of her cold, wet clothes. Louisa's eyes opened the moment we had her out of her dress and stockings. "Miss

Cooper? Where am I?" She had only a thin slip on, and her skin was blue from cold.

"Hi, Louisa, you're at the Barneses' home. We found you in the snow."

"I needed to find food." She wrapped her skinny arms around her waist.

"Let's run her a hot bath," I said.

Merry sprang up and was out of the room before I even finished the sentence.

"A bath?" Louisa asked.

"Yes, warm water will feel good."

"Warm water?" she asked, as if I were speaking another language.

"We'll get you clean and fed, and then you can tell me what happened."

I wrapped a blanket around her and took her across the hall to the steamy bathroom. As we helped her into the water, I saw skinny purple bruises on her lower back and buttocks. Bruises that could only come from a belt or a switch. They were in multiple shades of purple from different beatings. This poor child. She would not be going home to that bastard if it was the last thing I ever did.

With Merry on one side and me on the other, we gently scrubbed her skin and lathered her hair. I searched for nits in her fine white-blond hair, but found nothing. After a few minutes in the warm water, she stopped shivering. When we had her scrubbed properly, I helped her out of the tub and dried her with a soft towel.

"I'll go see about a tray of food for her," Merry said.

Josephine had left a flannel nightgown hanging on a hook behind the door. Louisa sagged against me as I slipped the night-gown over her head.

I carried her back into the bedroom and pulled the covers over her. Louisa trembled and let out a small, sad sigh.

"Are you sleepy?" I asked. "Do you want to eat first?"

She nodded. "I went to town for food," she whispered. "But the butcher shop was closed. We have nothing at the house to eat. Pa's been asleep since last night."

Asleep? Passed out was more likely.

Merry came in with a tray of chicken soup and some of Lizzie's freshly baked sourdough bread.

"Is that for me?" Louisa asked.

"It is. Can you eat it all up for me?" I set the tray over her lap.

"Yes, Miss Cooper."

Her hand shook as she brought a spoonful to her mouth. She took a timid sip, then another, then another. I buttered a piece of bread for her, and she gobbled that down next.

When she'd had enough, I set the tray on the dresser and returned to the bed. I adjusted the pillows, so she was less upright. "Louisa, why didn't you go home after you came to town?"

"I was out looking for food," she said. "Sometimes I can find berries or a dead bird."

A dead bird? Goodness, this poor child.

Louisa's gaze never left my face. It was as if she were watching to make sure I didn't leave. "If I come home without anything, Pa gets mad."

"Does your pa beat you if you don't bring home food?"

"Yeah. And other things too."

"Like what?"

"We play the hunter game. He chases me through the woods. I'm the deer."

Chills traveled the length of my body.

"If he catches me, I get a beating. I deserve it because I'm not fast. He says he's teaching me how to survive."

"Does he ever shoot his gun at you?"

"Sometimes. Just to scare me. He thinks that's fun." She shuddered. "One time he almost hit me. I felt it go right past my ear. He laughed and laughed when I fell to the ground."

I tried to steady my breathing, but my pulse raced. *The hunter game.* What if he'd been playing that the night Samuel was killed? Had he been firing his gun to scare his little girl and killed Samuel by mistake? Did he know he did it?

"Did you ever see any other people during your game?" I asked.

"Only once. A man in a black jacket was out by a shed."

"Did he see you?"

"I think so. He shouted something, but I didn't stop. I was too afraid." A shadow of a smile crossed her face. "That night I got away. Pa shot two times, but he didn't get me. I got to the house and hid under the bed, but he never came home. I fell asleep. The next morning, he was back."

I drew in a deep breath to steady my nerves. "Was that the same night the bullet whizzed past your ear?"

"No, that was a different time. These shots seemed far away. I was running fast and not looking back because that's when the enemy will get you, like Pa taught me."

I got up from the bed and went to the window. This bedroom faced the barn. The doors were open, and I could see Harley brushing the horses. "You're going to stay with us for a while."

"I can't. I need to go to Pa." She sat up and pushed back the covers. "He'll beat me real bad if I don't come home with food."

"We'll let him know where you are and that you're going to be a guest for a few days."

"But he needs food. I was supposed to bring it back to him."

"Would you feel better if we took some meals out to him? Would that get you to rest?"

She nodded, but her face remained pinched and worried. "I guess so."

"Now lie down and close your eyes."

Louisa turned on her side and tucked her hands under her chin. "This is such a soft bed." Her eyelids fluttered, then closed. I tucked the covers more securely around her small frame and sat watching her. She twitched as she drifted off to sleep. What would become of this poor, hunted child?

I PACED IN FRONT OF THE FIREPLACE AS I DESCRIBED TO Alexander and Jasper what the little girl had told me. I'd never before seen Jasper sink into anything, always stiff and formal, but for the first time, he collapsed onto a chair. "Dear God," he said.

"It's like something out of an Edgar Allan Poe story," Alexander said. "We have to get her away from that man."

Neither of them seemed to have grasped the other possibility. "What if they were out in the woods the night Samuel was killed? What if Kellam shot him by accident?"

What was left of Alexander's color drained from his face. "Kellam's shack is not far from their property."

"He might not have even known he did it," I said.

"There were two shots," Jasper said. "Aimed right into the middle of his chest."

"It can't be accidental then," Alexander said.

My mind raced ahead of the two men. "Samuel saw them. He saw what he was doing to Louisa. She said Samuel called out to her. Then there was shouting and two gunshots. Kellam shot Samuel because of what he saw."

"Rachel didn't hear voices," Alexander said.

"Didn't you tell me she was playing the piano?" I asked. "She might not have heard voices, just the gunshots."

"Yes, and the music room is on the other side of the house," Alexander said.

"What do we do?" I asked.

"We go into town and tell the sheriff what we know," Alexander said. "And pray he'll do something about it this time."

"Not in this weather," I said. "We'll wait until morning. There's nothing he can do between now and the time this storm passes."

Alexander

The next morning, we woke to clear skies and five feet of new snow. Harley hitched the horses to the snowplow, and the two of us went into town. We cleared our driveway and the road that led to town. He dropped me at the sheriff's office, promising to return for me after he plowed the streets of town.

Through the window of the sheriff's office, I spotted Lancaster asleep with his feet up on the desk. I startled him awake when I burst through the door.

"What? What the hell, Barnes? You scared me."

I hid how pleasing that was to me with a quick apology. "I've got some information for you." The sheriff's office also contained our jail, which consisted of a small cell behind steel bars. Most of the time, it remained empty. Today was no exception.

"You know, Barnes, your obsession with Cole's death has become tedious. Aren't you busy enough seducing the school-teacher to let this alone?"

I've never wanted to punch someone as badly in my life. "Keep Miss Cooper out of this."

He shrugged. "Everyone knows she's living with you. Tongues

wag, you know. Most folks think she's no better than a common whore at this point."

"That's not true," I said. "Every parent in this town loves her."

"Not what I hear from the boys down at Carter's."

"We've already established their lack of moral character," I said, "when they wanted a man dead for marrying the woman he loved."

"What do you want?" he asked. "I've got a game over at the saloon in a few minutes."

I laid out the entire story. "We have her at the house and have no intention of sending her home to that murderer. I hope you'll take it seriously this time and go out and question him."

Lancaster took one of his rolled cigarettes from his pocket. "See here, Barnes. It's not our job to take a young one from her father."

"Her father killed Samuel Cole. She has bruises from beatings. He hunts her like an animal." I gestured toward his unlit cigarette. "He burns her with his cigarettes. Isn't that cause enough?"

He struck a match against the rough desk and lit his cigarette. "We don't know all that to be true." He took a deep drag, then let out the smoke as if we had all the time in the world. I wanted to strangle him with my bare hands.

"Thing is, no one here cares about how Cole died. As far as I'm concerned, a man has the right to do with his daughter whatever he pleases. Also, it seems to me that this is nothing more than coincidence. We have no evidence it was his gunshots that killed Cole."

I couldn't believe what I was hearing. "You're going to do nothing about this?"

"Can't say as there's much to do."

"Listen here, you can arrest me, but I'm not letting Louisa go home to a man who thinks it's a funny game to hunt his own child."

He laughed the phlegmy snigger of a heavy smoker. "Barnes, what happens between you and Kellam is your own business. You think you can steal his kid and get away with it, then by all means, take your chances."

I leaned over the desk and snatched the foul cigarette from his mouth. "Listen here, you son of a bitch." I put the cigarette out on the sleeve of his cowskin jacket. He flinched as the tip burned a hole through the thick material. I pulled back before it burned his skin, even though I would have loved to see him yelp in pain. Tossing the cigarette aside, I drew closer, inches from his face. "You can bet your corrupt ass I'm going to take my chances. As far as you go—I'd suggest you start thinking about a different town to do absolutely nothing in but drink whiskey and play cards. This is my town. The people in it deserve a fair sheriff."

"What exactly are you going to do about it? I was sent out here by the governor. He's a friend of mine, Barnes. We go way back. Unlike you, we belong in America."

"Let me put it to you this way. When I offer a large donation to the cause of his choice, I have a feeling he'll do exactly what I want." I straightened, unable to stomach his rank breath for another moment. "Start packing your bags."

"Get out," he said through gritted teeth.

"With pleasure." I shoved a pile of newspapers across his desk. "Burn in hell, Lancaster."

BACK HOME, I TOLD QUINN AND JASPER ABOUT MY interaction with the sheriff.

"I can't believe a man of the law would behave this way," Quinn said.

"He's not a man of the law," Jasper said. "He's nothing but a coward."

We had to stop talking when Josephine came into the library.

"Papa, Miss Quinn, would it be all right if we all went to the barn? Lizzie's had enough of us in the kitchen."

Alexander gave her permission.

"I'll go with you," Quinn said. "And keep an eye on the little ones. Care to join us, Alexander?"

"I have a few letters to write," I said. "When I'm finished, I'll have Harley take them in to the post office."

"Very well, then," Quinn said. "We'll see you later."

When I was alone, I went to my desk with the intent to write two letters. The first was to Quinn's mother.

Dear Mrs. Cooper,

I'm writing to ask permission to marry your daughter. If you're in agreement to our union, which I pray you will be, I'd like to have you and Annabelle come live with us. I'm including a check for travel expenses and anything else you might need. I can assure you this is a match made of love and mutual respect. I promise to always take care of her and her family. I await your response with hope and prayers. Also, if possible, I'd love for you to come before Christmas. I can't imagine a better gift than your presence at our Christmas dinner. My daughter Josephine and I will pick you up at the station in Denver and ride with you the rest of the way to Emerson Pass. According to your daughter, that was a harrowing passage, and I wouldn't want you to be scared.

Yours truly,

Alexander Barnes

On the way home, I'd remembered the governor's passion for higher education. My letter to him was short and to the point. Replace Lancaster and accept my donation to build a library at the college in Boulder.

Quinn

꧁꧂

W ednesday during morning recess, I added a few logs to the fire while the students played outside. The Cole children hadn't come to school today. After everything with Louisa and the sheriff's lack of interest in protecting the Coles, I worried about them. I'd sent Harley out to check on them. He returned with news that they all had colds. I'd sighed with relief and gone on happily with the rest of the morning.

I'd just twisted the stove handle closed when a man stormed through the door. He wore dirty overalls over a stained gray flannel shirt, and a greasy-looking cap. Small, mean brown eyes peered at me from under thick, unruly eyebrows. From a few feet away, I could smell the foul odor of cheap alcohol. I knew who he was without introduction. Kellam. Instinctively, I picked up the iron poker I kept next to the stove.

"May I help you?" I spoke as stoutly as I could, pretending to be brave. My heart beat fast, and perspiration coated the palms of my hands.

"I'm Louisa's pa. I hear you've been sneaking around this town, poking your nose into things that don't concern you. The boys at Carter's shop told me you have her locked up at Barnes's mansion. I come here to get her and bring her home."

"She's not going back to your house ever again."

"Where is she?" He slurred slightly, his voice as unsteady as the rest of him, which swayed and lurched like a puppet. "Tell me where you're hiding her."

Had he not seen her outside with the others? Maybe he hadn't recognized her in the coat we'd found in Josephine's old clothes or with her hair freshly washed and braided.

"We know what you do to her," I said.

"Louisa belongs to me, and I'll do with her what I please." His teeth were stained brown, matching his cap. "My wife died, Miss Cooper." He spit my name out as if the words were foul inside his mouth. "She died giving birth to Louisa. That girl's all I have to take care of me."

"You've hurt her long enough," I said. Inside, I was screaming silent instructions to Louisa. *Run away. Run to Alexander's office. Anywhere he can't find you.*

"You stay out of my family affairs. I don't need no uppity schoolteacher telling me what to do." He drew close, his breath rank with chewing tobacco and whiskey. "If you don't, I'll make sure you're sorry. You want to end up dead, Miss Cooper? You think anyone in this town's going to care if something happens to you?"

I stared him down, holding my breath against his foul odor. I'd survived the streets of Boston. I'd be damned if I'd let this cowardly man intimidate me. "Like you killed Cole?"

"Cole should've minded his own business."

"You killed him because he saw the sick game you played with your little daughter. Everyone knows it. You're going to prison." Anger drove away any fear. Over my dead body was he taking Louisa anywhere.

"You one of them suffragettes?" He sneered at me as he stepped closer. "All about how women going to rise up?"

I gripped the poker tightly. I'd swing if I had to.

"She's mine." He snarled at me with his teeth bared like a rabid dog. "A child earns their keep. What did you tell her? That she didn't have to listen to me? That she could sneak out of my house and lie to my face every night? And then to keep her at Barnes's house like a prisoner? Like I wasn't good enough to be her father?"

"You're not good enough to be her father. You've treated her like an animal. I'd love to see you running through the forest with a man pointing a gun at your back. Or how about a cigarette burning your skin? What's wrong with you?" I was spitting mad by this time and wanted to ram the poker straight through his chest.

"Shut up, bitch." He knocked my arm, and I dropped the poker. It made a horrible clattering noise on the wood floor.

He lunged toward me. I backed into the wall.

"Don't feel so brave now, do you?" His thick fingers grasped the collar of my necktie and pulled it tighter, making a noose around my neck. "All that'll be left of you is this man's tie you wear around your skinny neck." He pulled tighter, choking me. I could feel myself going purple as I strained against his grip. *I'm going to die without saying goodbye to my family or the children or Alexander.* Just when I'd found love, this was how it would end. After all the struggle, I would die in the hands of this drunken idiot.

Just as I was about to lose consciousness, the door flew open and the children ran inside, with Josephine in the lead. "Get your hands off her," she screamed, her voice high-pitched. "Get away from her." Those light green eyes flashed with rage as she led the rest of the children in a wave toward my captor and me.

The Johnson sisters were right behind her. "Stop it—stop hurting Miss Cooper." Martha's shrill words pierced through my fear. They'd seen what was happening through the windows and organized themselves into an army.

Like a swarm of wasps, they rushed toward Kellam, carrying kindling pieces in front of them like swords. Their expressions were crazed and furious as they shouted various cries of war. For a moment I feared one of them might try to stab our villain in the chest. Right before I passed out, Kellam loosened his grip and tossed me against the wall.

I fell to my hands and knees, gasping for breath and coughing. It felt as though he'd broken my neck, but I knew that somehow, through the grace of God and a pack of very fearless children, he had not.

"Get him," Flynn shouted.

"Knock him down," Isak said.

The sound of stomping feet as they ran en masse toward Kellam only just penetrated my brain. For a second or two, I remained crouched on the floor, gulping for air. Black spots danced before my eyes. Afraid I might faint, I concentrated on taking deep, steadying breaths until I could make out the grains in the pine floor.

I rose to my knees and swallowed against the ache in my throat.

They trapped him in the corner of the room. When he tried to push through the wall of small bodies, Isak jumped on his back at the same time Flynn kicked him in the shins. The bulky man tumbled to the floor. Viktor shoved his boot into Kellam's side. Shannon and Nora leapt on top of his legs and sat on him as though he was a park bench. Theo sprawled over his chest. The Johnson sisters each stood on one beefy forearm. Flynn pressed into his throat with his small hands.

"How do you like it?" Flynn asked.

Kellam struggled, but he was no match for my wild band of students.

Alma, in the meantime, ran to my desk and came back with the rope we'd used in the blizzard. She dropped to her knees and hog-tied Kellam's hands over his head. When she was done there, she did the same with his feet. I'd never seen a child move as fluidly and quickly. Despite her little body, the girl was as strong as a horse. The days on her father's farm had taught her a skill I couldn't.

"Elsa, go to Father," Martha said. "Tell him to bring the sheriff."

"And my dad," Theo said. "He'll know what to do."

Elsa, without a word, took off running.

"Miss Quinn," Josephine said as she knelt next to me. "Are you hurt?"

The tears in her voice broke the spell. I looked up, then sat against the wall and scanned the faces of my students, as if the answers to my dilemma could be found in their frightened eyes. Martha and Josephine knelt next to me. The rest of the students gathered around, flushed from their efforts.

All but Louisa.

She stood in the middle of the room, small and thin in her new coat. Tears spilled from her eyes and made a pattern like a river down her cheeks. "Pa?" she whispered. "What have you done?"

"You. You'll pay for this, you little brat." He struggled to raise himself, but the hog-ties were too strong. "You belong to me, not these people."

The twins each offered a hand and helped me to my feet as Louisa drew closer to her father. "Why were you trying to hurt Miss Cooper?"

"It's your fault," he said. "You went against my word."

Just then, Alexander and the sheriff burst through the front door. For a second, they halted at the sight, clearly shocked to see Kellam on the floor trapped by my small band of students.

Alexander looked at me first, and I nodded to let him know I was fine.

Lancaster took his gun from the holster around his waist. "Looks to me we've got ourselves a prisoner." He and Alexander yanked Kellam to his feet. "Let's go have a talk down at the jail."

"Untie his legs," Lancaster said to Alexander. "He's going to have to walk."

Alexander knelt and untied Alma's knot. The rope hung from his wrists and trailed down his backside like a tail. How appropriate, I thought, for an animal.

As Lancaster dragged him out the door, Kellam growled and glared at his daughter. "You did this to me."

Louisa sobbed but didn't say anything. The girls had all gathered around her. Josephine slipped her hand into Louisa's. "It's all right," Josephine said. "We're all here."

The other girls held hands and created a protective circle around Louisa. "Don't watch," Martha said. "Just look at us. Do you see us?"

"Yes," Louisa said. "I see you."

"Always protect one another," Cymbeline said.

The boys huddled together in the corner of the room, cowed for once. They sank to the floor in a heap of exhaustion after our ordeal.

"Children, you did well," I said, faintly. "Teamwork was never better demonstrated than this afternoon."

"What do we do now?" Flynn asked.

"Stay here with Miss Cooper for a few minutes," Alexander said. "Just until the sheriff can do his work."

"I think going home early might be a good idea," I said. "Just this once."

I went into Alexander's outstretched arms, shaking from the adrenaline. "My brave girl," he whispered. "Are you all right?"

"I'm fine. You should have seen this pack of wolves we're raising. They were fierce."

"Like their teacher," he said.

I smiled up at him. "I wasn't sure I'd have another chance to tell you I love you," I said as I lifted the tie from my neck.

His cheeks reddened, which told me the bruising had already started. "He could've killed you."

"But he didn't. It's over now," I said.

"Not for Louisa," he said. "It'll never be fully over for her."

It was then we heard a gunshot. For the second time that day, my blood froze.

Alexander

"Stay here with the children," I said to Quinn. "I'll go see what's happened."

"Yes, yes. Go. We'll be here."

"Lock the door," I said.

I ran out the door and down the steps in the direction of the gunshot. It had come from the main section of town. Near the jail, if I had my guess. I was right. There, in the middle of the street, was Kellam's body, facedown in red snow. Lancaster hovered over him. The air smelled of gunpowder. Dr. Moore stumbled out of the saloon with his doctor's bag in his arms and ran toward them.

"What in bloody hell happened?" I asked Sven Johnson, who stood in front of his shop holding a broom.

"Kellam made a run for it, and the sheriff shot him in the back," Sven said.

Anna Johnson, wearing her shop apron, came to stand beside me. "Are the children at school?"

"Yes. I left them with Miss Cooper. Go to them, please. Keep them inside until I come back."

"I'll just get my coat," she said.

I turned back to the gruesome scene in front of me. All the

shop owners had come out to the street to watch. But I couldn't. I wanted no more to do with either the sheriff or the man who'd hurt his child and my Quinn.

I walked back toward school, thinking about Louisa. What would happen to her now? Who would take her in? Not me. God knows we had our hands full already. My feet seemed to have an idea of their own, because they led me to the rectory instead of the school. I knocked on the front door, and soon Pamela appeared.

"I heard gunshots," she said. "I was too afraid to come out. Simon's gone to visit a sick man."

"It's safe now. But let me tell you all about it."

She ushered me inside and poured me a cup of coffee and put a slice of fruitcake in front of me while I told her everything.

"That poor child," she said. "Where will she go?"

"I don't know."

"You aren't thinking of taking her in?" she asked.

"I've got so many of my own. And Quinn and I are getting married."

"Oh Alexander? Really?"

"Yes. She'll want more children. By the end of this, God only knows how many I'll have."

Pamela beamed at me. "I'm happy for you." She stirred milk into her cup of coffee. "Have I ever told you how much I wanted a child? But God never blessed us, so I focused on being the best pastor's wife I could be."

Was it my imagination or was this leading somewhere?

"I could talk to Simon. If he were willing, maybe we could take her in."

"She's a sweet little thing, but she's been through a lot," I said.

"Her own father hunting her. I'd say so," she said.

"Talk to Simon. For now, we'll keep her with us."

We said our goodbyes and I walked over to the school. I looked through the window, gathering myself. Anna was applying salve to Quinn's bruised neck. The children were all at their desks licking candy canes Anna must have brought from her store.

Surges of powerful anger and also fear overwhelmed me. I'd almost lost her. What the children and I would do without her seemed impossible to muster. I shook off the feelings. She was fine. The children were fine. Christmas was coming, and I had a surprise for my bride.

Quinn

❦

A t home, I sat with Louisa on the window seat of the spare bedroom as she sobbed into my lap. I smoothed her hair from her damp cheeks and let her cry. When she stopped, she sat up and looked me straight in the eye. "What's going to happen to me now?"

"You'll stay with us until we can find a new home for you."

"Who will want me?"

"Don't worry. All will be well." I said it but was unsure myself. The only people who would want her would take her in only in exchange for working on their farm or business. I wanted more for her. A warm, loving home with parents who cared for her.

"Did they shoot him dead?" she asked. "Tell me exactly."

"He tried to run away, and the sheriff shot him."

"Did he really kill Noah's dad?"

"Do you remember that night he was chasing you and you heard the bullets?" I asked.

"Yes." Tears rolled down her cheeks.

"He killed him. We're not sure why."

"Because he saw Pa chasing me, wasn't it? Pa didn't want anyone to know what he did to me."

"I believe that's right."

"Does it mean I'm a bad person?" she asked. "Because Pa was bad?"

"No, you're not a bad person. You're a little girl who has had to overcome a lot just to survive. You'll never have to be chased or go hungry again."

"How do you know?"

"Because Lord Barnes and I are going to make sure and find you a nice family. We're always going to look after you."

She put her head back in my lap and wept fresh tears until she finally fell asleep.

Alexander

I knocked on Rachel's front door late that afternoon. Would knowing what happened to Samuel give her some peace? I couldn't be certain. I knew only how much I dreaded telling her.

Rachel opened the door herself and stepped outside, squinting in the sunlight. "The kids are all sick. I don't want to expose you." She buttoned her coat.

"Theo too," I said.

"Is he all right? I can see on your face that something's happened."

"He's fine. In fact, Quinn sent this over with me." I reached inside my jacket for the herbal concoction Mrs. Wu had made. "Put a teaspoon of this in tea and have them drink it all. I can't swear to it, but I think it saved my boy."

She eyed it suspiciously but put it in her coat pocket.

"We know who killed Samuel," I said.

She drew in a long breath. "Tell me."

As much as I hated to tell the foul story, I relayed everything I knew, ending with Kellam's death. "He tried to run, and Lancaster killed him. Finally that idiot did the right thing."

She crossed her arms over her chest and looked out toward the woodshed. "It wasn't about me or the kids, after all. He was killed because he happened to be there just at the moment Kellam came through chasing his poor child. I've no doubt that he would have tried to stop him. He *did* try to stop him."

"He died trying to protect an innocent child," I said. "Which makes him a hero."

"He was always my hero," she said. "I miss him every moment of the day."

"I know."

Rachel shuddered. "That poor girl. What will happen to her?"

"We're trying to find a family for her. If not, we'll keep her."

"You can't be an orphanage, Barnes," she said, smiling. "First the Wus and now a little orphan."

"I will be an orphanage if I have to be."

"You and Samuel had a lot in common," she said. "Both a couple of fools."

"Will you be all right?"

"Eventually," she said. "Not yet, but someday."

Just before supper, Jasper announced the arrival of Simon and Pamela Lind. I asked him to bring them into the library where Quinn and I had been chatting about the Linds' interest in adopting Louisa. Quinn was overjoyed by the idea, as I knew she would be.

I invited them to sit on the couch. Jasper promised to return with tea as Quinn and I sat across from them.

Simon and Pamela held hands and exchanged a nervous glance before Pamela blurted out their intention.

"We've talked," Pamela said. "And we'd like to meet Louisa."

"If she likes us, we thought we could take her home," Simon said.

"She's a very sad, damaged little girl," Quinn said. "She thinks of herself as an animal, only worthy of shelter and food if she provides something in return. Convincing her otherwise may take time."

"She'll be slow to trust," I said. "Especially you, Simon."

"We understand." Pamela looked into her lap. "My mother died when I was young. I was raised by a stepfather who hurt me."

Simon handed her his handkerchief, and she dabbed at her eyes. "He's the reason I could not have children."

"Pamela, no," Quinn said.

"Yes. When I ran away at sixteen, I was blessed to find Simon. His devotion and love changed me. He taught me to live and breathe and love. Otherwise, I don't know what would have become of me." Pamela looked up at Quinn. "There's no one better than Simon and me to take her. I know the particulars of what it's like to be raised by an evil man. And Simon knows how much patience and fortitude it takes to love a girl after years of torment."

"We've prayed and the answer seems clear," Simon said. "We're meant to take her."

"Would you like me to get her now?" Quinn asked.

"Why not?" Simon said. "No time like the present."

Quinn scampered out of the room promising to return with Louisa.

"We have a room for her," Pamela said. "And I can sew her a few new dresses."

"We'll pack up some of Josephine's old things in the meantime," I said.

A few minutes later, Quinn came in with Louisa, guiding her over to sit between us as she introduced her to the Linds. "This is Louisa."

Quinn had her dressed in one of Josephine's old dresses. The light blue color highlighted the child's pretty eyes and fair hair, which Josephine had plaited into a braid that hung down her scrawny back. "This is Mr. and Mrs. Lind."

"Hello, Louisa. It's nice to meet you," Pamela said.

Louisa gave them a shy smile. "I seen you at church a few times."

"You were at church?" Simon asked.

"I looked through the windows. Pa said church was for weak people."

Simon nodded gravely, but a twinkle in his eyes hinted at his amusement. "I'm afraid I'll have to disagree."

"Would you like to attend church?" Pamela asked.

"My friends from school go there, so yes," Louisa said.

"That's a good enough reason," Simon said, laughing.

Louisa's gaze darted to Quinn. She'd obviously sensed she'd said something wrong but didn't know what. Quinn gave her an encouraging nod.

"Louisa's one of my best students," Quinn said. "She loves to read."

"Miss Cooper taught me. Now I can go on adventures whenever I want."

"Isn't that the very best thing about books?" Simon asked. "I have wanderlust myself, so books take me to places I'll never be able to go."

A light of recognition went off in Louisa's eyes. "When Pa was real bad, I'd wait for him to fall asleep and then I'd read and forget all about my real life."

"We'd like to give you a new home," Pamela said. "One where you didn't have to be afraid."

"One where you could have a few adventures of your own," Simon said. "Would you like to come live with us?"

"I can cook for you and keep house." Louisa's hopeful tone and earnest face were enough to break a man's heart. "And take care of the garden."

Pamela and Simon were silent for a moment as they looked to Quinn for help.

"Louisa, as a member of a family, you would have chores, as all children do. But it won't be like with your pa. Pastor Lind and Pamela want you to be their child, which means you're taken care of, not the other way around."

"Pa said I had to earn my keep or he'd kick me out to get eaten by a bear." Louisa's bottom lip trembled. "What do I do at your house so I don't get eaten by a bear?"

Pamela held out her hand. "Come here, Louisa."

Louisa once again looked up at Quinn for reassurance. "It's all right," Quinn said.

The child crossed over to sit next to Pamela, who put her hand on top of Louisa's head. "I'm going to promise you something, Louisa. If you're our child, we won't hurt you, and we'll do our very best to protect you from harm."

"But what will I need to do?" Louisa asked in a panicked, high-pitched voice. Her shoulders had lifted to her ears, and her gaze went from one of them to the other and back again.

"What specifically would you like Louisa to do?" Quinn asked.

Simon cleared his throat. "We expect you to be respectful and kind to us and anyone who visits. You'll help Pamela by sweeping the floors and setting the table for meals."

"Make your bed each morning. And help do dishes after supper," Pamela said. "In the summer, you'll help me in the garden."

"Attend church, of course," Simon said. "Keep up with your studies at school."

"Keep your hair and clothes tidy," Pamela said.

Louisa's shoulders softened. "Is that all?"

"Yes, Louisa," Pamela said. "That is all."

"I love to work in the garden," Louisa said under her breath.

"Do you really?" Pamela asked. "Because it's my favorite pastime. I grow tomatoes, beans, squash, and cucumbers to make pickles."

"What about potatoes and turnips?" Louisa asked.

"No turnips," Simon said. "I dislike them immensely."

"I haven't grown potatoes before," Pamela said. "But we could plant them together."

"I like potatoes," Louisa said.

"Me too," Simon said.

Louisa wrapped her arms around her middle and took in a long, shaky breath. "I understand now. I'm ready to go with you."

"We've made up a bed in your new room," Pamela said. "Would you like to see it?"

"Yes, ma'am," Louisa said, brightening. "My own room?" She looked over at Quinn as she slid from the couch. "Miss Cooper, my own room."

"I'm glad for you," Quinn said.

We all stood then. For a moment, an awkward silence filled the room until Louisa ran to Quinn and wrapped her arms around her teacher's waist. "Thank you for everything," Louisa said.

"You're welcome, dear one," Quinn said. "You can breathe easily now. No one's going to hurt you from here on out." She put her hands on the little girl's shoulders. "Are you ready to go with the Linds?"

"Yes, Miss Cooper." Louisa stepped out of the embrace and walked over to where Pamela and Simon waited by the couch. Pamela offered her hand and after a split second of hesitation, Louisa took it, and they walked toward the door together.

"Tomorrow we can look at fabric to make you some new dresses," Pamela said. "I've always wanted a daughter to sew for."

"Will you teach me how to sew?" Louisa asked as they passed into the foyer.

Simon and I shook hands. "I may need some advice as we go along." He chuckled. "A daughter when I'm already an old man."

"It's the best and hardest job you'll ever have," I said. "Although possibly easier to manage when there's only one instead of five."

"God hates a coward, isn't that what you told me?" Simon asked.

"Yes sir," I said. "Which makes him particularly proud of you tonight."

Quinn

✿

A fter the excitement of the last few days, our household
settled back into routine. Friday night, Alexander had
asked Clive to call on Lizzie. Clive, being a kind man,
and also much too young for Lizzie at only twenty years old, was
only too happy to help in the ruse. To help her get ready, Merry
and I joined Lizzie in her room. She had to look particularly
inviting this evening.

I coaxed her unruly hair into a bun, but tendrils escaped at
the back of her neck and temples. "Oh, why won't my hair ever
behave?" Lizzie asked.

"Never mind that," I said. "The curls are pretty."

Merry powdered Lizzie's nose and gave her a hint of blush on
her cheeks and lips.

"I'm not sure I've ever seen you without your apron and cap,"
I said as I stood back to admire Lizzie. She wore a sapphire-blue
dress with a white sash that flattered her curves and brought out
her eyes. "You're always pretty, but tonight you're simply
breathtaking."

"Do you think?" Looking at her reflection in the mirror,
Lizzie patted her hips. "I'm so plump."

"No, you're just right," Merry said as she sat on Lizzie's bed, looking fetching in a pale green dress. Her hair, usually braided and wrapped around the top of her head, was twisted at the nape of her neck.

"I agree." I looked small and skinny next to Lizzie's hourglass frame and Merry's tall, muscular build. "Anyway, it takes all kinds."

Mrs. Wu was in the kitchen making supper, and the smell wafted into Lizzie's room. "What is she making that smells so divine?" I asked.

"Some kind of bun with meat in the middle," Lizzie said. "Her mother taught her all the family recipes when she was a girl in China."

"Aren't we a peculiar household?" Merry said. "Everyone from somewhere else."

"That's America," I said.

"Isn't it strange to think of our children's children?" Merry asked. "They'll not know about the old worlds we came from, only here."

"All of our differences merged together by then," I said. "Into what, I wonder?"

"Harley's asked to marry me," Merry said.

We both whirled around to look at her.

"When did that happen?" I asked.

"Last night after class. When we dropped you off, I went with him to help with the horses. We were talking and then all of a sudden, he kissed me. He asked if I'd ever consider marrying him."

"What did you say?" Lizzie asked.

"How was the kiss?" I asked at the same time.

Merry smiled. "I said yes, and the kiss made my legs shaky."

"Oh, my," Lizzie said.

"That's the best kind of kiss," I said, as if I were the expert now that Alexander and I couldn't seem to stop kissing.

"It's all because of you, Quinn. If we hadn't started going to night school together, then I'd never have had the chance to talk to him. I might not have ever had the courage otherwise."

We all jumped at a knock on the door followed by Alexander's voice. "Ladies, Clive has arrived."

I squeezed Lizzie's hands. "Let's go make someone jealous."

ALEXANDER AND CLIVE WERE SITTING IN CHAIRS BY THE FIRE and rose to their feet as we entered. Jasper was across the room tidying the already-tidy liquor cabinet. His jaw clenched when he saw Lizzie. There it was, I thought.

We joined the gentlemen by the fire.

"I...I like your dress." Clive blushed red.

Alexander had coached Clive to give Lizzie a compliment. He might need a little practice.

Lizzie flashed Clive one of her best smiles. "Thank you."

Jasper left the room, the clicking of his heels on the floor louder than usual. We got him. This would shake him into action.

We all sat and made small talk about the weather and various other subjects. I noticed movement just outside the library doors. Was Jasper eavesdropping?

"Will you all excuse me a moment?" I asked.

The men stood.

I went out to the foyer and sure enough, Jasper stood just outside the door. He appeared too upset to even seem embarrassed by his lack of decorum. He gestured for me to move into the parlor that remained unused most of the time. Another one of Alexander's quirks. He preferred his library for entertaining.

"What in God's name is that boy doing here?" Jasper whispered.

"He's calling on Lizzie."

"How could you let this happen?" he asked.

"What do I have to do with it?"

"I don't know. It's just that since you arrived everyone's running around acting like lovesick debutantes. We've got Merry and Harley kissing in the barn and you and the lord carrying on like animals in springtime. And now this. Do you know she's asked the lord for her own cottage? Her own cottage. I mean, this is simply not done."

"Jasper, what does it matter to you what Lizzie does? You've already told her you don't love her."

"Because there is a right way to do things and a wrong way to do things. Cooks do not have their own cottages."

"Alexander does as he pleases with his money and his property. He has enough of both and wants to thank her for years of service."

"I won't have it. I'm supposed to run this house. We've got strangers living downstairs and perplexing food coming out of our kitchen. Does Lizzie even cook any longer, or is it dumplings every night now?"

I laughed. I couldn't help it.

"What's funny?" he asked, eyes flashing.

"I'm sorry, but you're funny. You know what's going on here, don't you?"

"Whatever do you mean?"

"You're jealous. You want Lizzie for yourself."

"I want things run the way they were," he said. "This has nothing to do with that Clive person calling on my Lizzie."

"Your Lizzie?"

"For heaven's sake, you're an annoying woman. Like a herding dog."

"Excuse me?" A herding dog? That made me laugh even harder, imagining nipping at the heels of this entire household.

"Nothing." He let out a long sigh. "You have a quality that makes every person you meet want to be better."

"I'll take that as a compliment," I said.

"It's meant to be one."

"Lizzie's spent her adult life waiting for you to see her—to love her. She wants that cottage to move away from you—from the idea of you two being together. Do you understand? If you love her, now is the time to tell her and to take action. Otherwise, she will find someone else. This town is full of single men. And she's a beautiful woman with her own money. Think about what you want. Do you want to grow old alone while everyone else is happily coupled simply because of principle? Because you can't let go of the old ways? I think that's just about the saddest thing I've ever seen."

I walked out of the parlor and downstairs to the kitchen, where Mrs. Wu was feeding the children, silently praying that I'd gotten through to him.

Alexander

I received the letter from Quinn's mother a week later.

Dear Alexander,

Your request came as no surprise. Quinn had written to me of her deep feelings for you and your children. In her last letter, she'd mentioned the possibility of marriage. I'm overjoyed.

We'd hoped to come west when we'd saved enough money. Your generosity makes it possible for us to come now, and for that we are grateful. Without Quinn, there has been a hole in our lives.

We have tickets to arrive in Denver on December 23 and will be expecting you and your sweet Josephine at the train station. We cannot wait to meet you all. I've been daydreaming of how much fun it will be to be a grandmother.

Love,

Your soon to be mother-in-law, Mrs. Cooper

A WEEK LATER, JOSEPHINE AND I TOOK THE TRAIN INTO Denver. Our aim was to pick out a ring for Quinn and to bring back her mother and sister.

We disembarked at Union Station around noon. Josephine

exclaimed over the welcome arch and reached for my hand as we walked across the street amid motor cars and people on bicycles. The noise and bustle of the city jarred my nerves, but Josephine was enthralled. Cables ran all over downtown, and she studied them as we waited for the streetcar, asking questions about how they worked and when they were built, none of which I had precise answers for.

She pressed her nose against the window as we traveled down Sixteenth Street, exclaiming over the buildings and the women's dresses and hats. We passed by the Metropole Hotel where I planned to take us all for a meal after the Coopers arrived. A sign in front of the hotel read: "Metropole. Absolutely Fireproof."

"Why would they say that?" Josephine asked.

"Just reassuring us," I said. Josephine was too young to remember the fires that devastated cities, including Chicago and Seattle. Or the one that burned our own Emerson Pass. "Do you see the brick?" I asked after telling her about the fires of the past. "That's an example of man learning from his mistakes."

The jeweler's name was Mr. Finney, and he had a sharp, thin face with a large nose, which made him look a bit like a mouse. He showed us a variety of rings in both ornate and simple settings. In the end, we agreed on a slim band with a diamond solitaire. "It's delicate yet shines, like Quinn," Josephine said.

We had another two hours before the train from Denver came. I took Josephine to the City Park and sat on an iron bench to watch the skaters on the frozen lake. "It's so big compared to ours," Josephine said.

"Would you like to move to the city when you grow up?" I asked.

"I don't think I would like it here. There's a lot of noise. I'd rather stay home and make a library."

"A library?"

"I read about it in the paper. Mr. Carnegie will give money to start one as long as the town agrees to fund it afterward."

"Really?"

"I could be the librarian, and then I'd get to be with books all day long."

I wrapped my arm around my little bookworm and held her close. "As long as you're happy, I'm happy."

"Same, Papa." She rested her cheek against my shoulder. "Do you think you and Miss Quinn will have babies?"

"I don't know. These things aren't always up to us. Would you want us to?"

"Do you think she would still love us if she had a baby of her own?"

"The human heart has capacity for a great many loves. Especially Miss Quinn."

"What would Fiona think if she were no longer the baby?" Josephine asked, laughing.

"For that reason alone, we should have more."

We sat watching the skaters go by, quiet and comfortable together until it was time to meet Mrs. Cooper and Annabelle.

I KNEW THEM THE MOMENT THEY STEPPED OFF THE TRAIN. Annabelle was tall and more robust than Quinn, with red hair and green eyes. Mrs. Cooper was small and slight, like Quinn, with white hair tucked under her hat.

"There they are, Papa," Josephine said.

I held up a hand in greeting as we walked toward them. "Mrs. Cooper?" I asked.

"Yes, yes, it's us." Mrs. Cooper's eyes were a lighter shade of brown. Faint lines etched her skin. "You're as handsome as she said you were." She turned to Josephine. "She told me so much about you in her letters, Miss Josephine. What a big, brave girl you are to take care of your sisters and brothers."

Josephine blushed. "Thank you, Mrs. Cooper."

Mrs. Cooper pulled Josephine in for a hug. "You have to call me Granny."

"Granny," Josephine said as they parted. "We've never had one of those."

"And this is Annabelle," Mrs. Cooper said.

The girls exchanged shy smiles. "Miss Quinn talks about you all the time," Josephine said. "She thinks you and I will be fast friends."

"I think so too," Annabelle said. She turned to me. "Lord Barnes, we're so very grateful to be here."

"We're family now," I said. "You must call me Alexander."

We had several hours before the train to Emerson Pass. After we collected their suitcases, I took them all out to a meal.

We dined on steaks, potatoes fried into crisp wedges, and crunchy salad with creamy dressing and bits of bacon. Josephine sat up straight and was polite and grown-up. I imagined her as a young woman. How soon that time would come that I'd have to agree to a man's request for marriage.

Both the Cooper women seemed to enjoy the meal immensely, exclaiming about everything. Mrs. Cooper fretted over the prices. I reassured her by saying it was a special day. "It's not every day you meet your bride's family."

"You've been able to keep our arrival a surprise?" Mrs. Cooper asked.

"Only Papa and I know," Josephine said. "Well, and Jasper and Lizzie. They know everything about our family. It's been so hard to keep the secret, hasn't it, Papa?"

"Very much so," I said. "However, I'm a romantic and want to have you both at the house to help us celebrate tonight. I've been imagining it for weeks now." I pulled the ring box from my inside jacket pocket. "Would you like to see the ring?"

Annabelle squealed when I opened the top of the box. "My sister will love it."

"I'm taking her on a sleigh ride away from the house. When we return, we'll have a party to celebrate, and you'll be her surprise."

"What if she says no?" Annabelle asked, deadpan, before

bursting into peals of laughter. "I'm just teasing. We know for a fact she's saying yes."

"I certainly hope so," I said. "Or it's going to be an awkward party."

THAT EVENING, I TOOK QUINN OUT FOR A SLEIGH RIDE. THE stars were bright overhead, and a sliver of a moon smiled down on us. Oliver and Twist nuzzled as they clomped through the snow. When we reached a spot in the middle of the meadow where the stars were particularly bright, I stopped them and adjusted in the seat to face Quinn. She had her head tilted back, looking up at the sky.

When we returned from Denver, we'd hidden Mrs. Cooper and Annabelle in Harley's cottage.

"I think about my mother and sister on nights like these," she said. "And wish they could see the stars from right here."

She turned toward me. In the shadowy light, I could only just make out the outline of her face. I knew every inch, though. Every freckle and the exact color of her eyes and the way her nose wrinkled when she laughed.

I took the ring from my pocket. "I fetched you a trinket in Denver."

"A trinket? Do you mean a ring?"

I didn't answer as I lifted her hand from under the blanket and tugged at her glove, which stubbornly refused to come off her slender fingers.

"Here, let me," she said, giggling. "There's a trick to it." She gracefully slid the glove from her hand and waggled her fingers at me. "Would you like to put the ring on, or shall I?"

"I have to ask first."

"You're taking a very long time," she said.

"Perhaps I'll just put it back in my pocket?"

"No, no. I'll be quiet now." She pressed her fingers against my mouth. "See, it's ready for you."

I laughed and kissed each one of her fingers. "Will you wear this ring and be my wife?"

God bless the sliver of the moon, for it took that moment to shine a little brighter and made the diamond sparkle. "Yes, I'll wear your ring and be your wife."

I slipped the ring on her finger and kissed her. Somewhere in the night, a wolf howled as if giving his approval. "Marry me on Christmas Eve?"

"Christmas Eve?"

"Yes, Pastor Lind will do the ceremony. We'll invite the whole town."

She laughed. "What about my mother and sister? If I marry without them here, they'll never forgive me."

"All right, then. As soon as we can get them out here, we'll marry. Can you promise me that?"

"Oh, Alexander, I love you so."

"Let's go back to the house. Jasper's opening champagne."

We drove back to the house, laughing and kissing as the bells chimed merrily, and the horses shook their manes as if celebrating with us.

IN THE FOYER, I HELPED QUINN OUT OF HER COAT. THE sounds of chatter and laughter came from the library.

"It sounds like they've started without us," she said.

"We're back," I called out. The room hushed.

Quinn's brow furrowed. "Why'd they get so quiet?"

"Come with me," I said. "You'll see." I tucked her arm against me and opened the door to the library. Her mother and sister stood together by the window.

She went rigid with shock at the sight of them. "Mother? Annabelle?"

Mrs. Cooper came forward with her arms out. "Come here, my girl, and hug me."

Quinn, crying, ran to her mother. Her sister joined them, and they all hugged and laughed and cried at the same time. When they parted, Quinn looked over at me. "How did you do this?"

"They took the train," I said. "Surprise."

She turned to the children, who were huddled together on the couch, watching the entire affair with big eyes. "Children, were you in on this?"

"Just Josephine," Cymbeline said, sounding put out. "Until a few minutes ago."

Quinn went to the couch and knelt down next to them. "Do you know how happy I am that now all the people I love will be under one roof?"

"Do you love us as much as Papa?" Cymbeline asked.

"I love you as much," she said.

"I love you too," Cymbeline said.

"And you won't ever leave us?" Fiona asked.

"I'll never leave you," Quinn said.

I looked over at Josephine. "I told you it was meant to be," she said. "We knew it from the start."

"*You* knew it and told us," Flynn said. "I'm glad you were right."

"We have a grandmother and an aunt now," Fiona said as if this were new information. "They're going to live here with us."

"And a mother," Theo said softly.

"Yeah, a mother." Flynn grinned. "The best, toughest mother in the whole world."

Jasper popped a bottle of champagne and poured a glass for the adults and cider for the children.

We gathered in a circle and lifted our glasses. "To the happy couple," Jasper said. We all toasted, and there were more congratulations and happy tears from the female members of my family.

"Tomorrow there will be a wedding," I said. "A Christmas Eve wedding."

Quinn laughed as she looked up at me. "I promised the minute Mother and Annabelle were here, we'd do it, so I guess we're getting married tomorrow."

Harley cleared his throat, then tapped his glass. "I have an announcement as well. Merry and I went to see Pastor Lind this morning, and we've married."

Both Lizzie and Quinn pounced on a blushing Merry. She held up her hand to show off a gold wedding band. "It was Harley's mother's," Merry said. "And Poppy's graciously let me have it, even though it was meant for her."

Poppy grinned. "I'm never getting married anyway."

"And why not?" Harley asked.

"Boys are disgusting," Poppy said. "And anyway, I'm going to be a veterinarian and won't have time for a husband."

"I think that sounds like a splendid idea," Quinn said. "But if you're like me, you might find a man despite your other plans."

"Papa, turn on music, please," Josephine said. "So we can dance."

I turned on the phonograph, and the children pranced around the room. Jasper stood by the fire looking miserable. Lizzie sat on the couch drinking her champagne and looking equally despondent. For such a smart man, Jasper was making a terrible mistake.

I took Harley aside and poured him a whiskey. "Congratulations. When will she move into the cottage with you?"

"We wanted to check with you first," Harley said. "Is it all right?"

I slapped his shoulder. "A man should be with his wife."

Abruptly the music stopped. Jasper, near the phonograph, lifted his glass. "I have something to say."

Everyone paused what they were doing and turned toward him.

"I've been a fool," Jasper said. "Lizzie, I don't want you to marry Clive Higgins. And you might like him because he's a butcher and you're a cook and all that, but you belong with me. We belong to each other."

She stared at him.

"I want you to be my wife. I have money of my own, thanks to the lord's generosity. I can take care of you."

Lizzie's mouth had dropped open a smidge, but she continued to stare at him as if he were a ghost.

Jasper crossed over to her and dropped to one knee. From his pocket, he pulled out a round diamond with tiny emeralds surrounding it. His grandmother's ring. She'd left it to him when he was only a kid. I'd forgotten.

"Please, Lizzie, will you marry me?" he asked.

"I...I thought you didn't love me."

"I lied. I was afraid."

"Of what?" she asked.

"Of not being enough for you. I'm boring and old-fashioned, and you're the opposite."

"I've loved you since we were children. It's not like you've changed." Lizzie smiled as she reached out to caress the side of his face. "I don't find you boring."

"Is that a yes?"

"It's a yes," she said.

The children all cheered. Poppy and Josephine held on to each other by the hands and galloped around the room.

I put the music back on, and we poured more champagne and danced and laughed and talked deep into the night.

Quinn

❦

The morning of Christmas Eve I woke next to my sister in the bed in my room. We'd agreed that she would take the room when I came home later as Lady Barnes. The night before, we'd been too tired to unpack her trunk, so now I was sitting on the bed watching her move around the room in her dressing gown. She'd had a bath and washed her hair. Her damp, loose hair dried as she hung clothes in the wardrobe.

Watching her, I decided she seemed older than when I left home just a few months ago. Living alone with Mother had given her a self-assurance she hadn't had before. It hurt a little to see how life had robbed her of any childish tendencies, but I supposed it was for the best. The world was a hard place and courage our only map.

She showed me the new dress she'd made for herself in a light green organza. "A day dress or a sister-of-the-bride dress," she said. "Are you mad I spent the money on fabric?" she asked.

"Never," I said. "It was time for a new dress."

"It's just you sent so much money and then Lord Barnes wrote and sent more, so I didn't think you'd begrudge me or Mother a few new clothes."

"I'm glad you had enough to make something nice for your-self," I said.

Annabelle bounced on her feet. "I've brought something for you, too. When you wrote a month or so ago that Alexander had stated his intention to marry you, I started to worry about a wedding dress. I made this for you." She pulled from the trunk a high-waisted white organza gown with a tiered skirt and tight sleeves that stopped at the elbows.

I leapt from the bed and grabbed the dress. "Annabelle, how did you ever do this?"

"It's nothing. I used a pattern. Although I tweaked it a bit to suit your small frame. Making this wedding dress was the most fun I've ever had."

"I adore it." I placed the dress on the bed and stared at it with great reverence. I couldn't believe such a pretty dress was mine. "And I adore you."

"There's one more thing." She lifted a lace veil from the trunk. "I made this from a piece of lace Mother had kept for years and years, hoping one of us could use it for a veil. Do you like it?"

I fingered the delicate lace my sister had cut and sewn onto a small cap. "Making this from an old piece of lace. You're such the clever one."

"Aren't I though?"

We hugged, laughing and crying at the same time. A knock on the door followed by Merry's voice interrupted us from our sisterly reunion.

"Quinn, I've come to help you get dressed." She gasped when she saw the dress. "Where did it come from?"

"My sister made it," I said.

Merry couldn't keep the envy out of her voice. "It's the pret-tiest dress I've ever seen."

We spent the next hour getting dressed. Merry powdered me and blushed my cheeks while Annabelle twisted my hair and fixed the veil with pins. Finally, I slipped into my gown.

My sister fussed with the material, smoothing it with her fingers. Merry simply watched, shaking her head. "You're like a princess," she said.

Another knock on the door, and my mother entered wearing a light gray organza gown I'd never before seen. My sister's seamstress fingers had been busy. "Oh my goodness, will you look at you. The dress is even prettier on." She wheezed and thumped her chest.

"Mother, are you all right?" I asked.

"Yes, yes. I'm fine. It's the first I've felt it since we left that dirty city. All this fresh air's going to cure me." She pointed at Annabelle, who had fixed her hair but not yet put on her dress. "They're ready for us downstairs. We must go."

Annabelle quickly slipped into her dress, and we all went downstairs together. Alexander and the children were waiting in the foyer, wearing their Sunday best.

Alexander met me at the bottom of the steps. "You, my love, are a beautiful bride." Tears moistened his eyes as he held out his hands. "Are you ready to be my wife?"

"Yes, but there's one last thing." I motioned for the twins to come near. "I have a question for you two. My father is in heaven and typically he would walk me down the aisle. I was wondering if you would do it instead?"

"What do we do?" Flynn asked.

"Will people be looking at us?" Theo asked.

"You'll each take one of my arms, like this." I tucked their small hands inside my elbows. "And then we just walk toward your father."

"And no one will be looking at anyone but Quinn," Alexander said. "You can trust me on that."

The little boys each nodded their heads and exchanged proud looks with each other. "We will do it," Flynn said.

Cymbeline stomped her foot. "What about us? We want a job."

"You and your sisters are to wait at the front of the church with Papa," I said. "Make sure he doesn't run away at the last minute."

Both Fiona and Cymbeline giggled.

"He won't run away," Josephine said. "And you can trust me on that."

Quinn

That night of our wedding, I lay in Alexander's arms for the first time. Given my inexperience, I'd been surprisingly calm about the expected coupling. I'd wanted only to be with him. He'd taken his time with me, gentle and courteous, and had promised that it would be better the second time. He was right.

Nearing 3:00 a.m. and physically spent, I nestled into the crook of his arm.

"I had no idea it would be like this," I said as I breathed in the scent of his skin.

"We'll have many more nights like this one. My only desire is to give you everything you ever dreamed of."

"You already have." I ran my hand over his broad chest, marveling at the feel of him. It occurred to me that I was now allowed to touch him any time I wanted. I was his wife.

"Will you want a child of your own?" he asked.

"I already have five of them. They're mine in here." I tapped my chest. "They've owned my heart since the very first time I saw them."

He chuckled and pulled me tighter against his hard frame. "I can only imagine what you must've thought—all of us staring at you like that."

"I thought I'd died and gone to heaven with the angels. And I was right."

"I'm not sure I'd describe them as angels," he said.

"Won't it be wonderful to watch them grow up? I wonder what kind of remarkable lives they'll have."

"They have more of a chance now," he said. "With a mother to love them and nurture them."

"Someday, they'll have weddings and babies. Think of it, Alexander. All the fun we'll have."

"We might have more children, Quinn. You should prepare yourself for that."

I smiled into the darkness. "I'd be pleased. But we'll see what plans God has for us. He might think we have more than enough for one couple."

"I'm a blessed man," he said.

"And my mother and sister are here. I can't imagine how any person could be happier than I am."

"Did you see how Clive looked at your sister at dinner?" he asked. "I had to remind him she's only sixteen."

"Well, if he can wait a few years, who knows? Clive's a good man."

"I was thinking as I looked around our table tonight about the children Harley and Merry and Jasper and Lizzie will surely have. The thought of them all growing up together on my land warmed my heart. Someday our children and the others will have children of their own. Do you think our descendants will be as happy here as we are?"

"Only time will tell," I said. "But I have a good feeling that this community will grow into a place of love, friendship, and tolerance. You set the foundation with your generosity and fair-mindedness. We have only to head further in that direction with each year that passes."

"Ah, my love. What did I do to deserve you?"

"And I, you?"

I turned on my side and nestled against Alexander, unable to predict the future but full of hope. Of course, I couldn't know then that the years would indeed bring much joy to Alexander and me. Our children and the children of our beloved friends did grow up to have love stories of their own and children and grandchildren. As is true in life, the paths to their true norths were not without a few bumps and twists. However, they were armed for any battle because of the depth of their spirits and goodness of their characters. They knew from our example that love was the only thing worth fighting for, the only thing that can fight darkness and evil. But those stories are for another time and not mine to tell.

I knew only this as I drifted off to sleep. Courage is truly the only map to a satisfying life. We must not shy away from that which frightens us. For if we do, we might not fulfill our destiny, our true callings. Without bravery, we might miss those who will fill the hole in our hearts and for whom we are the missing piece.

Step off the train, dear ones. Your life awaits.

READY FOR JOSEPHINE'S LOVE STORY? HER TALE OPENS TEN years later in The Spinster. Download here from your favorite retailer now and escape into another sweet historical.

Sign up for my newsletter over at my website at www.tess-writes.com and never miss a sale or new release, plus you'll get a free ebook copy of The Santa Trial. You can also join my Face-book group Patio Chat with Tess Thompson for fun giveaways and sneak peeks.

I appreciate you helping to spread the word about my books. Thank you for sharing a recommendation with friends and please leave a review on the retailer of your choice.

Sending love from my home to yours, Tess XO

More Emerson Pass!

Josephine's story opens ten years later in The Spinster of Emerson Pass. Get it here: The Spinster

Theo's story is available now! Get it here: The Scholar.

Pre-order The Problem Child for its November 9th 2021 release.

Pre-order The Musician. Fiona's story will be coming May 17, 2022.

The first of the Emerson Pass Contemporaries , The Sugar Queen , starring the descendants of the Barnes family is available at your favorite retailer.
The second in the contemporary stories, The Patron is also available. Will Garth and Crystal ever find a way to leave the past behind to embrace each other and the future?

For more Emerson Pass, download the historical books in the series. Travel back in time to meet the original residents of Emerson Pass, starring the Barnes family.

The School Mistress
The Spinster
The Scholar

Sign up for Tess's newsletter and never miss a release or sale!
www.tesswrites.com. You'll get a free ebook copy of The Santa
Trial for your subscription.

The Spinster

*Her love died on a battlefield. He carries a torch for a
woman he's never met. Can the tragic death of a soldier
entwine the souls of two strangers?*

Colorado, 1919. Josephine Barnes wrote every day to her beloved
fiancé battling in the trenches of the Great War. Devastated
when he's killed in action, she vows never to marry and buries
her grief in the construction of the town's first library. But she's
left breathless when she receives a request from a gracious
gentleman to visit and return the letters containing her declara-
tions of desire.

Philip Baker survived the war but returned home burdened with
a distressing secret. Though he knows it's wrong, he can't stop
reading through the beautiful sentiments left among his slain
comrade's possessions. Plagued by guilt, he's unable to resist
connecting with the extraordinary woman who captured his
heart with her words.

When Josephine invites Philip to join her gregarious family for
the holidays, she's torn by her loyalty to a ghost and her growing
feelings for the gallant man. And as Philip prepares to risk everything by telling her the truth about her dead fiancé, he fears he
could crush Josephine's blossoming happiness forever.

Will they break free from their painful pasts to embrace a passion meant to be?

The Spinster is the second book in the heartwarming Emerson Pass historical romance series. If you like staunch heroines, emotional backdrops, and sweeping family sagas, then you'll adore Tess Thompson's wholesome tale.

Buy *The Spinster* to read between the lines of destiny today!

The Sugar Queen

The first in the contemporary Emerson Pass Series , The Sugar Queen features the descendants from the Barnes family.
Get ready for some sweet second chances! To read the first chapter, simply turn the page or download a copy here: The Sugar Queen.

True love requires commitment, and many times unending sacrifice...

At the tender age of eighteen, Brandi Vargas watched the love of her life drive out of Emerson Pass, presumably for good. Though she and Trapper Barnes dreamed of attending college and starting their lives together, she was sure she would only get in the way of Trapper's future as a hockey star. Breaking his heart, and her own in the process, was the only way to ensure he pursued his destiny. Her fate was the small town life she'd always known, her own bakery, and an endless stream of regret.
After a decade of playing hockey, a single injury ended Trapper Barnes' career. And while the past he left behind always haunted him, he still returns to Emerson Pass to start the next chapter of his life in the place his ancestors built more than a century before. But when he discovers that the woman who owns the

local bakery is the girl who once shattered his dreams, the painful secret she's been harboring all these years threatens to turn Trapper's idyllic small town future into a disaster. Will it take a forest fire threatening the mountain village to force Trapper and Brandi to confront their history? And in the wake of such a significant loss, will the process of rebuilding their beloved town help them find each other, and true happiness, once again?

Fast forward to the present day and enjoy this contemporary second chance romance set in the small town of Emerson Pass, featuring the descendants of the characters you loved from *USA Today* bestselling author Tess Thompson's The School Mistress.

The Patron of Emerson Pass
She's afraid to take risks. He's an incurable daredevil. When tragedy throws them together, will it spark a lasting devotion?

Crystal Whalen isn't sure why she should go on. Two years after her husband's death on a ski trip, she's devastated when a fire destroys her quiet Colorado mountain home. And when she can't keep her hands off the gorgeous divorcé who's become her new temporary housemate, it only feeds her grief and growing guilt.

Garth Welty won't be burned again. After his ex-wife took most of his money, the downhill-skiing Olympic medalist is determined to keep things casual with the sexy woman he can't resist. But the more time they spend with each other, the harder it is to deny his burgeoning feelings.

As Crystal's longing for the rugged man's embrace grows, she worries that his dangerous lifestyle will steal him away. And although Garth believes she's his perfect girl, the specter of betrayal keeps a tight grip on his heart.

Will the thrill-seeker and the wary woman succumb to the power of love?

The Patron of Emerson Pass is the emotional second book in the Emerson Pass Contemporaries small-town romance series. If you like lyrical prose, unexpected chances at happiness, and uplifting stories, then you'll adore Tess Thompson's sweet tale.

Buy *The Patron of Emerson Pass* to rebuild broken hope today!

Acknowledgments

As always, I have to thank my assistant, MaryAnn Schaefer for her undying loyalty and friendship. She manages so much for me and I'd be lost without her.

Also, I'd like to thank my author sisters in our Facebook reader group, My Book Tribe. They're such an inspiration to me, not only as writers but as people. We do a lot of giveaways and author interviews. If you'd like to join our reader group on Facebook, click here.

Thank you to my street team. My street team, Tessers, is the absolute best early reader group in the world. I love every one of them!

Thank you to my fan group Patio Chat With Tess Thompson. We have such fun in there. We have contests and live chats. If you'd like to join us, click here. Every new member gets a free ebook from my catalog.

Thanks to my four kids for being independent enough to help with dinners and errands so that I have more time to write. My beautiful daughters are my pride and joy. My bonus sons light up my heart.

Finally, thank you to my husband. Cliff Strom is the love of my life, my biggest fan and best friend. When I was first starting out, he would always say, "Not if, honey, but when." Those words have encouraged me every step of the way.

And finally, to my readers. Thank you for the privilege of writing for you. Thank you for spending a few hours inside my stories. It's truly an honor.

Also by Tess Thompson

CLIFFSIDE BAY

Traded: Brody and Kara

Deleted: Jackson and Maggie

Jaded: Zane and Honor

Marred: Kyle and Violet

Tainted: Lance and Mary

Cliffside Bay Christmas, The Season of Cats and Babies (Cliffside Bay Novella to be read after Tainted)

Missed: Rafael and Lisa

Cliffside Bay Christmas Wedding (Cliffside Bay Novella to be read after Missed)

Healed: Stone and Pepper

Chateau Wedding (Cliffside Bay Novella to be read after Healed)

Scarred: Trey and Autumn

Jilted: Nico and Sophie

Kissed (Cliffside Bay Novella to be read after Jilted)

Departed: David and Sara

Cliffside Bay Bundle, Books 1,2,3

BLUE MOUNTAIN SERIES

Blue Midnight

Blue Moon

Blue Ink

Blue String

Blue Mountain Bundle, Books 1,2,3

EMERSON PASS

The School Mistress of Emerson Pass, Book 1 (First historical installment).

The Sugar Queen of Emerson Pass, Book 2 (First contemporary installment).

The Spinster of Emerson Pass, Book 3 (Second historical installment).

RIVER VALLEY

Riversong

Riverbend

Riverstar

Riversnow

Riverstorm

Tommy's Wish

River Valley Bundle, Books 1-4

CASTAWAY CHRISTMAS

Come Tomorrow, Castaway Christmas, Book 1

LEGLEY BAY

Caramel and Magnolias

Tea and Primroses

STANDALONES

The Santa Trial

Duet for Three Hands

Miller's Secret

About the Author

Tess Thompson

HOMETOWNS *and* HEARTSTRINGS

USA Today Bestselling author Tess Thompson writes small-town romances and historical romance. She started her writing career in fourth grade when she wrote a story about an orphan who opened a pizza restaurant. Oddly enough, her first novel, "Riversong" is about an adult orphan who opens a restaurant. Clearly, she's been obsessed with food and words for a long time now.

With a degree from the University of Southern California in theatre, she's spent her adult life studying story, word craft, and character. Since 2011, she's published over 20 novels and a five novellas. Most days she spends at her desk chasing her daily word count or rewriting a terrible first draft.

She currently lives in a suburb of Seattle, Washington with her husband, the hero of her own love story, and their Brady Bunch clan of two sons, two daughters and five cats. Yes, that's four kids and five cats.

Tess loves to hear from you. Drop her a line at tess@tthompsonwrites.com or visit her website at https://tesswrites.com/ or visit her on social media.

Made in the USA
Middletown, DE
12 April 2022